The terrible roar of gunfire pulsed outward, grabbed hold of me, and held me crouched in a tight ball. But the capture was only for an instant, until the desire to live proved stronger than the fear of dying, infusing a powerful strength into my legs. My thighs tightened as I rose from the hard-packed ground and pushed off with the toe of my boot.

I didn't look back to see if the others still stood, if my escape had been noticed, if guns were trained on me even now. I didn't look back because I didn't want to know. I didn't want to know if Franz or Amos or Fat Shorty, who thought to shield me with his own big body, lay sprawled out like Uley.

Two more shots followed, and I felt a split in the very air I breathed. Just ahead of me, the tall snowy white crown of a Queen Anne's flower exploded. Willy's taunt, "Outrun the bullets!" screamed in my mind, and I pushed harder, lifting my knees and hitting the ground solid with my boots.

Outrun the bullets!

Praise for *OUTRUN THE BULLETS*

"I always anticipate a trifold reading experience in the tales spun by Steele. Characters to cheer and cry for, fully immersed in language, time, and place, with a passel of historical knowledge. Enjoyable!"

~Ira Amos, Author

~*~

"In *OUTRUN THE BULLETS*, M. Carolyn Steele expertly blends the challenged lives of a northwestern Arkansas family during the closing months of the Civil War. As the family's blunt Irish mother observed, fighting one another brings the ugliness out in mankind."

~vehoae, Author

~*~

"This captivating story is a fascinating read—a real page turner. It is rich with historical details, colorful characters, and surprising twists and turns. Steele uses masterful descriptions and vivid details."

~Nikki Hanna, Author

Outrun the Bullets

by

M. Carolyn Steele

Outrun the Bullets

Cover Art by *Rae Monet, Inc. Design*

The Wild Rose Press, Inc.
PO Box 708
Adams Basin, NY 14410-0708
Visit us at www.thewildrosepress.com

Publishing History
First Mainstream Historical Edition, 2019
Print ISBN 978-1-5092-2680-1
Digital ISBN 978-1-5092-2681-8

Published in the United States of America

Dedication

To my father, Gath C. Fears, who had stories to tell,
and, to his great-grandsons,
Cameron Henderson and Cayden Henderson

Acknowledgements

I have many people to thank for getting the novel *Outrun the Bullets* to the point of publication. Before the writing classes, conferences, critique groups, and hours at the computer comes the seed of an idea, and for that I have my father, Gath Fears, to thank. A Civil War historian, he delighted in passing on tales from his childhood of the grandfather who outran a Confederate bullet. As the youngest of four siblings, Dad felt a kinship with his grandfather, who was also the youngest in the family.

Ancestor legends are near and dear to me. This one grew from a creative nonfiction short story to a full-fledged novel and, except for Catherine Fears and her four sons, is filled with fictional characters. Those readers who are curious about what is real and what is imagination need only ask.

I thank the many who came and went from the Crossroads Writers' Group, led by Steve Amos, for their insight and encouragement. Excellent writers themselves, Carla Stewart and Becky Eagleton took time to critique and advise. Julie Kimmel-Harbaugh put her stamp of approval on the story and told me it was time to march forward, as did my daughters, Teri and Traci. Among many others who helped with research, a Civil War reenactor at Pea Ridge filled my brain with nuggets of information about a soldier's lot.

Last, but not least, a big thank you to my patient editor at Wild Rose Press, Allison Byers, the final link in this adventure.

Chapter 1

"You've been down to the ticky place, haven't you?"

It wasn't the tone of Ma's voice that could have brought a dead man to life, it was the look on her face, all screwed up and sour. It cut through me like I was a mound of churned butter. How did she know where I'd been?

"And, Ebenezer Fears, lest you forget, I can hear a lie rolling around your head, trying to wiggle out of your mouth right now."

"Ah, Ma."

She put a finger to her pursed lips, which was the unspoken warning to think before I answered. Ma's red hair glowed fierce in the fading sunlight that spilled through the cabin door. It always turned darker when she got mad, a sure sign of a wind-spout getting ready to rip through our little corner of Arkansas.

A fish line, strung through the gills of four brown bass, pressed deep across my palm. I held up the fish, scales layered and shiny, black round eyes seeing nothing, mouths gaped open in silent pleading to be let go. Maybe she'd forget the ticky place when she saw such a fine catch.

"I saw those fish dripping all over me floor the minute you come through the door. Now, where'd you get the crawlers that caught those brownies?"

Well, maybe she wouldn't forget. Ma was like a hound dog on the trail of a opossum once she got something in her mind. No, there wasn't any way around fessing up. Like Willy says, it's how you fess up that takes the mad out of Ma.

"Yes, ma'am. I reckon you're right to be thorny at me. Didn't mean any disobedience." My hand ached where the weight of the fish line threatened to cut through the flesh. I glanced down to see if I was bleeding yet. The sight of blood always softened Ma a bit. No blood. When I looked up, she stood, arms folded across her chest, green eyes boring holes into my soul.

I took a deep breath. "You know all we have are skinny, half-starved crawlers in the dirt around here. A fella can hardly get them strung on a hook. Down in the holler, where the sun doesn't dry things out, the dirt's moist and full of fat wigglers."

Ma didn't flinch—didn't even bat an eye.

"Ah, Ma, I can't abide one more meal of pork rind and greens. All we've had to eat is some kind of pork since the boys took the rifles and joined up with them Union fellas."

Ma blinked straight-off with the mention of the boys. It was her biggest worry that something would happen to one of my brothers. Maybe she was weakening.

"Yesterday, Big Jolly said him and Little Jolly caught the biggest mess of fine fish over at Natural Dam. Used wigglers from the ticky place and could hardly keep the line in the water for the fish snagging hold of the hooks."

"Ebby." Ma sighed and relaxed her stance a bit. She kept her arms folded, which meant she was still angry. "You know full well ticks don't cotton to Indians like they do to us white folk. Big Jolly could crawl around bushes and such all day and not get more than a tick or two. You, they smell your Irish blood and come crawling fast as their little legs can carry them, ready for a feast."

When Ma was right, she was as unmovable as a stone fence. Talking only built the fence higher. I shook the line, and the brownies slapped against each other, increasing the fishy smell that followed me through the door.

"What's done, is done, I reckon." For the first time, Ma took her hard stare from me to settle on the catch. "Big Jolly was right about one thing. Those are mighty fine fish. You aren't the only one been wishing for something besides turnip greens and poke salad. Don't suppose you picked up that salt from old man Flanagan, did you?"

"No, ma'am. I sure enough had it on my mind. Guess I forgot."

She sighed again. "Um-hum. Be that forgetting come on you before or after Big Jolly squeezed the chores out of your mind with stories of fat crawlers and fish?" She didn't wait for an answer, which pleased me proud, since it was after Big Jolly came along I forgot Ma's salt. "Well, go on. Get them fish ready for the frying pan. I'll get bathwater heating."

"Bathwater! What for? It isn't Saturday, Ma."

"No, it isn't. I just reckon you'll have two baths this week, unless you go back to the ticky place. Then you'll have three. I'm not opening a boarding house for ticks."

Ma pulled a blackened bread pan from the bottom

of the cupboard and held it out. "Put the fish in here once you get 'em cleaned. Then strip off your clothes out there on the porch. We'll boil those overalls."

She lifted her skirt and bent to examine the floor like a chicken looking for bugs. "I swear, I hear them little blood suckers crawling 'round right now. Skiddy, skiddy, skiddy. Looking for another fine Irish meal." She shivered and stomped several balls of dirt into dust. That's all they were—little balls of dirt. I know, because I was drawn to look, too.

"Aren't any skiddies down there, just dirt you're stomping between the boards, Ma. Besides, you know you can't kill those bitty critters by stomping them."

All four feet ten inches of Ma rose up to five feet. Her hair glowed orange. She put both hands on her hips. "I said I heard them. Stomping will make 'em think twice before taking root. Now, get on out of here before any more of those ticks let loose."

She reached for the broom leaning against the door jamb. I took both porch steps in one bound before she could lay that broom across my back. When I looked over my shoulder through the open door, Ma was hopping around on one foot, and then the other, stomping the floorboards like she was doing an Irish jig. She was temperamental about spiders, ticks, and such. And one thing Crawford County had an abundance of was spiders, ticks, and such.

Willy always teased her, bringing buckets of long-legged spiders back from Salem Cemetery. Said it was worth a rap on the noggin, just to see her jump. The house has been duller than a winter night since my three older brothers signed up with the Union Army, leaving me to take care of things.

The fishy odor of the brownies grew more powerful. Sally, Ma's mouser, curled around my leg, long tail high, purring and rubbing against my overalls.

I circled the house, hung my catch on the corner post of the chicken yard, and slit the gill of the first brownie, releasing it from the line. The fish lay pale and sickly across the foot-wide tree stump. So many animals had been gutted and skinned there, it was permanently stained brown. One swift blow of the ax separated the head. It fell to the ground, and I kicked it under the fence wire.

Flip and Dip, Ma's last two remaining Dominicker chickens, fluttered toward the offering, wings flared and necks craned forward. Each tried to out-cluck the other as they tousled with the fish head, pecking at the eyes and stripping flesh from the bones. Some thief, whether four-legged or two, stole our rooster months ago. Poor old Flip and Dip kept laying an egg a day, like they knew their life depended on producing.

The two chickens grew loud in their gluttony, raising their heads so a morsel could slide down their long necks. Then they dove back for more.

"No need to argue, girls. I believe, for a change, there will be plenty to go around." I kicked a fish head toward Sally, and another one under the fence. The chickens attacked the fresh contribution to their dinner with renewed fury. "Guess you critters were getting about as tired of left over greens as the rest of us."

Ma was waiting on the porch with a butcher knife when I got back to the house. She pointed to the laundry bucket simmering over a fire in the front yard. "Your clothes nay be welcome in me house, laden as they are with vermin. Drop those breeches in the water, and we'll drown the critters."

I'd no sooner got a towel wrapped around me, when she drug me to the fireplace. I knew I was in for it.

"Sit. Twenty ticks sucking on your blood and, come a fortnight, you'll be laying in your bed, sweating with fever. Mark my words, it's so." Ma pulled my big toe near off my foot. "Ah ha, here's one." She plucked a wooden spoon from the honey crock I held.

Thick, amber-dark honey glistened, as she allowed a dollop to drip between my toes. The drop began a slow maddening tickle down the bottom of my foot. The decision of digging for fat wigglers in the ticky place seemed downright stupid while sitting in front of the fireplace with nothing but a towel covering my unmentionables.

Ma moved to the other foot. She was on a tick hunt and driven to find every last critter.

"Ma, I can search for those ticks. It isn't seemly to be here in my all-together. I was sixteen last birthday, and that's pretty near grown."

"You got eyes in the back of your head, hmm?"

"No, ma'am. I haven't, but…"

"Well then, looks like we haven't got any place for seemly, do we? I raised you and your brothers alone since the day you were born. If you had a pa, which you haven't, since he got himself killed fighting down in Mexico, he would be doing this. If you had one of your brothers, which you haven't, since they all went off to fight Rebels, one of them would be doing this."

The wooden spoon, shiny with its coating of honey, wagged before my eyes. "All you got left is me, so don't talk of seemly."

Wood crackled as flames lapped at the dry timber stacked in the fireplace, stirring a pleasant warmth to the early evening air. Ever since my three brothers signed up in the First Arkansas Cavalry, Ma had taken to heaping all the mothering, which used to be divided four ways, onto me. It hardly left a fella room to breathe.

"Smother it, and scrape it when it comes up for air," Ma muttered as she scraped at every freckle along my arms, back, and neck. I knew the chant by heart since she said it each time she found another tick.

"Ow!" I protested in a useless effort to shake her hand loose. Pain radiated through my ear as she stretched it out a mile.

"Shush! Don't move a muscle, lad. Be a shame to lose an ear now, wouldn't it? What's the use of taking the critter's body and leaving its head to suck your blood?"

Whether it was digging a splinter from a finger or a tick from my flesh, Ma was not given to unnecessary coddling. She rested the sharp edge of the butcher knife in the bend of my ear and scraped the flesh.

I sucked air through gritted teeth.

"Now, that makes the thirteenth tick." She shook her head and ran the knife blade along the stone hearth. The tiny varmint's body bubbled and hissed in the heat like a balloon losing air. Ma continued the hunt, lifting handfuls of hair. Yes sir, I was cured of the ticky place. Honey dripped from my hairline, down my neck and back. I waited for another scrape that would lift several layers of skin with a fat tick.

"Fourteen. Thank the stars, it wasn't just thirteen. That be an unlucky number."

"Yeah, Ma. Thank the stars. Don't want any unlucky number of ticks."

"Here," she said handing me the honey spoon and butcher knife. "I've checked as far up as possible and as far down as possible. Now, it be for you to check possible." She nodded toward the tub in the corner. "Bathwater should be nigh on to tolerable. Scrub good. Don't want to draw ants. Can't abide ants."

I watched Ma pause at the door and turn back to smile at me. Sleeves rolled to her elbow, she pushed a lock of red hair back into the thick knot at her neck.

"Those fish are going to taste mighty fine, son. Now, don't forget…"

"I know, Ma. Smother those bloodsuckers and scrape them when they come up for air."

Chapter 2

The trees were whispering. I paused at the porch steps, sat the milk bucket down, and listened. Listened for the familiar night sounds—the snort of our old hound, Abner, as he pawed a resting spot under the porch, the bellow of bullfrogs down by the creek, and the soft rustle of little critters through the grass as they started their nightly prowl. We had all sort of trees— hackberry, elm, apple, oak, and such—surrounding the cabin. When a breeze stirred, it set them all to talking. Ma called it night music.

An owl hooted nearby. If the Jolly twins had been sitting on the porch, they would get up and chase the bird away, declaring its presence an omen of bad luck, maybe even death. Cherokee Indians have lots of superstitions.

June was too early in the summer for katydids to trill from the trees. Their shrill song was a comfort, proof nothing crashed around in the dark night ready to do mischief. It wasn't the four-legged critters that were a worry. It was the two-legged kind, those that carried weapons and a heart full of hate.

The owl hooted again. It sounded closer, even though I knew it wasn't. Soon, some fool field mouse or rabbit would think so, too, get worried, and make a dash for a better hiding place. Patience, that's all the night bird has to have, and a fat meal would present itself.

"Good luck, Mr. Owl," I said. "I'm about to have a fine supper myself."

Clean overalls chafed my legs. It would take two days of wearing to soften them to tolerable. I picked up the bucket and, once again, studied the deep shadows for anything that shouldn't be there. The aroma of frying fish met me at the door, setting my mouth watering.

Ma squatted in front of the fireplace, arms encircling her knees, and watched flames lick up around a large iron skillet. Pieces of fish turned golden brown in a sea of bubbling lard. She reached for a spatula and lifted one piece to peer under it.

"Perfect," she said and looked up. "You have the uncanny ability to know just when supper be ready, Ebby. 'Tis like your pa, that way. How was the milking?"

"Right poorly. Hardly worth the effort." I set the bucket down and reached for two empty fruit jars. "Not enough for churning. Might as well drink what there is. Reckon the cow's getting too old? She hasn't calved in two years now."

"No." Ma wrapped a towel around the skillet handle and swung the heavy pan onto the table. "Most likely, she's unhappy. She can't abide the hog. Never could. Him snorting and grunting all night unsettles her digestion. Ever since you took to locking the two of them up in the shed at night with the Dominickers, she's been showing her displeasure in the only way she knows how. Never mind she can't much calve without a bull, now can she?"

I settled myself at the table. It was no use pointing

up Betsy's shortcomings. Ma had a blind spot when it came to that cow, born like it was with a white star on its forehead between large brown eyes. A sign of Divine Providence some said. I expected something wonderful to happen. Like she would birth three calves at once. Instead, Civil War came to Crawford County, bringing hungry times and a terrible meanness in folks we didn't even know and some we did.

A plate of cornmeal-dusted and fried brownies slid in front of me. Grease oozed from the fish and pooled in the rim. One steaming bite made me forget Betsy and her stingy measure of milk. I lolled the mouthful of food from side to side and swallowed, feeling the warmth travel down my throat to my chest.

"Ma, no one can cook fish like you." I stabbed another hunk and stuffed it into my mouth.

"Um-hum. Most folks don't know it's the crushed rosemary mixed with corn meal gives it that special taste." Ma's fork paused in mid-air. "Of course, a touch of salt would have been nice, too."

A piece of fish stopped halfway down my throat. I coughed and reached for a glass of milk.

"Yes, ma'am, about that salt. Tomorrow, soon as the sun comes up, I'll get on over to the Flanagan's. Right after I walk the field for weeds."

"Um-hum. You know the hog's got to go. It isn't just because Betsy doesn't like Horace. He's fat enough, seeing as how he's rooted all the acorns hereabouts. We haven't got more than one ham left in the smokehouse." She lifted an eyebrow and looked straight at me. "I can't preserve any more pork until I get salt."

It seemed best to change the subject from salt.

"Been meaning to ask why we can't eat that ham, instead of having nothing but greens and rinds, and maybe fish, when they're biting?"

Steam burst from a piece of fish as Ma poked it with a fork, flaking the meat in search of bones. "It's for a celebration, Ebby. First one of your brothers to grace me front door gets a fine welcome home."

Ma glanced up from her plate again. "That doesn't change the fact 'tis time to slaughter that old hog. Hams are a sight easier to hide than Horace, what with his nasty disposition, growling and carrying on like he does."

I decided against pointing out that Betsy was bigger than Horace and no easier to hide from the ruffians scouring the countryside. Locking up our remaining livestock at night provided Abner with enough time to smell rotten no-account thieves and let out with a howl.

"Ma, Big Jolly says his pa looks to move them up to Fayetteville. Says it isn't safe anymore with all the bushwhackers roaming hereabouts. I've been thinking…"

"Save your breath, Ebby." Ma straightened her shoulders and stared at me. Her eyes, usually green as creek ferns, were gray in the dim cabin light. "Years ago, your pa died to get us this piece of land. Buried in some lonely grave down in Mexico, all on account of the government promising a bounty of a hundred and sixty acres for fighting. He was a fair and tolerable man. Haven't found any better than him, and plenty come around wanting to please. I'm not letting any rabble run me off my place. I be for dying here, if I have to."

I shoveled another fish from the skillet onto my plate. Pa died sixteen years ago, barely a month before I was born, and Ma never let us boys forget that our land, payment for Pa's services, was bought with his blood. No man, including her sons, could ever live up to his memory.

"I don't mean to leave here forever, Ma. Just until the war is over. Valentine Matlock had his smokehouse raided two days ago. Took everything he had while he was out in the fields. Stole right from under his nose, too. He's not but spitting distance from here."

"Um-hum. Perhaps you should build a cache box for hiding vittles. Trees in full leaf now. Settle it high in grandfather oak over by the creek. 'Tis a truth, it will be a bit unhandy, but safe." She glanced at me and frowned. "Safe, unless you loosen your tongue about it."

The fish sat heavy in my stomach. Each brother, before they signed up nigh on to two years ago, charged me with the duty of protecting Ma and keeping up the chores. I was of a mind to ask how they expected me to do much protecting without so much as a flintlock, but I didn't. The only thing I could do to protect Ma was word-best her into going someplace safe until the rebels got tired of having the stuffing beat out of them.

"That might keep our vittles safe for a while, at least until some tree-furry finds a way to break into the box. But how am I to keep you out of harm's way?"

Maybe I could scare her into listening to me. "I wasn't aiming to tell you about Othella Thompson over on Lee's Creek, but I suppose you would hear soon enough. A couple of Confederate bushwhackers accosted Othella and ordered her to fix a fine supper for them. Of course, that old woman refused, and those no-good Sesech up and killed her mouser. They told her that was what they'd do with her if she didn't do as they wanted. Said they hadn't had a home-cooked supper in a month of Sundays, and plump as she was, she looked to be a fair cook."

"Killed her mouser?" Ma gasped and leaned back in the chair.

I nodded. "Of course, that was only a cat. It could have been worse." It weighed on my conscience to fret Ma, but she was a stubborn woman and only the whole story would convince her of the wisdom of leaving. "It could have been Othella that got her neck wrung. Even after she filled their bellies, they stole all her quilts, set her shed on fire, and made off with her crap-critter."

Charred wood collapsed into ashen piles in the fireplace, sending tiny sparks spiraling up the chimney. Ma pulled the lantern across the table and turned the wick up. A circle of light warmed the rubbed-oak surface. We sat in silence. It was always best to let Ma ruminate on things awhile.

"I reckon the joke is on those Sesech, stealing Othella's crap-critter."

Ma's voice was soft, and I stared at her trying to figure the joke.

She smiled. "That mule was the stubbornest animal I ever did know besides Horace. Othella said she could feed him a cup of oats and get two buckets of crap. He sat down when you said to pull, and pulled when you said to sit. I once saw him roll in the mud like Horace, then shake like Abner when he comes padding up from the creek. Mud went everywhere, all over her line of washing. That notch-eared mule's a gobshite, I reckon, just plain brain-addled."

Ma sighed and added, "'Tis a truth. Those boys did her a favor making off with her crap-critter. He won't be anything but trouble for them." Her voice hardened. "But can't abide a man that would steal a poor woman's quilts and fire her property. Old Beelzebub will be waiting at hell's door for those hooligans, sure as I'm sitting here."

She shook her head. "Fighting one another brings the ugliness out in mankind. A person does things against their nature with all sorts of mischief, stealing and even killing. The *why* of the war gets forgotten. Men get eat up with hate, and soon they hate even themselves. They aren't human anymore, just creatures with the devil burning hot inside them, bursting to get out."

I pushed my plate away and reached for Ma's hand. It was small and boney, with a scattering of freckles across her skin. "Ma, it isn't safe here. Big Jolly said his pa would most likely make room in his wagon, if we want to ride up to Fayetteville with them."

"When they be for going?"

"End of the week."

"Now, I'm not saying I'll go, but if we should go up to Fayetteville, will you get it shook out of your mind about joining your brothers? Three of my lads are enough to be off fighting."

I felt Ma's eyes bore down on me. She didn't blink or smile. She just stared and gripped my hand, hard as a plow handle.

"Promise me, Ebby."

The only way I could keep Ma safe was promise the one thing I'd been thinking on for the past two years. I'd have to give up joining my brothers in the First Arkansas Cavalry, the best unit in the whole Union Army. My stomach twisted the fish I had eaten minutes before into a tight knot.

"It isn't even much in my mind, Ma, to join up."

She nodded. "Then I'll ponder on it some. I'm not afraid of any hooligans, mind you. But 'tis a pity to see those worry lines on your face." She released her hold on me and smiled. "I'll still be needing the salt, you know."

"Yes, ma'am." I flexed the blood back into my fingers. "Tomorrow, I'll fetch it home first thing after chores."

It looked like I was going to be the only boy in the county that didn't take up arms. The notion just about broke my heart.

Chapter 3

The noonday sun came close to the earth, bright, with nary a cloud. I had to shade my eyes to peer at the two figures jogging toward me. There was no need to see their faces to know who they were—Big Jolly, running smooth as a lazy stream, with hardly a break in his stride, and Little Jolly, limping along with his arms flailing in all directions.

Some folks said Big Jolly twisted his twin brother's foot to hold him back and prevent him from being born first. I figured that might have been the truth, for nobody in Crawford County was more determined to win a race regardless the wager, unless it might have been me.

Ma said Little Jolly's deformity was, most likely, the Lord's doing—a reminder to their ma of some offense committed in the past. The Lord has a harsh way of dealing with sinners, which was something a man needed to remember.

"*Osiyo*, Ebby," Big Jolly yelled as he trotted up. A wide grin spread across his bronzed face. "We go fish. You come, too?"

"Hello back." I returned the Cherokee greeting. I knew a few Indian words, but they always got tangled up in my mouth, so I didn't much try the language. "Aw, wish I could go fishing. Been over to old man Flanagan's for the salt he owed us." I shifted the small sack that was draped across my shoulder.

Little Jolly staggered toward us, his right foot turned inward causing him to lope along with a clumsy gait. He sank to the ground and rested his arms and head on his knees. Sweat beaded down his bare back, soaking the waistband of his pants.

"You been racing your brother again?" I asked, knowing full well the answer in advance. The two boys competed against each other in everything—running, hunting, fishing, girling.

Little Jolly looked up, brushed strands of black hair from his face, and nodded. He smiled, looking just like his brother. It was as if they were mirrors of each other.

"Well, what'd you bet this time?"

With a shrug, Little Jolly pulled a string of dried possum grapes over his head. He tossed them to his brother, who caught the necklace in midair and added it to the collection around his neck.

"Seeing as how you got that ill-formed foot, why do you race your brother?" I didn't understand my friend at all. "You know he's going to win."

Little Jolly raised one eyebrow, looked skyward as if in deep thought, and rocked his body back and forth. Like it was a signal, Big Jolly squatted, too, removed a string from around his neck, and pulled a small dried grape off with his teeth.

I groaned and sat right down in the dirt. Might as well rest a bit, too. A story was coming on, sure as the sun was up in the sky.

"Long time ago," Little Jolly said, "before Maker of Breath created ancestors, animals ruled earth. There were many. Big ones, like bear and buffalo. Not so big, like wolf and fox. Little, like ant and bee and snail.

Small creatures had four legs like big and not so big. One day, Mother Earth see small creatures."

Little Jolly raked his fingers through the dirt, making a wide trail. "Snail's legs were short and fat. He slow and could not run like big animals. He complained to Mother Earth. He not know why she gave him such useless legs.

"Ant struggled with his burden on four thin legs. He not stop. He not complain." Little Jolly nodded toward a large anthill at the road's edge, piled high with crumbled dirt. Dozens of ants scurried in and out. "Ant ran everywhere, back and forth, to home in ground. Store lots food for winter.

"Bee, too, ran up flower's stem and back down and up tree to hive and back down. Over and over, bee did this and not complain. Hive was heavy with honey. Still, bee not rest."

Little Jolly paused with his storytelling, face all somber-like, and looked at us.

I pulled my knees up, wrapped my arms around them, and waited. No use hurrying the boy. He answered most questions with a story. It was just his way.

Bees buzzed over a dense carpet of clover in a patch of sunlight, and Little Jolly pointed toward them. "Mother Earth was pleased with bee and ant. She said to ant, 'You make home in ground. Because you not complain and work hard, I will give you two more legs to help carry burden.'

"Then Mother Earth called to bee, 'I will give you two more legs like brother ant. Because you make home high in tree, I will give you wings to reach hive. Since I give you more than ant, you must share food with first people when they arrive.'"

A breeze stirred through the trees, cooling the sweat on my face and back. I stared at the storyteller. The snail—what happened to the snail?

After a short pause, which was part of the story to make sure you paid attention, Little Jolly continued. "Snail waited to see what gift he would receive. Ground trembled when Mother Earth turned to him. She was not pleased. Snail became frightened and pulled into his shell. She said, 'You do not value what you have, so I will take legs away.' " Little Jolly's brow furrowed. He leaned near. "To this day, snail has not grown legs and must creep upon stomach to find food."

I bent forward until I was close enough to smell the boy's sweaty odor and waxy hair pomade and to peer into his dark eyes. "I surely do hope to be here to see Mother Earth give you two more legs. That I do, for a fact."

"Aiyee, brother, you waste good story—" Big Jolly snorted, pushing me backward, "—on *this* white man."

"Do not!" I shoved back with my elbow. "You want to hear a good story, wait until Josiah gets home and tells about the battle he had with those Rebs. They're wild-eyed crazies. Josiah totes one of those miniè balls around in his body." I poked a finger in Big Jolly's muscled shoulder. "Right there. Doctor wouldn't take it out. Said it was too dangerous. Josiah wrote as how, at night, he can feel that ball rolling around his body. Guess the thing is restless to get back in the battle."

I puffed myself up to sit taller than the brothers. "Didn't read that part of the letter to Ma. No use worrying her, seeing as how Josiah isn't sure the devil got shook off the miniè ball before it hit him."

The two Indians stared at me. For once, I'd left them speechless, most likely impressed, about Josiah being in a fight and being wounded. Battle wounds were big medicine to Indians.

"Fish restless," Little Jolly said at last. He patted the pouch strapped around his waist. "Have plenty of line, plenty hooks. You come, too, Ebby."

"Aw, I don't know." I stood and brushed dirt from my pants. "Ought to be getting on home with Ma's salt. She's been in a fit for it lately. Besides I'm not of a mind to go crawling around the ticky place again. Already had my bath for the week."

"We dig little crawlers by creek, maybe. Not many ticks by creek."

"Well, those brownies did taste mighty fine." I glanced up through the hackberry and elm branches sheltering us from the heat of the sun. "Too hot to be doing chores for a while. Would be cool down to the Natural Dam."

I picked up the sack of salt. "Reckon wouldn't take long to hook a few brownies. Ma probably be glad to have them, too. She's bound and determined to save that last ham we got in the smokehouse for when one of my brothers comes home."

"Come," Big Jolly said, tossing a string of dried possum grapes to his brother and one to me. "I catch more fish than anyone."

"Oh, yeah." I pulled several grapes free with my teeth. The dried fruit, withered to small wrinkled lumps, wrapped around a tooth, filling my mouth with a tartness that caused my eyes to water. "Betcha can't."

By the time we finished trying to coax fish onto

our hooks, the trees cast long shadows across the road, and the sun had slipped low in the sky. With home an hour's walk down the road, Ma was going to be a mite bad-tempered at the late arrival of her salt. I looked down at my two small brownies, hardly a good mouthful for one person.

Big Jolly strode ahead, a string of seven brownies slung over his shoulder, bouncing with each step. At least he wasn't boasting his luck. Just walking a few paces in front, so I was sure to see his catch.

I turned to Little Jolly, who was limping along next to me. "I would have caught more, if I had my own pole, instead of that old crookedy one I cut off that sapling. A man needs to have his own pole and hook when he fishes."

"Humph. Brother not need own pole. He carry fish charm."

"Fish charm? What in thunder is a fish charm?"

"Long time ago, bear stole much fish from old uncle. Uncle kill that greedy bear. Uncle say he share one fish, not all fish. Work chant over arrow and now, it charmed. Brother carry arrow in pocket. Always catch lots of fish."

"A fish charm! I'll be danged. Why, doesn't hardly seem fair, a charm and all."

Big Jolly stopped and turned. "Ebby, how 'bout we race. Me and you. Betcha I win."

I shook my head. "Can't. Not toting these fish and this sack of salt."

"I carry fish and salt," Little Jolly offered. "I carry brother's fish, too."

It was a tempting challenge, and I looked down at my pitiful catch of fish. Tempting, for sure, since I'm fast of foot and can beat just about anyone in the county. Anyone, except for, maybe, Big Jolly. Last time we raced, the Indian worried me a bit.

"If we race, whatcha want to bet?"

"Humm, if I win," Big Jolly scratched his chin. "Salt!"

"Salt! Jehosephat! I'm not betting my ma's salt."

"You afraid? Maybe we not race, you afraid."

"I'm not afraid of losing to you!" I felt heat crawl up my neck. "I can beat you any time. It's just you don't have anything to bet, so why get all worn out in this heat?"

Big Jolly held up his long string of brownies. "Fish."

"My salt is worth more than your puny fish. What about, uh…I know, what about, if I win, I get your fish *and* that fish charm you didn't tell anyone about."

Big Jolly's eyes widened, and he touched his pant pocket. "Fish charm?"

"Why, sure. Unless you're afraid of losing to me."

The Indian squared his shoulders and jutted his chin out. "I bet." He pointed down the road toward a lightning-struck oak at the top of the hill. "We race to spirit tree."

"Deal!" I shifted the salt and my fish into Little Jolly's arms.

Me and Big Jolly crouched down, shoulder to shoulder. I bunched up my leg muscles, ready to spring.

"Go!" Little Jolly shouted.

It was the last thing I heard. I pushed against the ground with my toes and sprang forward, a big leap ahead of Big Jolly. My feet hit hard, jarring all the way up to my teeth. Pretty soon, my thigh and calf muscles burned. I held my elbows in close, churning my arms back and forth like wheels on a train engine. My breathing turned ragged, but I kept my eyes focused on the spirit tree ahead.

Next to me, Big Jolly ran close enough to spit on. I could feel him crowding my space, threatening my lead.

My heart thumped so hard I feared it would fracture my ribs. Pretty soon I tasted the dust we stirred and gritted my teeth 'cause, by now, I was surely sucking air.

Ancient, gnarled, and blackened, the barren spirit tree lurked over the road, a reminder of the deadly power of lightning. It stood as a sentinel under which travelers passed. I knew I had to focus on that tree.

Even though sweat watered my eyes, I noticed four riders top the hill. They passed under the tree and started toward us at a trot.

Then, I heard it plain as day—the shrill squeal of Horace, the bawling of Betsy.

Chapter 4

The riders, black shadows against the glare of the western sun, crowded the narrow road. They reined their horses and sat four abreast, as if they owned that part of the country, as if it were the most natural thing in the world to intimidate the progress of citizens going the opposite direction.

Nothing to do but skid to a halt and bend, hands on my knees. My muscles twitched at being brought up short. I swallowed deep breaths of air, trying to gain my voice. The hair along my arms prickled with fear the instant I glimpsed the riders come over the hill and under the spirit tree. When my heart stopped thumping, I straightened and studied the grinning horsemen.

They were strangers, wearing butternut trousers, and dressed in an assortment of mismatched clothing. Must be Confederates. Worse yet, maybe bushwhackers, men with no allegiance to anyone but themselves, damn cowards and scoundrels, with an unnatural longing for their neighbors' goods and chattel.

Trailing behind the riders, Betsy bellowed. Petted and coddled, the cow was plainly unhappy at being dragged along with a rope. She protested with pitiful bellows. The hog let out a shrill squeal, before snorting like a dog with a fly up its nose.

Big Jolly wasn't but a couple steps behind and near

ran me over. He was heaving hard, too, and dropped to one knee.

"Mister," I gasped, still winded from the race. I squinted to study the unfamiliar faces and cleared my throat. "Mister, must be some mistake. That, there, is my ma's cow. She must have gotten loose for you to find her, but I'd know Betsy's whining anywhere." I strained to see around the horses. "And I swear that sounds like our old hog, Horace."

A rider, tanned to a leathery brown, nudged his roan forward a few steps to block the view. With one arm resting on his saddle pommel, the other on his hip next to a holstered Colt revolver, he stared down, dark eyes peering out from under a battered gray hat, and worked his jaw from side to side.

"Cow? Hog? I don't hear no cow or nothing." A stream of tobacco juice hit the ground in front of me. "You boys hear a cow?"

Several men snickered and looked from one to another, shaking their heads in unison, as if struck deaf as fence posts.

One rider, curly-headed and smooth-faced, looking no older than me, mocked in a girlie voice, "Ohhh, aren't them little birdies I hear tweeting? Must be something wrong with your ears, youngster."

Youngster? I set my teeth tight and studied the kid whose feet barely reached the stirrups. There wasn't much difference between him and me, except a mule, a gun, and a real smart mouth. If the odds were even, I could beat the living daylights out of the little puke jerking the rope and bedeviling Betsy like he was.

It was then I noticed the big mule the kid straddled—its left ear notched and flopped over like a hound dog, upper lip curled under. Othella Johnson's crap-critter!

The dark-eyed rider pointed to Big Jolly. "Hey, Indian, you don't hear a cow, do you? Or you got something wrong with your ears, too?"

Big Jolly, mouth clamped shut, drew himself up and crossed his arms. He slid a glance over the riders and back to the man on the roan but didn't utter a sound.

"Mister, thank you kindly for fetching along that cow and hog. I'll take them off your hands now. In fact—" I glanced back at Little Jolly, who was limping toward us "—we got some fine brownies caught fresh this afternoon. Give 'em to you for all your trouble."

"Hear that, boys? Going to give us some fish for all our trouble."

Sweat trickled down my back and armpits, even watered the palms of my hands. Othella Thompson came out on the short end of the stick, arguing with bushwhackers, but she always was a bossy old woman. Most likely she scolded, didn't try to best-talk them into what she wanted.

"Yes, sir. I'm beholding to you gentlemen for catching Betsy and Horace up. Plenty of folks wouldn't take the time to be so obliging." My mouth was parched as a summer creek, and I tried to swallow the lump in my throat. "Listen to Betsy bawl. She's nigh on to dry, pretty near worthless, but she's my ma's pet."

"I said I don't hear any cow." The dark rider straightened in the saddle. "Like Curly says, you need your ears cleaned out."

His foot slipped free of the stirrup. Next thing I know, he kicked out and caught the side of my head. A burst of pain blocked out the sun and trees, and I saw a rainbow of shooting colors. I felt myself spin forever, hit the ground, and roll, head over heels. Shards of agony screamed through my brain with a power that wrapped itself around my eyeballs and shot out my ears. I could hardly catch my breath—couldn't even cry out—which was probably a good thing. If tears squeezed out my eyes, I'd have never got them stopped.

Nothing to do but cradle my head in my hands, as much to hold it in place as to contain the pain. I pulled up on my knees and tried to focus my vision. Then, I caught sight of my pig again.

Horace lifted his long snout, tested the air, and looked straight at me.

The horses chomped at their bits and pranced in place as the hog fought the rope imbedded in its neck, long strings of spittle looping in all directions. Horace squealed and churned the dirt with his hooves, one minute balking stiff-legged at the rope's tug, the next, charging between the horses' legs and spooking them. He put on quite a show.

Above the hoots and hollers, the dark man's voice growled, "Told you once, Indian, don't move. Not going to tell you again." The click of metal, ratcheting into place, punctuated the command.

"Jolly!" I yelled, bringing a fresh throb of pain. "Jolly! It's all right." I forced my legs to push up, to stand and hold my body upright. "I'm not hurt much," I lied. Nobody's a match for a gun.

Big Jolly, fists clenched, stepped back.

"Murphy, can't you hold that blasted pig?" Curly whined and jerked the reins in an attempt to control the crap-critter. The rope tethering Betsy was wrapped around his hand, and as the cow resisted being yanked, the boy struggled to stay in the saddle.

The mule went stiff-legged, leaned back as if to sit, and then bucked. With a howl, Curly hit the ground. The mule bolted forward past the other riders and galloped down the road.

Horace continued to charge back and forth, bumping everything in his path. The horses panicked. Curly rolled clear of the hog's rage and lost his grip on Betsy's rope. She turned and trotted back up the hill, most likely heading for home.

In the blink of an eye, the dark man twisted in the saddle, aimed his Colt, and fired. The sound echoed through the trees. Startled crows screeched and flapped into the sky. Horses reared. Horace went wild, churning and thrashing at the end of the rope. Again, the man pulled the trigger.

As if they had discovered a new game, the other two riders aimed at the pig. A torrent of bullets thudded into Horace's body, each hit causing him to jump and squeal. Bright red spots sprouted fountains of blood.

I was so dumbfounded I just stood, frozen to the spot, as my old pig thumped to the ground, let out a low groan, and stared right at me with tiny black eyes. With a last accusing look, Horace closed his eyelids, his short legs still pawing the air. Finally, his body sagged. Blood, streaming from his snout and dozens of wounds, pooled in the dirt.

Horace dead? I felt my chest tighten at the horror of such meaness, thought I might choke in the acrid smoke of gunpowder.

Silence, save the snorting of the horses as they calmed down, settled over the riders. The air cleared.

Curly stood, slapping dirt from his pants and shirt. "Blasted pig. Look at what you done." He reared back with one leg and kicked the carcass, then hopped on one foot. "Blast it all to perdition!" he cursed. "Blast it, blast it, blast it!"

The dark rider blew across the barrel of his Colt, spun the chamber, and checked the load. Without looking up, he ordered, "Curly, you lost her. Now get on after that cow." He nodded to another rider. "Fetch up that no-good-poor-excuse for a mule, 'less you want the boy riding double with you. Kid hasn't had a bath in a month of Sundays."

A chuckle rumbled through the men. One of them spurred his horse down the road after Othella's crap-critter.

Curly cast a dirty look at me. "Blasted old cow." He adjusted his holster on his hip and patted the gun that hung nearly to his knee, before turning to limp back up the hill. "Ought to plug her full of holes. See how she likes that."

I clamped my teeth tight. Ought to plug you full of holes, you hind-end-of-a-jackass. See how you like it. It would considerably improve your looks. I took a deep breath and said, instead, "She'll come along if you don't jerk her." Seeing one killing in a day was all I could stomach.

"Hey, you there, hand over them brownies." The dark rider motioned Little Jolly forward with his pistol. "Fish'll go good with a side of ham. And I want that sack, too."

Little Jolly didn't move. He stood, holding the sack of salt on his shoulder with one hand and the strings of fish in the other. It was as if the violence had shaken all the speech out of him.

"Is that cripple deaf? Or doesn't he understand good English?"

Little Jolly's knuckles went white. He didn't say anything. And he didn't give up his hold on the sack and the fish, neither.

"He's not dumb, mister, and he understands English," I said. Even though the action of speaking sent another ripple of pain through my head, my tongue kept forming words, like it had a brain of its own and didn't mind the agony it caused. "I reckon he's just never seen thieving bushwhackers murder a pig before." I bit my lip to silence my tongue and tensed, ready to dodge another blow.

The rider scowled, lifted his leg as if he might kick out again; then, he settled back in the saddle and roared with laughter. "Hear that, boys. We've all done sunk to pig murdering." He leveled his Colt at Little Jolly and said without a glint of humor in his voice, "Won't take but a pull of this trigger to up that distinction a bit."

Big Jolly took a step forward, and I grabbed his elbow. There was no doubt these men wouldn't think twice about gunning down anyone that stood in the way of what they wanted. And, right now, they wanted Ma's sack of salt. The fish were no big loss, but the salt was another matter, and losing it wouldn't be anybody's fault but my own.

"Mister, that's nothing but a little old sack of salt. You've already got our animals." Not likely these men would be charitable with my own goods.

I glanced at the other rider, lounging atop his mount with one leg hooked over the saddle horn. He fished pickles from a jar with two fingers and popped them into his mouth. Bulging gunnysacks hung on either side of his horse.

"Salt?" The group's leader shifted his wad and spit again. "I haven't had salt in my beans since we come down from Missouri. What say, Skinny, must've been when we camped with old Bloody Bill last winter, we last had such a treat. Only thing better would be sugar or coffee, and since you don't appear to have any of that, I reckon salt will do." His finger rubbed back and forth across the curve of the Colt's hammer.

On my worst day, and today was certainly the worst in my memory, I could outrun these ruffians. Big Jolly, too. But not Little Jolly. He couldn't outrun a turtle.

I took a deep breath. "Go on, give it up to them."

Little Jolly frowned. Hugging the salt up to his chest with one arm, he held out the string of brownies. The odor of fish, too long out of water, grew powerful.

"Yeah, them, too," the bushwhacker murmured. "Skinny, fetch them up."

The man with the pickles sighed and stuffed another pickle in his mouth, until his cheeks puffed fat in contrast to his thin face. He nudged his horse forward, reached for the fish, and secured the string around his saddle horn.

"Gimme," he said, bits of pickle escaping his mouth. Then pointed to the sack.

Little Jolly stood holding the sack, as if it were filled with gold instead of salt. His jaws worked, but his mouth remained firmly shut.

Most likely, a story was forming. Only, no story I ever heard could make a thief give back what he stole. I ran a hand over the huge lump that had popped up on the side of my head. Blood smeared my fingers.

"I said give it to them, Lil' Jolly. No salt is worth a bullet."

The Indian hefted the bag up and shoved it toward Skinny.

"Smart kid." Skinny inclined his head toward his boss and added, "He's got a short fuse. We don't cross him." He looked down the road and turned in his saddle. "Hey, Murphy done caught up the stupid mule. Let's get out of here and make camp. I've got a powerful hunger, and looks like we got the right good makings for a feast."

Murphy, leading the mule, trotted through the milling group and trailed up the hill after Curly and Betsy.

"Now," the dark rider leaned forward, resting his arm on his saddle horn again. His gun dangled in his hand. "Lest you think harsh of us, I might explain something to you. These are your ma's animals? Then, your ma is the Widow Fears, and she's raised herself up a passel of Yankee boys. I hear tell as how she's got three sons serving with those criminals that call themselves Union soldiers. That right?"

My throat clenched up. How'd they know about my brothers? About Ma?

"What's wrong? Cat got your tongue?" The bushwhacker grinned, exposing teeth the color of Ma's weak coffee. "Doesn't matter you don't want to answer. We pretty near know everything in these parts. It's treason what she's done, raising up pups that succumb to Lincoln's blasphemy, telling free Southerners what they can and cannot do."

A wave of weakness spread up my legs. Horace

hadn't broken free and strayed down the road rooting for acorns with Betsy trailing after him in search of tender grass. These men had been to my home. Knew about Ma and the boys.

"Now, son, you're young. There's still hope for you." The rider looked at his gun, polished the dull gray barrel with his sleeve, and slipped it back into its holster. "Why don't you redeem the family name, come along with us like Curly done?"

Ride with bushwhackers—miserable skunks that went around stealing from widows. My tongue pushed against my teeth. I bit my lip again, before my tongue started listening to my brain and lashed out.

"How about it?" The rider leaned forward as if telling a great secret. "The South is going to win. Oh, we may be a little down right now; things not going good. But the South will win, never you doubt it. Right is on our side, you know. Now, how about riding along with us?"

I swallowed back a mouthful of curses.

When the bushwhacker didn't receive an answer to his question, he jabbed the air with one finger. "We're not going to forget those that had their chance to come over and didn't."

Skinny tipped the pickle jar to his lips and drained the liquid dry. He grimaced, let out a loud burp, and wiped his mouth with his sleeve. "Aww, leave the kid be. Yonder comes Murphy and Curly. We don't need any more wet-behind-the-ears boys. If you ask me, Curly hasn't been anything but trouble since he joined up with us."

With a fury, the rider snapped at Skinny. "Well, I didn't ask you." He turned, brows furrowed into a scowl. "Think on what I said. And tell your ma Shilo Riddle and his boys will be back sometime for that chicken dinner she didn't fix us." Then, flicking the ends of his reins against his horse's withers, he proceeded down the road.

Shrugging, Skinny tossed the empty pickle jar into the bushes and wrapped the rope tied to Horace around his saddle horn. The pig's carcass jerked as the rope pulled taut and disturbed a blanket of flies drawn by the blood. Murphy trotted past and joined the group that was now stirring a cloud of dust.

Slouched in the saddle, Curly trailed behind on the stubbornest mule that ever lived. "I'm leading your old cow easy," he mumbled to me as he passed.

With her head pulled high by the tethered halter, Betsy rolled large soft brown eyes at me and let out a sorrowful bawl.

The plea might as well have been a knife. Throat tight, I watched as the star-kissed cow and the unfortunate Horace disappeared down the road. All of a sudden, I couldn't breathe. My legs just wilted out from under me. I dropped to the ground. The bittersweet taste of possum grapes visited my mouth, and I near gagged.

The twins knelt. "You all right?" they both asked at once.

"I'm not ever going to be all right." I looked up, and the motion renewed the throb in my head. "Horace, killed, right before my eyes."

Little Jolly spit into his palm and held it out for his brother to do the same.

"And Ma. You don't reckon they've done harm to Ma, do you?"

Little Jolly didn't answer, just scooped a measure

35

of dirt up with his fingers, sifted it into his palm, and stirred a thick paste of spit and dirt with one finger. He pressed the mud against my wound to staunch the ooze of blood. Even his gentle touch hurt powerful.

I pushed to my feet and fought a new wave of nausea as I started up the hill. The spirit tree loomed, black and ugly, at the top.

"I got to get home. Got to find out what's happened to Ma."

Chapter 5

No matter how wobbly my legs claimed to be, I had to get home. Each thud against the dirt road sent daggers into my aching head. The bushwhackers had threatened Ma, most likely stole Horace and Betsy right in front of her face. And Ma wouldn't give up Betsy without a fight. Horace, maybe, but not Betsy.

Normally, when I hadn't been knocked silly, I could run a fair piece, but not now. By the time I got to the top of the hill, I had to stop and catch my breath. Only then did the throb behind my eyes ease. A long spindly branch of the old spirit-tree loomed overhead. It dangled in the breeze, as if to point a charred and crooked finger and accuse me of leaving Ma unprotected. Catching a bushel of fish couldn't make up for the worry I felt twisting my gut into knots.

Big Jolly skirted the reach of the tree's shadow and waited a few feet away. Indians feared the lightning spirit that lived inside. Maybe they were right. The branch moved like it wanted to slap me for my sin of selfishness. I gulped a big lung full of air and pushed away from its grasping arms.

Light green oak, maple, and hackberry leaves, and silvery-blue cedar needles blurred to a tunnel of color closing in tight along the road. I could feel Big Jolly's presence running alongside. It was a comfort—a comfort to know that, if the throb in my head struck me blind, or worse, struck me dead—someone would check on Ma.

The road widened and split in two directions. We turned north toward Cedarville and passed the Everlasting Church at the Crossroads, paint weathered, windows boarded, and door barred. It was a sad reminder of Sunday morning sermons and afternoon picnics under the sheltering shade of ageless oaks. It had been two years, maybe, since a minister of the gospel dared travel in these parts. Three large stones, stacked one on top of the other, marked the path toward our cabin.

Just when home was close, a wave of nausea pushed into my throat, and my knees went soft. The fear of what I'd find near doubled me over.

Big Jolly grabbed my arm. "You all right?" He was gasping, too, with the seriousness of the run.

"Not likely." I struggled to breathe. "Feels like the devil laid his boot to the side of my skull." By now, I was on the ground. Blood oozed again from the wound, and the ache mushroomed into my eyes. "My belly feels a mite clabbered, too."

"Look." Big Jolly pointed toward the marker stones. I blinked hard to focus my eyesight on the pillar of rocks.

Two feathers danced atop the big rocks and swirled into the air. Several more lifted to join them and then fluttered to the ground when the breeze stilled. As the wind rose and fell, so did other bits of fluff, twirling up and around, catching on tall stalks of grass, landing in bushes, layering the ground.

Feathers—some pure white, others tinged with brown or black—trailed from the path onto the road.

They trembled as if exhausted from their flight; yet never quite settled, always ready to lift into the air again.

Big Jolly looked at me and shrugged. I pushed to my feet and started walking. Dozens of feathers became hundreds that fluttered with each step we took past rambling blackberry bushes boasting greenish berries not near ripe and guarded by needle-sharp thorns.

The path curved around a hillock covered by a grove of apple trees. Trees planted when I was a babe, trees that had grown with me and were now mature and strong. They sheltered the cabin from the blazing afternoon sun in summer and buffered it from cold winds in winter.

It was then that I heard it—a song that seemed to rise from the very earth. High pitched and quivery, but definitely my mother's voice. Were my ears deceiving me? Ma never sang. She laughed, she teased, she scolded, but she never sang, except on Sundays. And that, she said, was so the Highest of High would remember she was still here. She said song left her soul the day my father died.

Around the bend of the hill, the woods parted, opening into a small clearing. A two-room cabin, built for the Widow Fears by friends and neighbors, sat framed by tall hollyhock stalks on one side and an herb garden, crowded with all manner of remedies—rosemary, sage, horehound, basil, dill, and fennel—on the other. Our wide porch, sagging with age, ran the width of the house.

Mounds of feathers covered the ground. There, in the middle of them, sat Ma. Solitary feathers floated in the air, aimless, like the first snowflakes of winter. She reached to catch one in her hand. Patches of late afternoon sunlight sliced through long shadows cast by the trees, firing Ma's red hair with a golden glow. Surrounded by feathers and wearing her gray dress, she looked, for all the world, an angel—an angel come down to earth, shedding her wings and singing the praises of God.

I stopped up short. Relief flooded through me. Ma didn't look hurt, but there she sat, singing. *Singing!* And it wasn't even near being Sunday.

Big Jolly touched my shoulder. When I turned to look at him, I could see in his eyes the same puzzlement that churned deep in my chest.

I fought the urge to run and gather Ma in my arms, but something held me back. It was as if doing so would shatter the spell, like a fine china cup dropped on the hearth. Instead, I walked, slow and deliberate, toward her.

"Be thou my vision, O Lord 'o my heart," sang Ma, her wobbly voice rising and falling with each intake of air. She paused to study a feather, dusted it with her fingers, then dropped it in her lap and resumed the chorus to the ancient Irish hymn, "Naught be all else to me, save that thou art."

"Ma? Ma, you all right?"

She looked up, mouth poised to begin a new verse. Instead, her lip trembled, and she sucked it in between her teeth. Tears welled in the corners of her eyes. For a moment, I thought she was going to cry. It was a show of emotion reserved only for the death of close relatives, one I had seen only a couple times in my life. Ma was not the sort of woman to blubber and take on.

"Ebby!" She scrambled to her feet, spilling feathers

from her lap, grabbed me around the neck, and pulled me close. A fluffy cloud floated up, hovering for a moment before settling around us.

I held Ma tight. I was taller and had been for at least two years, but just now, I felt confused—like a child wanting the comfort of his mother's arms and like a protector ready to do battle.

"You were singing, Ma."

"Aye, and praying, too," she whispered. "I been singing for the Lord's attention for ever so long, and I feared He nay liked my song." She released her grip on me and looked down. "Oh, I dropped them. Help me. They're flying away." She squatted and scooped handfuls of feathers into the folds of her dress. "They're making an awful mess."

I took her hands and looked straight into her eyes. For the first time in my life, they were dull. Little Jolly limped into the clearing and joined his brother standing a few feet away. Neither boy said anything. Ma didn't seem to notice they were there.

"Are you hurt, Ma?" She looked fine, but clearly, she wasn't. "What happened? Are you hurt?"

"Hurt?" She glanced down at the blush of bruises on her wrists and hands. "Nay. 'Tis naught but a small matter. Betsy, now, be another matter." She shook her head and frowned. "They took Betsy. Horace, too. The spawn of Beelzebub, himself, came and took her. 'Tis my fault. I let them loose to graze."

"Nothing is your fault, Ma. Animals got to eat, and nobody knows when bushwhackers choose to come around stirring up mischief. If anybody is to fault, it's me. I should have been here."

"Oh, no." Ma's eyes grew wild-looking. "'Tis a

blessing you weren't. Told me they'd learn me better than to raise up Yankee boys. No." She lowered her voice. "They would have done you harm if you'd been home."

"I should have been here. I can take care of myself."

"Can you now?" She pulled one hand free, reached up, and ran her fingers across my forehead. Even her light touch pained me. "'Tis a wicked look you have there, Ebby. You come across those hooligans, did you?"

"It's nothing. Nothing more than an accident." I waved her hand away. No use upsetting her any more than she already was. "Those bruises on your arms may be a small matter to you, Ma. But they aren't to me. How'd you come by them? I don't recollect them being there this morning."

Ma relaxed onto the ground, scooping and cradling feathers in the skirt of her dress again. "Why, it must have been when the leader took offense. He was a big man, with eyes like burned out pieces of coal. Not a bit of light in them. He marched himself into the smokehouse and fetched out that big ham I've been saving for the boys and the last of the cornmeal we ground at the mill last fall. Took the jar of apple butter and my quince jam, too. Even took me last jar of pickles. The one with a big dose of alum in it. Remember, eat too many, and they double back on you?"

"Ma! I'm not interested in those pickles." When Ma didn't want to talk about something, she always talked around the subject. "How'd you get those bruises?"

"Well, one of those other hooligans rounded up the Dominickers, told me to fix 'em dinner." She frowned with the memory. "I started to tell them they could starve. Then I remembered Othella Thompson and how they killed her cat and made off with her crap-critter, so first time in my life, I bit me tongue. I knew Betsy be lazing about in the shade of those trees yonder, and I didn't want them finding her."

She rolled her eyes toward the house. I followed her gaze and felt my stomach lurch again. I'd been so intent on Ma, the gruesome sight escaped my notice. Both chickens hung by their feet, upside down, in the entrance to the cabin. It wasn't the fact that they were limp and headless, with their wings sagged open, that bothered me. I'd beheaded chickens since I was old enough to swing an ax. It was seeing them hanging in the doorway. The church bell didn't have to fall on me to know a threat when I saw one.

What had Shilo Riddle said? He'd come back for that chicken dinner Ma didn't fix. Now, there was no doubt about the need to leave with the rest of the neighbors and head north to Fayetteville. Whether or not Ma wanted to go.

"I had hold 'o me tongue until the big one came out, dragging Grannie McDonald's wedding ring quilt. He wadded it up and stuffed it in his toting sack. Grannie McDonald's quilt! And, Lord forgive me, I wished him to burn in hell for his thieving ways. He was an angry man, and 'tis a fact, I lit a fuse with those words." She shook her head. "That evil devil took to shaking me and shouting unmentionables, his face darker than a storm cloud. Don't rightly know why, but old Horace came charging out of the woods. Caused such a commotion, the hooligan let go me arms and roped poor old Horace and took to dragging him about instead of me."

Gathering another armful of feathers in her lap, she continued, "And before I knew it, they dragged me mattress out, split the ticking, and run their horses back and forth. Feathers flew everywhere." She shook her head again. "Looked like Christmas, it did. Put them in a cheerful mood, laughing and joking. Then they were gone, with most everything we had. Me darlin' Betsy, gone. And poor Horace. Poor, poor Horace." Her shoulders slumped, and she let out a sigh. "Got nothing left but feathers."

I let Ma go back to retrieving feathers from the dirt and walked over to the twins. "Have your pa stop for us on your way north. We're not going to be here when those thieving brutes come back for their chicken supper. I've never seen Ma like this. Reckon she needs a doctor?"

Little Jolly put a hand on my shoulder. "One day, brother wolf have fine rabbit for meal. Wolf settle down to eat, and along come hungry mountain lion. Mountain lion is big, with long teeth, sharp claws. He snatch rabbit from mouth of wolf. Wolf never see mountain lion before. Wolf run like coyote with tail between legs. Spirit broken and body shaken. Soon, brother wolf hungry again and hunt for rabbit. Only now, wolf smart. Watch for mountain lion before settling down to eat."

Ma hugged the mound of feathers up to her chest. Her voice, heavy with the land of Ireland, sang mournfully in the stillness of the late afternoon. "Thou be me best thought, by day or by night, waking or sleeping, thy presence me light."

Ma's spirit was broken all right. I just hoped that it would right itself like brother wolf. But if Shilo Riddle was the mountain lion, it would take more than a sharp eye to outsmart him.

Feathers caught in the fabric of Ma's sleeves. Watching her pluck at them, I knew what I had to do, and Ma wasn't going to like it. Not one little bit.

Chapter 6

Clouds of dust rolled from under the wheels of Levi Standing Corn's loaded wagon as it rumbled along the dirt road. Ma sat in her old rocker, perched on the back of the wagon bed. She gripped the wooden arms each time the wagon hit a rut, threatening to spill her and the rocker onto the road. It was the only piece of furniture taken when we said our goodbyes to the cabin seeing as how she wouldn't consent to leave without it.

Ma rocked all four of us boys in that rocker. Childish teeth-marks marred the oaken arms, which were worn dark from years of use. The carved headrest sported a crack across its width, put there when brothers, Willy and Jim, rocked so hard it tipped backward and crashed to the floor.

Little Jolly and me fanned the air to rid ourselves of the plague of mosquitoes hungry for our blood. "Darn gallnippers," I said and slapped his arm, killing two bitty tormentors with one blow. I nodded toward Ma. "She's better today, don't you think?"

Little Jolly rubbed his arm and studied Ma for a minute. "Sometimes wolf lay in sun, eyes closed. Look asleep to me and you. Inside, ears hear, nose smell, claws ready for fight."

"Yeah, well, I dunno. Just wish Ma would eat something. I had to pluck those chickens and fry them up, myself. She wouldn't touch them. Said they were unclean because the devil had laid hands on them."

It wasn't like Ma to let vittles go to waste, just like it wasn't like her to be talking about dying. That morning, she said she never intended to be buried anywhere but on her land. Then she sat in her memory chair and started rocking, like she was waiting for the event.

I dabbed sweat from my forehead with cautious fingers. A dull ache still lived in my temple. My left eyelid, which had taken offense at being jarred silly, turned a deep purple. It swelled up like a horny toad and near scared me to death when I looked in the mirror.

If Ma had been in her usual frame of mind, she would have smelled my excuse of hitting my head on a rock as the lie it was. I studied her, sitting in the rocker with her eyes shut tight, red hair curled in moist ringlets around her face. Like, if she didn't see the miles fall away, she wouldn't have to admit we were leaving home.

The tingle of pain in my head was punishment, plain and simple. Served me right. I'd promised my brothers to see after Ma, and I'd failed. Without a weapon, I might not have been able to stop their thieving, but Shilo Riddle would never have laid filthy hands on Ma. Somehow, I would have seen to that.

Big Jolly skirted the wagon and jogged back to where me and Little Jolly herded two milk cows down the center of the road. If Ma weren't so fragile-minded, I'd be out scouting the countryside, too, looking for sign of an ambush. A lone wagon was a sure invitation to ruffians out for easy pickings.

"Hey, Jolly, any sign of those bushwhackers up

ahead?"

He shook his head and fell into step beside us.

If Shilo Riddle and his boys were anywhere within a mile or two, he'd know we were coming for sure. Metal cooking pans swung from pegs on the side of the wagon, clanging against each other and keeping a loud rhythm that, along with the groans of an overloaded vehicle, would most likely raise the dead.

The two cows, tired after a long day of travel, bawled their need for water and rest. More than once, I wished they'd lose their hollering boxes. It wasn't because they added to the commotion, but the constant complaint was sure to remind Ma of Betsy. And Betsy was best forgotten.

Heavy timber cast deep shadows when the wagon slowed at a clearing and turned off the rutted road. The smoke of woodfire hung in the air. The cattle, sagging utters swinging, picked up their pace and trotted toward a bubbling creek.

Another wagon occupied the clearing. It was guarded by a bearded old man with a rifle nestled in the bend of his arm. Two young boys peered out from behind the skirts of a gray-haired woman.

"*Osiyo*," Levi Standing Corn said, calling out the Cherokee greeting. "Mind we stay the night?" The twin's father sat, reins threaded between his fingers, dark complexion belying the fact that his mother was rumored to have been half-white.

"Sir, I think that be old man Casey from over to Lee's Creek," I said. The Caseys were known to keep to themselves. They were suspicious of outsiders and none too personable. Of course, most hill people tended to be that way.

"Depends," Mr. Casey said and walked toward us, leather straps flapping against his boots.

"Depends on what?" Levi questioned.

"Depends on whether you are Yankee or Secesh?"

The two men stared at each other. My palms went to sweating. In truth, I'd never heard the twin's father voice an opinion. One thing I did know, old man Casey was as Union as Abraham Lincoln. He'd proclaimed his sentiments at the last church revival, along with the fact that God would smite the South a mighty blow. Then he'd sat and not said another word, while friends and neighbors argued the righteousness of each side.

"Well," Mr. Casey demanded. "Which side you favor?"

"Neither."

"What's that you say?" The old man lifted his head and cupped his ear, trying to hear the answer.

"Neither." Levi's deep voice was flat, without tone, just matter-of-fact. That was the thing about Indians, unless you knew them personal, it was hard to tell whether they were friendly or otherwise.

"Neither." Mr. Casey's bushy eyebrows shot up. "Whatcha mean, neither?" the old man roared, his long beard dancing over his chest. "A man's got to know where he stands, leastwise he gets blasted to the Everlasting."

Levi shrugged, rose from the wagon seat, and jumped down. Tall and thick bodied, he was an imposing figure next to the bent old man, who stroked the barrel of his rifle like a favorite cat. The threat seemed entirely lost on the twin's father as he turned his back to unhitch the two mules. Impatient for water, they snorted and shook their heads, long ears perked forward.

"I said," Mr. Casey raised his voice, "I got to know where you stand as regards this confounded rebellion. Not gonna let no Rebel sympathizers share the night here. No, I'm not." He ceased caressing his weapon, balanced the barrel in one hand, and slid the other hand back to the trigger. "Why, that'd just be asking to get whipped up on and robbed. And I'm not of a mind to be whipped up on."

The twin's father unsnapped the last buckles on the harnesses, slapped the mules on the rump, and sent the animals toward the creek. He squared his shoulders and turned to face the old man.

Goosebumps flashed along my scalp. For an instant, I saw the fierceness of Cherokee ancestors in Levi's glare. Strong. Not intimidated by an unspoken threat.

"Your kind war upon ancestors before my eyes know light of day. Many years ago, grandparents come, settle on land here, no more to fight with white man. Here, trees thick, rocks many. Grandparents think your kind not want to set plow to ground in this place. They wrong." He stopped for a moment to look at his sons, then back to Mr. Casey. "This time much trouble boils up in white nation. It not our fight. It *your* fight. Levi Standing Corn on neither side. I wait, maybe I lucky. Maybe white man kill each other off."

Levi waved toward the wagon. "My animals, these women tired. Need rest, need water. We stay." With that, he turned and walked to the other side of the wagon to help Martha Standing Corn down.

Mr. Casey's mouth wavered as if he wanted to say something but couldn't think what. Finally, he cleared his throat and relaxed his hold on the rifle. "Humph. As long's you know I'm not abiding any blasted Rebels, I reckon you can spend the night. Better we company up. Safer that way." He glanced around at the trees and headed back for his own campfire.

For a minute it was quieter than prayer time at church, and then the Jolly brothers blew air through clamped lips. I released a lung full of air that I had holed up in my mouth, too.

"I reckon that's the longest speech I ever heard your pa give."

Big Jolly nodded. "Me, too."

"Reckon that old coot would have shot your pa?"

Little Jolly shrugged. "When only one rooster in chicken yard, him strut big. Another rooster come along, stretch neck high, puff feathers out, first rooster sometimes not so brave."

"Tarnation. Can't you ever answer a question without making a man think? Are you saying the first rooster was old man Casey, there, and the second rooster…"

A deep throat-clearing sounded behind us. We all swung around. Levi Standing Corn held a large blackened kettle in one hand and a wooden crate under the other arm. He didn't say anything. He didn't have to. Both Jollys turned and hurried into the brush, picking up sticks as they went.

"I was, uh…" I backed toward the rear of the wagon. "I'll get Ma, sir. Then, I'll be about helping gather up wood for the night."

Ma sat in her rocker, looking at the heavens. "'Tis a right pretty sky. Nary a breath of rain in the air. Should be nice for sleeping under the stars."

For the moment, the setting sun's orange blush held darkness at bay. The effort was futile. Already, inky fingers crept in from the east.

"Ma would say someone left the door to heaven ajar, and the Lord's glory slipped out to color the night and remind us His love be eternal." She sighed. "For a truth, 'tis a right pretty sky."

"That it is, Ma. Remember the Caseys? They live over by Lee's Creek."

Ma rested both hands on my shoulders and let me lift her down. She frowned.

"Sure, you remember, don't you? They come to the Reverend Bullard's Revival two summers back. Two wagons of 'em. The old man wasn't over talkie, but reckon the others were friendly enough."

Ma nodded. "Mrs. Casey puts pe-cans in her sweet potato pie. I remember that. Not many lavish such treats on a sweet potato pie."

"They're camped over yonder." I slid the rocker off the wagon, turned it upside down, and balanced the seat on top of my head. "You might want to say your howdy-dos. I'll put your memory chair right by the campfire. You go on over for a visit."

"No." Ma shook her head. "Haven't got anything to say."

I stared at Ma. She stood, brushing out wrinkles in her skirt. In my lifetime, I couldn't ever remember her being at a loss for words. Not even last winter when her throat seized up painful. She just coughed and wheezed her way through telling me what to do.

I carried the rocker around to where Levi arranged stones for a fire and set it down, then guided Ma to it. Martha stopped in the middle of transferring a handful of ground corn into the kettle and smiled. She had been taught to read and write. A waste of good learning in some people's mind, since she had only a thimble of white blood in her veins. Educated like she was, Martha had taken up the habit of talking freely, even when not being spoken to first.

"How you feeling, Catherine? Imagine you glad to be on firm ground for a piece."

Ma nodded, settled back in the rocker, and set it in motion.

Martha dusted the cornmeal from her hands and looked up at me. I couldn't do anything but shrug. She and Ma had been friends for as long as I could remember, and when one stopped talking to draw a breath, the other took up the conversation.

Now, Ma acted like doing anything other than rocking was more than she had energy for. It wasn't like her. I kicked a rock toward the campfire and turned to join the twins who were gathering firewood. Blast those bushwhackers, scaring the words right out of Ma's mouth. A bruise to the head was a sight easier to get over than a bruise to the soul.

After dinner, I was so tired even the hard ground was a comfort. I'd barely closed my eyes, when a hand clapped down on my shoulder, and I thought sure Shilo Riddle had come back. I was about to give out a holler until the glow from the smoldering campfire lit up Little Jolly's face. He frowned and bent close.

"Your turn," he whispered and shoved several pieces of kindling in the fire.

"Already?" I stretched to work a kink out of my back and yawned so big my jaws all but come unhinged. "Seems like I hardly got to sleep."

"Look." Little Jolly pointed to the moon, nearly straight overhead. "Your turn." He jerked the blanket off my shoulders.

"Hey, give that back. Want me to freeze to death while I'm standing guard?"

"Shush!" Little Jolly hissed again. "Cold is good. Keep sleepyhead awake."

"Well, what if it doesn't? I can hardly keep my eyes open."

"Here, take this."

It was then I noticed what Little Jolly was holding. A sure-enough Indian weapon. Three long bear claws, imbedded at one end of a stout handle and secured with rawhide strips, curved out in a wicked threat. No doubt about the meanness it was meant to deliver.

"Goose gravy. What am I supposed to do with this?"

Flames jumped along the fresh timber. Little Jolly held his arm out in the radiance. Long scratches whelped his skin. "Feel sleep come, pain wake up."

"If I want pain, I can poke the side of my head." I took the weapon and turned it in my hand. It had a nice feel, with a bit of heft to it. The sharp claws glistened in the light. "Don't have to go marking myself to keep awake." I gripped the wooden handle. "Still, this might make a good 'nipper bat."

With a shrug, Little Jolly yawned and wrapped the blanket around his shoulders. "Belong to grandfather's grandfather." He pushed skimpy bunches of grass into a mound with the toe of his foot, settled down, and pulled his knees up. Within minutes, his breathing eased into a steady rhythm.

I shoved my feet into my boots and stood. Big Jolly

curled up on the other side of the campfire. Levi and Martha slept under the wagon, sheltered from the dew that already gathered on blades of grass.

I tiptoed to the back of the wagon and allowed my eyes to adjust to the dark. A mass of curls poked from beneath a quilt. Ma slept peaceful enough, although I didn't know how. She'd barely eaten a bite of Martha's steaming bowl of cornmeal pudding. I'd gulped down two bowls, savoring the bits of wild onions and peppers that flavored the meal.

Being careful not to step on the boys, I retraced my steps past the campfire and crossed the clearing toward the trees.

Levi declared the need for night watchers, and no one, not even old man Casey, disputed the necessity. The fires had been too large, billowing too much smoke in the air; the cattle, horses, and mules too noisy; loaded and poorly guarded wagons too much of a temptation.

Mindful of where I stepped, I threaded my way around the animals, their tails in constant motion against night insects. One cow glanced at me, her jaws working a cud of grass. The mules and horses were hobbled to prevent them from straying into the forest, as well as to slow down any thief that might think to make off with our animals.

A large hickory tree cast great arms over dozens of willowy seedlings that had grown two feet high. Without sun and robbed of moisture by the giant tree, most would wilt and wither by the time midsummer's heat struck. But now, young and energetic, they slapped at my pant legs as I waded through them.

I tucked the bear claw weapon under my belt and jumped for a low branch. Bark crumbled beneath my grip as I swung up, straddled the limb, and reached for a yet higher branch.

When I judged myself to be about seven feet up, I searched out a perch that afforded a view through the jumble of leaves—one where several branches attached to the trunk and formed a suitable sitting space.

The blaze of the campfire illuminated Levi's wagon and the sleeping twins. Old man Casey's fire had dwindled to a bare glow. The entire family had climbed into the covered wagon and pulled the flap tight against the night air.

Moonlight filtered through the foliage, and I stretched to catch a good look at the silvery orb which was half its usual size. Little Jolly said the moon fasted now, soon to become only a skeleton, before it feasted and appeared again with a fat round face.

Sometime in the distant past, Levi's grandfather's grandfather had stood guard with this same bear claw weapon. Probably against bloodthirsty savages from the east. Maybe Mohawks with their heads shaved, except for a strip down the middle, or Mohicans with scalps dangling from their waist. It was a comfort to have such a mighty weapon keep me company, and I choked back a yawn.

Grasshoppers chirruped in the tall weeds. Below me, a mule wandered near, nibbling tender shoots. Down the creek, bullfrogs bellowed, competing to see who could be the loudest. Any other time I would be out froggin.' Not tonight. Tonight, I stood guard.

I leaned against the broad tree trunk and crossed my arms, with the club handle tucked in my elbow. Another yawn stretched my mouth wide, and I fought the heaviness in my eyelids. Maybe I'd close them for just a minute.

A sharp prick shot through my arm, and I near yelped. Instead, I sucked air through my teeth and stared at the bear claw embedded in my forearm. Must be my arms relaxed, and the weapon slipped and fell forward. Stupid. Even the weapon was a better guard. I rubbed the puncture wounds with the heel of my hand, to dull the ache, and glanced out at the wagons.

Both campfires were near out. Spindly threads of smoke lazied from the ashes. Around the bend of the creek, one lone bullfrog still croaked. The grasshoppers were quiet. I sat straight up. It was too early for quiet—insects carried on until almost dawn.

A rustle sounded, stopped, sounded again. I held my breath, scanning the ground. The mule snorted. Below me a dark figure moved toward the animal, then it crouched, clucking in soft tones to entice the mule near.

Mule thief. A sneaking, good-for-nothing mule thief right below me. I gripped the handle of the bear claw. It warmed in my palm, and I could feel its power surge up my arm. Another figure passed below me heading toward the other mule. Two of them. Maybe more. I was afraid to swallow, afraid to move. They'd have guns, for sure.

Chapter 7

The hair on my head pretty near stood on end. From my perch high in the tree, I counted two and then four figures creeping along the ground. The two Jolly brothers lay curled beside the fire; Levi and Martha underneath the wagon; and Ma snuggled into a quilt at the back of the wagon. Everyone asleep—easy prey for cowardly thieves that walked on silent feet.

If I had a gun, I could make short work of the miserable mule thieves before they got to Ma and my friends. All I had for defense was the Cherokee bear claw. My thumb rubbed the smooth handle, and the weapon trembled in my hand. It was all I needed. I was sure of it.

Directly below, a fifth man clucked to the hobbled mule. The soft swish of a knife being drawn from a leather scabbard stirred me to action. If the hobbles were cut, the animal would bolt to freedom.

I pulled myself into a crouching position and sucked in a lungful of air. From deep within, a cry pushed its way up my throat and filled the night. A cry of revenge. Sharp. Piercing. Angry. A cry of Indian warriors rushing to battle.

I didn't know I had such a scream in me. It boiled my blood, and still screaming, I pushed off the branch and dropped down. For an instant, my breath was stolen, and the warrior's cry died as I fell right on top of the thief.

We rolled and slammed into the mule's legs. The animal hopped about and brayed in panic. Hobbled like it was, the mule couldn't get out of our way, and we sure couldn't get out of his. If the mule fell on us, we'd be crushed flatter than one of Ma's hard corncakes.

The knife flashed through the air toward me. There wasn't room to swing my weapon unless I released my hold on the thief. I had a wildcat by the tail, and to let go of the tail, I risked the teeth. The brute was all arms and legs.

It was a desperate move to make, but I wasn't at all sure how long I could hold on. I let go and rolled away in one powerful shove. The scream that died was refueled and tore from my throat again. We both got to our feet, and the thief lunged forward. I dodged. Like it had a mind of its own, the claw swished through the air and smashed into flesh. I felt the blow travel through my body and nearly fell backward.

With a shriek, the thief dropped his knife and clutched his cheek with both hands. For the first time, I got a good look at who I was fighting.

"You." I huffed and could hardly talk.

Shoulders heaving, Curly, the young blond-headed bushwhacker who had deviled Betsy, backed against the mule. He pulled bloodied hands away from his face and gazed at them. Three long gashes ran down the side of his face. Blood streamed to his neck, soaking his shirt.

I grasped the bear claw in both hands and felt the strength of warriors come on me again. "I'll knock your ugly head clean off your worthless body."

The air quivered with shouts and curses. A shot

thundered from somewhere, but I focused on the boy in front of me. I was intent on delivering another blow—a mighty blow to make up for all the misery of the past two days.

Curly covered his face with one arm and held the other up to ward off my attack.

It was then I heard Ma scream, and it stopped me in my tracks. For the first time, I glanced away because I knew, for certain, there were four other bushwhackers.

Ma stood at the back of the wagon, clad in her white nightgown, looking like a ghostly haunt in the moonlight. A man reached toward her. A glint of metal flashed in his hand.

The twins rose and fell, struggling with their attackers.

From the corner of my eye, I saw Curly lunge for his dropped knife.

The claw, grasp tight in my hand, took up the battle again and swung out toward the shadow.

Curly cried, grabbed his arm, and fled toward the woods.

My feet seemed heavy as anvils as I raced across the clearing, willing one foot in front of the other. Saplings grabbed at my legs threatening to trip me. I had to get to Ma.

Above the bray of the mules and the curses of the bushwhackers, I heard another scream. It gathered mountainous strength and shocked the air, echoing over and over.

Blood froze in my veins, and for an instant, I almost lost my footing with the terrifying cry. It wasn't Ma's, and it certainly wasn't mine.

Levi Standing Corn, faintly illuminated by the

glow of the campfire, stood stark naked with long black hair loosened around his shoulders. He shrieked as if calling his ancestors from their graves to join the fight. He lifted a bushwhacker off one of his sons, hoisted him over his head, and threw the man against the side of the wagon. The wagon rocked, causing the pots and pans hanging from its sides, to clatter. Ma lost her balance and tumbled into the arms of the renegade pointing a gun at her. Gunpowder flashed.

My feet sprouted wings, shook off the anvils, and flew at the wagon. I gripped the handle of the bear claw. As if called to action by the war whoop, the weapon swung in a wide circle, and I hung onto it for dear life.

Ma was a blur of motion—arms and legs flailing in all directions. The bushwhacker shoved her to the ground and turned, gun pointed straight at me.

Ma screamed, "No!" She lunged for the man's legs just before the gun roared, sending a blinding flash my way.

The bullet's hiss ripped a path through the air, and the burn of flying powder singed my ear.

In the next instant, I was on the man and loosened the power of the bear claw. The force of the blow fairly shook my arm from its socket and knocked the bushwhacker to his knees.

With a howl, the man fell backward. His gun, torn free of his grip, tumbled end-over-end and thumped to the ground. He regained his footing and spun around in search of the weapon.

Another man tore past us, nearly colliding with the fumbling bushwhacker. "Run!" he hollered at the top of his lungs. "Run!"

Still whooping, Levi charged around the end of the wagon after the escaping attacker.

Both bushwhackers fled across the road, with Levi close on their heels.

Old man Casey, clad only in his long johns, huffed up to the wagon. "Stand back, Indian!" he bellowed. "Let Ol' Hickory here blast them heathens to perdition."

Levi glanced back, saw the stance of the old man, and dove to the ground.

"Hell's coming to get ya!" Casey called after the fleeing figures. He hoisted his long rifle and with barely time for an aim pulled the trigger.

The barrel responded with a deafening roar, belching a cloud of acrid smoke. Across the clearing, several branches groaned and split away from their trunks.

The bushwhacker's lost pistol glinted in the grass, and I jumped to get it, but Ma scooped it up.

"One of you hooligans forgot something," she screamed toward the trees. "I'll be sending it your way." She struggled to pull the hammer back with both thumbs. Holding the gun out at arm's length, the four-pound heft of it strained a level aim.

Levi, who had pushed to his knees, saw her and flattened himself on the ground again, hands over his head.

"Ma, let me…" I shouted.

The gun's explosion knocked Ma off her feet and into my arms.

Flashes of light streaked back at us from the depths of the surrounding forest. A bullet slammed into the wagon bed which spit out a shower of splinters.

I pushed Ma down and fell on top of her.

Mr. Casey, struggling to reload his Springfield, hunkered on his knees. "Keep your top knots down," he ordered while ramming a paper of powder and a bullet down the muzzle.

The command was unnecessary. As suddenly as it had all started, it stopped. Even the panicked hee-hawing of the mules quieted. Powder smoke settled, leaving a sting to the air.

From the far wagon, the old man's wife called, "Gordon, you aren't killed, are you?"

"Hell, woman," he answered, "them tick turds don't have good enough aim to hit me."

Even though the ring of Ol' Hickory was still in my ears, the impulse to laugh was mighty strong. I clamped my lips shut to prevent its escape. The force was too powerful. It finally broke free the only way it could, through my nose.

Ma raised her head and grinned wide enough for her cheeks to dimple. It was the first time I had seen her smile in two days, and the sight couldn't have been more welcome than a squad of troopers trotting down the road.

"Hey, boy, what's that Indian's name?" Casey murmured, breaking the spell. "I didn't set it to memory."

Down on one knee, the old man rested his elbow on the other. His rifle was snugged into his shoulder and aimed at the stand of trees on the other side of the road.

"It's Levi Standing Corn, sir."

"Levi, I got a bead on them trees behind you. You want to quit hugging the dirt, I reckon its safe enough now. Any of them brigands want to shoot you in the back, me and Ol' Hickory'll be on 'em like a coon dog on a opossum."

Levi pushed up onto one elbow and looked around. Slowly, he stood tall, turned, and walked back to the wagon, almost as if to dare any shadow-thief to shoot.

"Merciful heavens." Ma gasped at the sight of a full-grown man, naked and proud-made. She buried her face in her hands.

Martha appeared and held out a blanket.

Levi snatched the offering from her hand and wrapped it around his waist. He turned to the old man. "They not be back tonight. Like coyote, they crawl off to lick wounds. Maybe—" he looked around the side of the wagon "—that one not so lucky."

"Wow," I said. "You mean you got one of them bushwhackers?"

A rush of excitement surged through me, and I plumb forgot my wrenched shoulder and the renewed throb to my head. I grabbed the bear claw up and followed the others to the campfire.

Sprawled out on the ground, as peaceful as a napping youngster, lay a long, skinny ruffian, eyes closed. Big Jolly stood, pointing the man's own gun at him. Little Jolly sat cross-legged next to the campfire, nursing a cut to his chin.

The old man's wife and two grandsons joined the gathering. They stood, in their nightclothes, staring at the intruder.

"Is he alive?" someone asked.

As if to answer the question, the man moaned and one leg twitched.

Little Jolly picked a broken branch from a pile of

kindling and tossed the wood into the fresh-stirred fire. Sparks flew with the added fuel, sending flames high, providing a wide circle of light.

"Yes," he answered and pointed. "Don't you recognize?"

I moved around to get a better view of the laid-out figure. "Why, isn't he the one they called Skinny?" I looked back at Ma. "He ate a whole jar of your alum pickles."

Ma lifted the hem of her nightgown, stepped closer, and frowned. She pointed her finger. "That's one of the hooligans who made off with Horace and Betsy."

Levi unwound a length of rope and bent to the task of securing the unconscious prisoner. He bound the man's arms behind him, bent his legs back, and finished off by tying the rope around his ankles.

I turned the weapon over in my hands and squatted next to Little Jolly. A smear of blood gleamed down the length of the claws. "You was right." I held my arm out to show the three small puncture wounds. "The thing slid off my shoulder, hit my arm, and woke me up just in time. Remember Curly?"

Little Jolly nodded.

"Well, he was trying to make off with one of your pa's mules right below where I sat up in that tree yonder. I was right glad to have this. I marked him up good. Every time Curly looks in a mirror, for the rest of his life, I reckon he'll remember me."

Old man Casey balanced his rifle in the crook of one arm and scratched through his bushy white beard with his other hand. "Was it you what let out with that holler?"

"Yes, sir. But that was nothing compared to Levi's war whoop. My blood ran cold when I heard it."

Casey puffed his chest out and looked at Levi. "Land sakes, man. I thought I was back fighting Indians in Georgia. I come up out of my blankets and grabbed Ol' Hickory here." He patted the polished gunstock affectionately. "Kept her loaded, just in case. No sooner got her in my arms when the canvas flap ripped off and a yellow-bellied snake come slithering through the opening."

"What'd he look like?" I asked.

"Pretty dark inside the wagon. Only saw his shadow and a glint off eyes black as midnight."

Me and the Jolly boys looked at each other, and we all nodded in agreement. It had to be none other than Shilo Riddle.

"Blast it all." Casey snorted. "Must have heard me slam the hammer back because he disappeared from sight just before I let loose. Powder caught ahold the canvas, and we went to slapping flames, else I'd have got him for sure. Good thing you hollered an alarm, young fella."

The old man's wife murmured an agreement.

"Yes, sir," Casey continued. "Don't reckon them bushwhackers figured on Ol' Hickory, nor having the fight scared right out of them with blood-curdling banshee screams." He looked over at Levi. "You decide to get in this fight, I hope to high heavens it be on the Union side."

Levi crossed his arms over his bare chest and nodded. That would be as close to acknowledging a compliment as anyone would ever get from him.

"Yes, sir." Casey looked up at the dark sky and

sighed. "Everyone might as well settle in for a bit. Won't be light for a few more hours. Doubt them brigands will show their faces around here again." He put a hand to his back and winced. "Best I stand watch. My turn anyhow."

"Let me," I offered. "My eyelids wouldn't stay shut now if I glued 'em."

With a nod of thanks, the old man hustled his wife and grandsons toward their wagon.

"Good fight." Levi grunted, turned, and crawled back under the wagon.

Martha put her arm around Ma. "You all right, Catherine?"

I jumped up and reached for Ma's hand. In truth, I'd been so taken with the fight and Skinny's capture that I plumb forgot Ma's fragileness.

"You needn't be fussing over me, you two," Ma protested as I led her to the memory chair and slipped a quilt around her shoulders. "I feel right as rain, I do, now I let loose all that fury been trapped inside. It was a black thing, eating me alive. I was afraid to open me mouth, worrying what would slip out."

Ma sank into the rocker and pulled the quilt tight. "Lord, it felt good to scream." She touched her throat and swallowed. "I fear me hollering box be a tad raw."

Martha raised one finger. "A hot cup of sage tea will take care of that. Maybe a little licorice root." She scooped up the empty coffeepot and moved to the water barrel.

I studied Ma, who had taken a sudden care to the state of her hair. She sounded like her old self. Indeed, acted her old self, smoothing a tangle of red curls through her fingers.

"You sure you're all right, Ma? Never knew you to handle a Colt before."

"What's to know, Ebby? Would take a gobshite not to know to level the hammer back and pull the trigger. Heavy as an iron skillet, it was, with a kick like a mule. But, may heaven forgive me, as soon as the thing roared, me soul felt a release of anger." She stopped rocking, and her eyes went wide. "I pray I nay hit anyone, though."

The attack might have been fearful, but it seemed to have brought Ma back to normal. A weight as heavy as a boulder lifted from my shoulders. I didn't even mind the assortment of aches and pains taking hold in my joints.

"Ebby," Ma said in her thoughtful voice, pointing to Skinny, now snoring in fits and starts. "How is it you come to know this hooligan's name and the fact he consumed a jar of me alum pickles?" She rocked forward, with both hands on her knees. "And you might as well tell me for truth, how you come to be wearing that gash in your head. I want no horse's hoof, either, for I can smell a lie as well as a fart."

Chapter 8

"Ye nay be thinking I'll take pity on ye, trembling and carrying on so." Ma's voice cut through the sounds of the camp, which was coming to life. Levi and his sons held to a low murmur as they moved away from the crackling campfire. Water sloshed in the barrel, and pans clanked.

I roused up. No use burying my head under the blanket. It would take a pile of blankets to muffle Ma once she got riled. By the sound of things, it was a pretty safe bet she was back to her formidable self, threatening the vinegar right out of a body.

I turned over and propped my elbows on the ground, chin in my hands. Ma stood, stretching her four feet ten inches to at least six feet tall over one miserable looking man. She was a sight, Ma was—hair so red in the morning sunlight that it looked ready to burst into flames. Hands on her hips, toe tapping the ground like it was hammering nails.

Trussed tighter than a Christmas turkey, the bushwhacker screwed his long face into a mask of misery—nose wrinkled, brows furrowed together over squinty eyes, mouth puckered tight.

"Honest, ma'am," Skinny whined, "the urge is most powerful. I'm not up to no tricks." He clenched his teeth and sucked air through them. "I've had the grunting miseries for a couple of days now. Haven't been this sick since I took down with the measles a few years back."

"Haven't you, now?" Ma stopped tapping and bent forward.

I sat up to get a better view. The bushwhacker was in for it. When Ma's toe went quiet, she was near to action.

"Haven't been this sick for a couple years, you say? Why you suppose this sickness come over you so sudden-like?"

"Aw," Skinny groaned. "I don't know, surely I don't. It comes and goes."

Ma stabbed the air with her finger. "Perhaps it be ill-gotten gains that made you sick?"

"Huh?"

"Did you consume a whole quart of pickles that you hooligans stole from out of me larder? Just answer that."

Skinny looked stricken, corners of his mouth pulled down. "Pickles?"

"Best answer truthful-like," I said. "Ma can smell a lie as well as a fart, which at the moment seems most in abundance." I fanned the air. "Besides which, if you don't remember, I saw you gulping pickles like they was buttered biscuits."

"I apologize, ma'am." Skinny grimaced. "I confess to thievery. My poor old mammy always did say my stomach was bound to get me into trouble." He wiggled about on the ground, straining at the ropes. "Oh, have mercy on a sinner. I'm about to mess my britches. And if that isn't the truth, I don't know what is."

"Ought not to take pity on you." Ma flapped a towel and wrinkled her nose. "Ebby," she ordered, "take him to the bushes. I'm not feeling sorry for this skunk, smellin' to high heavens like he is, mind you. I've just better respect for me nose than to have him trailing behind the wagon."

"My oldest brother, Willy, once ate half a jar of Ma's alum pickles," I said to Skinny as I reached for my boots, turned them upside down, and slapped the bottoms to dislodge anything that might have crawled inside during the night. "Yep. Had the runs for a week." I made a show of brushing the bottom of my feet and pulling on each boot just to devil the man.

"Oh, hurry, for the love of heaven." Skinny groaned.

I fumbled with the ropes, and for truth, I was having a mite of trouble with them. "Don't reckon Levi meant to have you slipping loose these ties."

Skinny's body was aquiver. "Hurry," he pleaded.

"Tied 'em real good, he did. There now. Got your feet free. Hold still while I get your hands undone." I called over my shoulder, "Ma, better hand me that pistol."

"Don't have to worry about me making a break for it. Just got to worry I'm not going to make it yonder in time," Skinny said, tearing at the top button on his pants as he struggled to his feet. "Oh, merciful heavens." He groaned again and collapsed, rubbing the circulation back into his legs. He cast a worried look toward the line of trees and scrubby brush that circled the small clearing.

Skinny held his stomach with one hand and pushed himself up with the other. Bent at the waist and taking locked-knee steps, he made a bee line for the timber, pants slipping farther off his rump until it gleamed in all its pasty-white glory. His pants were bunched at his knees by the time he plowed through the pokeberry bushes and dropped from sight.

"I'm not taking any pleasure in this," I called to him, tramping through the brush, gun aimed. "But I'd be a plumb fool to let you have your privacy."

Squatting, arms locked around his knees, Skinny looked up, eyes squinched and mouth pulled into a tight grimace. "Why didn't you tell me about those pickles when you saw me eating them?"

"Reckon it's 'cause most folks 'round here know about Ma's pickles. Old man Ewing sends for a few about once a month, every time he gets seized up. Besides, how was I to know but what you had a serious problem. Ma says a fellow that lets himself get backed up is just asking for heart and liver failure." The man's misery was a pure pleasure to see. "Only problem about getting dosed too heavy is, about the time you think you're all cleaned out, you find out you're not. The runs could go on for days."

Skinny let out another groan, and I looked away. Levi and Big Jolly emerged from the trees, waved, and walked toward us. Both stopped to stare at Skinny, still hunkered, red-faced and straining.

"Ma's pickles," I told them, but they could have guessed as much. By now, the whole camp knew about alum pickles.

"Humph." Levi snorted and walked on. "You watch 'em. Snake bite when not looking."

Big Jolly waved the air and stepped back. A large bruise blossomed across one cheek. "Here, find over by big tree. You earn right to keep."

He held out a knife, its five-inch blade, nicked and

worn thin. The handle looked to be, at best, hickory wood, with a hairline crack running the length. A wide strip of rawhide, glued in place, wrapped the blade's end. It was nothing special. Just a well-used knife with a crude "C" carved into the wood.

"Thanks. Must have been Curly's." I gripped the weapon with my free hand. "Didn't get a real good look at it last night." The memory of the struggle flashed in my mind. Yes, I reckon I'd earned the right to keep the weapon. To the victor go the spoils. A rusty old knife wasn't much, but holding it in my hand was a reminder that I won the fight. I felt proud as a young rooster and tucked the knife under my belt.

"Corncakes about done," Ma called. She waved to us from the campfire. Martha bent over a large blackened skillet, flipping cakes with a long-handled wooden spatula.

"You hurry up now," I ordered Skinny, just like the call of nature could be controlled by an order. "I don't aim to miss my breakfast on account of the likes of you."

"Don't reckon you have a supply of corn cobs to take care of the necessaries?"

"No, not for bushwhackers, we don't. I reckon a handful of leaves ought to do you."

Skinny reached for meandering vegetation crisscrossing the ground and ran a closed hand along one of the vines, stripping it of leaves as he went.

"You sure that's not poison ivy?" I kicked at a tendril with the toe of my boot. Maybe the suggestion of poison ivy might worry him a bit.

"Aw." Skinny huffed. "I guess I ought to know woodbine." He stood, pulling his pants up as he went.

"You're just thinking to be funny."

I shrugged and motioned toward the camp with the barrel of the gun. "Soon as you get those trousers hitched, best grab you a piece of air with your hands."

Little Jolly joined us as we trudged through the weeds, weaving around the scattered cows and mules and their leavings.

"Skinny big complainer," he said. "Wake me up complaining."

"Yeah, well a whole jar of Ma's pickles will do that to a glutton."

"Your ma better today. Her fuss like always."

"That she is. Wish Ma hadn't drug that promise out of me not to join up before we left home. With her back to her old self, I'm hoping maybe she won't be so dead set against me fighting for the Union. Fighting doesn't seem so hard." I nodded toward Skinny. "Not if they're all like that pitiful excuse for a thief."

Little Jolly frowned. "Frog come to puddle. Him wade across, no trouble. Frog come to creek. Him hop across, no trouble. Frog come to river. Him swim and swim and swim. Much trouble."

It was best to ignore one of Little Jolly's stories when they made too much sense, and I looked to change the subject. "Mmmm, nothin' better than the smell of fryin' bacon." We stopped to peer down at the simmering pans. Corncakes, edges browning in a sea of grease, popped and bubbled in the skillet as flames licked up the sides. Rashers of bacon, heaped in a tin plate, sat at the edge of the fire to keep warm.

Ma looked at us. "Your stomach still be rumbling, Sir Thief?"

Skinny hung his head. "Sure enough, my innards

feel a heap better."

"Do they now? Well, wait awhile, those grunting miseries will be around again. Best eat a tad while you can." With a long fork, she flipped a strip of bacon, dripping with grease, toward him.

"And while you wait," I told him, "we best keep you tied to the wagon." I pulled one of Skinny's arms through the wagon wheel spokes and secured both wrists, leaving the man to feed himself however he could.

"Ma, we sure chased those bushwhackers off, didn't we?" I reached for a piece of browned bacon and plucked a stiff black hair from the pork rind with my fingers. "I'm thinking they're not so tough after all."

Ma set a large coffee pot on a rock and rested both fists on her hips. "No, Ebby."

"No, what? I haven't asked you anything yet."

"Then don't. 'Cause the answer to whatever you want to ask is no."

Chapter 9

The sun, like a big glowing eye in the sky, blazed down, sucking the dew from the grass and drying the dirt to a fine powder. It kicked up behind the wagon wheels in our lumbering progress north toward Fayetteville. I walked on the side of the road, slapping a slender branch across the backside of the cows each time they stopped to nibble tender shoots.

Skinny, hands tied in front of him and tethered to the wagon by a length of rope, trudged along in the dust. Ma sat in her memory chair at the back of Levi's wagon, her heels slapping down hard with each rock forward. Every bump in the road interrupted the beat and moved the chair an inch closer to the end of the wagon.

The rocker had received its own wound in the previous night's clash. A bullet embedded in the headrest created a new set of cracks, a fact that didn't do much to sweeten Ma's temper.

Ma glared at the bushwhacker, with the stock of old man Casey's rifle balanced in her lap and the barrel leaned against her shoulder. No one doubted her resolve to use the weapon. It tried the mind to remember that, only yesterday, she was all pulled into herself, not saying a word.

I studied Ma, how her lips pulled tight. I'd heard it said that a good slap would bring a hysterical woman to her senses. Maybe a scare, like looking down the barrel of a pistol, brings a body back to life. It surely seemed to work with Ma, though I'd hardly want to be the one to try it should the incident ever occur again.

Casey's two young grandsons wandered back to stare at Skinny, who had taken to muttering to himself. He lifted his upper lip in a growl and snarled at the boys. They yelled and stumbled over each other in their attempt to flee back to their own wagon.

I had to laugh. Such little simpletons! Aching for a look at the man like he was the devil's disciple, wanting to be scared, to feel their flesh creep, then running when their hair prickles. Skinny was nothing to be frightened of, all tied up and fighting the grunting miseries.

"Ma'am, the cramps has done come on me again," Skinny pleaded, half stumbling as the rope jerked taut when the wagon lurched forward.

Ma ceased rocking and steadied the chair. She narrowed one eye and shot a withering look toward the man, like she expected to read his mind. "Ebby," she called, "how many times we stopped for this here miserable hooligan to empty his greedy gut?"

"Three times, not counting before we broke camp this morning." I hopped onto the back of the wagon and sat down, legs swinging off the back. I watched Skinny, brows drawn into a scowl. "Why you ask?"

"Did he accomplish much the last time he squatted?"

"Aw, Ma. Do you think I'd be wanting to look? I stood upwind a bit, as a matter of fact. Had the pistol on him the whole time. Wasn't any danger of him running."

"You're thinking I'm worried on him slipping

away. Nay. 'Tis the simple fact me alum pickles are good, all right, but he's had only a rasher of bacon. Those pickles can't clean out a gut that should be clean as a whistle by now. I'd allow he might have a twinge, now and again, but until he's had another meal, he nay be needing to squat."

Ma rocked back slowly and forward again. "Now, why do you think he'd be complaining so?"

I fanned a cloud of gnats from my face and studied Skinny, who couldn't seem to look me in the eye. He kept his head down, staring at his feet, which, given the rockiness of the road, was not a bad thing to be doing.

Why would a man want to drop his pants, if he didn't have to? Skinny did seem to take his sweet time hunkering in the weeds. But after all, it'd take a cold heart to hurry a man that's all cramped up.

"Most likely he's taking advantage of our good nature, Ma. Might be he's lazy, don't much like walking. There are those that'd ride a horse to cross the street."

"Think deeper, Ebby." She shaded her eyes to study the distance we'd covered.

I glanced down the road, too. A dusty haze hung over the ground, stirred by our passing. A variety of trees and shrubs alternately hugged the road and, then, thinned out, leaving patches of ground alive with henbit and buttercups, dandelions and wild pitch. Where the foliage was thick, shadows shifted with the blink of an eye. Lots of places for someone to hide if they were of a mind to conceal themselves.

"Maybe he thinks as how his friends might try to rescue him. Each time we stop gives them a chance to catch up to us."

"Aye, 'tis a fact a desperate hooligan might cling to. The simple truth is, fellows such as him seldom have a care but for themselves. I suspect his friends have crawled back to their lair to lick the wounds that have been justly accorded them."

She raised her voice to Skinny, "You've a care, you know, to look to yourself. You best be thinking on what you'll tell the authorities in Fayetteville. Like who leads that pack of scoundrels and where be their hiding place."

Skinny looked from me to Ma. "Don't reckon it's any secret, seeing as how the boy already saw me with Shilo Riddle, who blabbered his mouth off making threats."

I ran my fingers along the still-raw wound on my face. "I took his threats for gospel."

"Humph. You'd be a fool not to. I once saw him ride back through Union lines just to fire the house of a fellow that pointed Shilo's little brother out to the authorities. He's got nothing but hate in his heart."

Skinny stopped twisting at the ropes circling his wrists and glanced around at the trees. His voice lost its hard edge. "That's why we rode with him, you know. We're all afraid of him. He made us do those things. Why, ma'am, I never wanted to steal any widow lady blind. No, sir. But when Shilo Riddle says to teach the folks of those that go over to the Union a lesson, why, that's what you do."

His eyes widened, soft and amber brown like our cat's, and took on a weepy look. "I reckon you know what they'll do to me in Fayetteville, don't you?"

I looked at Ma, who stopped rocking and leaned forward. Wind loosened wisps of red hair fluttered against skin as smooth and white as the marble columns in the Van Buren courthouse. She was a looker, when she wasn't filled with Irish determination, which seemed to be most of the time.

Skinny swallowed. "They'll hang me, you know. All because I rode with Shilo. I swear, by all that's holy, I've never killed nobody. Any killing done has been on Shilo's head. And, mercy, we've been blamed for lots of stuff we haven't ever done. Sometimes we'd sneak into town just to get a newspaper and find out what all we'd be up to."

He twisted at the ropes securing both wrists. "Now, if you'd let me loose, I'd see that the good deed would get back to Shilo. He's right kindly to those that show a care to one of his boys. Like I said, I never killed nobody."

"So you say." Ma leaned back and took a deep breath. "You've a way with the gab, I'll give you that. But you did steal my larder empty and made off with Betsy and Horace. Which, by the way, where does Shilo have Betsy and Horace stashed?"

"Betsy and Horace?"

"Aye, me cow, Betsy, and me pig. A big mean porker that you boys hauled off."

"The pig. Well, it pains me to tell you that pig was tougher than a doornail, he was." Skinny shook his head at the memory. "Soaked him in brine for half a day and boiled him for half the night, and he was still tough."

I frowned at Skinny, trying to get him to drop the recollection of Horace's end, but Skinny paid no mind to me. He kept on recollecting the deed.

"Reckon it was because we pumped him full of

lead and drug him through half the county before we made camp. He was bled dry by the time we carved him up."

Ma's eyes flashed, and her mouth dropped. "You killed and ate Horace?"

I winced. It hadn't seemed necessary to tell her about the hog's violent fate, and here this idiot had to up and blabber the sorry end of Horace. Maybe the blow could be softened.

"Ma, we were down to one ham. We were going to butcher Horace ourselves. Remember?"

"It's not the same," she shot back. "One thing for a critter to come to his end by those that raised them—another to be massacred by hooligans. Where's Betsy?" She aimed the question at Skinny like a dagger.

The bushwhacker stared back at her, chewing on his lower lip. "Well, ma'am, I'm sure I don't know, seeing as how I'm trussed up here. But maybe I could find her and bring her back to you, if you'd see clear to looking the other way for a bit. One thing old Skinny has got is a soft heart. I can see Betsy is dear to you."

The front wagon wheels bumped down into a deep rut in the road and out again, setting the hanging pans to banging against the sides. Ma steadied herself. The back wheels traversed the hole just as roughly and jarred her up out of the chair and down again with a *whump*.

She settled herself and brushed at a lock of hair that had strayed from its pins. "'Tis a fact, I'd a heap like to have Betsy back. How would you get her from Shilo Riddle if I was to let you loose? I figured Betsy would be in the next county, by now."

I stared at Ma. She wasn't normally the trusting

sort. What had come over her? Maybe she wasn't as back to her old self as I thought.

Skinny looked around at the trees again, all the while twisting his hands against the pull of the rope. "Oh, Shilo isn't so far. Must have three or four hideouts in these parts. I don't reckon him to be more than spitting distance." He tilted his head, his long face drawn into a mournful stare. "Like I said, ma'am, I was against coming down on your place. Truly, I was. It was all Shilo Riddle's doing. I'd like to fix things right by bringing Betsy back to you."

"You were against robbing me?"

Skinny nodded.

"You must think me a gobshite, Mister Skinny. You were against robbing me, you say, but you enjoyed me pickles, sure enough, and poor old Horace."

Ma shifted the long Springfield rifle to balance it across the arms of the rocker. "Ebby, reckon this be a good lesson to ye. This bloke is going to hang for the company he keeps. Mind who you are friends with in this world. The wrong sort could see you to a short end."

Chapter 10

"Riders!" Big Jolly's voice carried from the top of the hill as he trotted back toward us. He waved both arms over his head and pointed north, the direction of Fayetteville.

"Hear that?" I called to Little Jolly and motioned him forward around the two cows we were herding. "Riders coming."

Levi pulled up on the reins, and the wagon bumped to a halt behind Gordon Casey's wagon. Both men jumped down from their high seats and waited for Big Jolly to reach them.

"How many?" Old man Casey grabbed hold of my friend as soon as he was within arm's reach.

"Six men riding by twos." Sweat beaded on Big Jolly's face. He pulled away to run his arm along his forehead and catch his breath.

"Two abreast." The old man's brows furrowed into deep crevices, and his eyes narrowed. "Union or Confederate?"

"Maybe they were bushwhackers." My voice, sounding like a scared girl, echoed in my ears. I cleared my throat. "I mean, could you tell if they're wearing uniforms?"

Big Jolly shook his head. "Don't know. Too far away. Disappear in valley, behind next hill."

"Wooeee!" Skinny whooped and stomped his feet

in a jig. "It be Shilo. Maybe even Buck Brown. He's been operating around Fayetteville." He pulled against the rope that tethered him to the back of the wagon to get a good look down the road.

"You'll be sorry, ma'am, you didn't listen to old Skinny. You've already missed your chance to be currying my favors. Yes, sir, already had your chance."

Uh-oh. I hurried to the back of the wagon. I knew Ma wouldn't like his fool taunting.

"Too bad." Skinny continued like he didn't have a lick of good sense. "Because I was feeling some tenderness toward a poor widder woman like you."

"Were you now?" Ma rose from the rocker, balanced the gun's stock on the floorboards, gripped the barrel with one hand, and perched the other on her hip. "Are you sure it wasn't my pickles you were feeling tenderness toward?"

"Oh, I was willing to forgive you for those pickles."

"Forgive me!" Ma huffed up like a banty rooster and leveled the rifle at Skinny.

"Ma! We got riders coming." I jerked at the rope's multiple knots. "No use letting them know we're here until they get over the rise. You just keep that gun trained on him until I get this rope loose."

Levi came around the wagon, reached for the rifle, and leveled it at the bushwhacker. "Catherine, you, Martha, hide." He nodded toward the jumble of hackberry trees along the road. Gordon Casey's wife and grandsons were already scurrying through the high weeds. "Ebby, make sure Skinny stays quiet."

He glanced at his sons and nodded toward the other side of the road. "Get cattle deep in trees. Out of sight.

Stay there. Good man, bad man, all look with hungry eyes at cow."

"Humph." Ma snorted and gathered her skirt tight around her legs, ready to jump from the back of the wagon. "I wouldn't have shot the hooligan. That'd be a waste of a perfectly good bullet."

"Woo-hoo!" Skinny laughed and called after Ma as she and Martha hurried for the trees. "I been in lots of fights. No bullet has found me yet."

I wiggled the last knot loose and pulled Skinny, hands still bound, toward cover. Insects, disturbed by our passing, whirred up from the weeds. Back in the trees, fresh foliage filtered the sun's light and warmth, leaving the earth to smell of mold and dampness.

Ma and Martha settled themselves close to the ground. I pushed Skinny down next to them and whipped the rope around a slender trunk, pulling the bushwhacker's hands tight to the tree.

"I think I hear them coming," Mrs. Casey hissed. She squatted deep in the shadows, arms around each of her grandsons.

Skinny grinned at Ma. "Like I said, I'll put a good word in for you, ma'am. I always did take a fancy to red hair and all."

Heat flamed up the back of my neck. Blasted Rebel making pretty talk to my mother. Ought to knock the words right out of his head. "Wish I had a towel or something to plug up his hollering box."

"Aye, you could hardly ask his word of honor to stay silent. Men such as him don't know the meaning of honor." Ma sat back, lifted her skirt, and ripped a strip of cloth from the bottom of her petticoat.

"Aw, ma'am," Skinny whined. "There you go

trifling with my sensibilities again."

Martha gasped. "Catherine, what in the world are you doing?"

"I'm contributing to the cause." Ma leaned over and dangled a length of frayed fabric in front of Skinny's face. "This hooligan will be tasting the dust o' me hem."

I grabbed the petticoat strip. "They'll be coming over the rise any minute. Get down and be quiet."

Skinny threw his head back. "Listen, you let me free, I'll see no harm comes to you and your ma." A chestnut brown hank of hair fell over one eye, and he blew upward to dislodge it. "I know most of the fellas riding these hills and I guarantee…"

I stuffed a length of petticoat into the bushwhacker's mouth while it was still open and wrapped the ends around his head.

Skinny jerked like he was snake bit, tossing his head back and forth.

It was a struggle to tie a knot.

"Don't make any difference who you know." I pushed Skinny down into the dirt and sat straddling his back. "I don't reckon you to be the type to put yourself out on our account."

When I peered out between the tree trunks, Levi Standing Corn and old man Casey had both climbed back into their wagons. They stood with their rifles resting in the bend of their arms.

The bushwhacker's body heaved beneath me. A deep growl made its way through the layers of cloth.

The thud of hoofbeats and groaning leather preceded the riders over the rise. I bent over Skinny's head and breathed in the stale odor of Doctor

Higgenbothem's hair tonic. "I got a rusty old knife here. It's not sharp enough to skin a rabbit, but I reckon it'll do a good enough job of cutting your throat if you don't hush."

Skinny ceased struggling, and I was proud of that. Much as I disliked the man, I wasn't sure I could poke someone all trussed up like a Christmas turkey.

"Whoa!" The loud command slowed the horses.

I stretched forward to catch a glimpse of the clothing the riders wore. Not that the clothing would tell me much. Most of the time, neither side had the proper uniforms. That caused no end of problems for honest citizens just looking to keep out of harm's way. Armies west of the Mississippi, especially in Arkansas, had to scavenge for themselves.

"They're Union." Ma sighed, relief etched in her voice.

"Shhh." I shook my head at the others to remain where they were and leaned toward Ma. "Buck Brown was dressed in blue when he raided over to Hedley's Ferry."

Old man Casey was the first to speak. He called out, "Well, shore am glad to see you boys. Out on patrol, are you?"

"Might be." The captain stood in the stirrups to look past the old man at Levi. "What are you folks doing?"

"Looking for protection, you might say. Heading to Fayetteville."

Another soldier veered off the road to walk his horse around the wagons. "That's what Fayetteville needs, sir. More refugees to strain the resources."

"Humph." Casey's voice lost a bit of its

friendliness, and he stiffened his stance. "If you fellows could manage to keep the countryside free of the likes of Buck Brown and Shilo Riddle, don't reckon I'd find reason to be leaving my homeplace. With those bloodthirsty outlaws still on the loose, a man hasn't got much choice in the matter."

The soldier lifted the flap at the back of Casey's wagon and looked in. "Seems to be household goods, sir." He spurred his horse to check out Levi's wagon.

The captain cleared his throat. "Well, do you men need assistance?"

"We got ourselves this far. I reckon we can make the few more miles into town."

"Very well. Carry on then. The road ahead is clear. Of course, you know that could change with the blink of an eye." He clucked to his horse and trotted past, followed by the rest of the riders.

I watched the blue-coat soldiers disappear down the road. Casey and Levi relaxed the hold on their rifles and nodded us forward as the sound of riders receded in the distance.

"Reckon it's all right to go out, Ma." I squatted to untie Skinny, who had managed to dislodge his gag. It hung in folds around his neck.

Fabric rustled as the women rose and shook dirt from their skirts.

"Thank the Lord," Mrs. Casey breathed. "I was powerful afraid it was a trick. I can't wait to get into Fayetteville where I can tell friend from foe." She grabbed each grandson by the hand and marched toward her wagon.

Skinny struggled onto his feet and wiped his mouth with his bound hands. "Ma'am." He bowed to Ma in an exaggerated effort. "I will forever treasure the taste of your petticoat in my mouth."

Martha stifled a giggle and shook her head. "He does have a way with words, doesn't he, Catherine?"

"The heathen doesn't fool me a bit, thinking to soften me heart with brazen words." She turned and stomped through the weeds, a strip of petticoat trailing along behind her.

I jerked the rope, nearly dragging Skinny along. "You like Ma's petticoat so well, how about I stuff it back in your mouth?" Loose-mouthed outlaw, taking liberties and talking in such a familiar manner.

Mr. Casey stood in the middle of the road stroking the wooden stock of his rifle and glared down the road after the soldiers.

"Why didn't you tell them about Skinny, Mr. Casey?" I secured the end of the rope to the back of the wagon again.

The old man scratched through his long beard and spit a dark wad of tobacco into the dirt. "Didn't like that young captain's tone. Besides, no need to let them get the glory of capturing a bushwhacker. A thing like that puffs a man up."

Chapter 11

Leather reins slapped across the withers of Levi's team of long-eared mules as they strained to haul the wagon up the steep hill. Fayetteville couldn't be more than a mile beyond. The air, heavy with the scent of smoke and the humanity of a few thousand souls, announced the fact.

I couldn't resist a grin. Despite the dust and weary muscles that two days walking produced, I felt as giddy as a schoolgirl. Fayetteville—home to churches, schools, businesses, and the encampment of the First Arkansas Cavalry.

"Ma, reckon any of the boys will be at camp? Sure would like to see one of them."

Ma gripped the wooden arm rests and planted her feet firmly to prevent sliding out of her memory chair. The wagon lurched along at an alarming angle. A rope, stretched the width of the wagon, lashed the rocker in place. "Aye, it will do me heart good to see one of the lads. I reckon it'd be better not to burden them with the mischief that's been done."

"These ropes are cutting clear through my hands." Skinny groaned. "Don't you folks have any milk of human kindness about you? It wouldn't hurt anything to loosen these bindings a notch." His thin face stretched a mile long, pulling the ends of his mouth down in a grimace. "I swear I can't feel anything in my fingers."

He loped behind the wagon at the end of a rope and stared hard at Ma, trying to melt her icy attitude.

The glare Ma had fastened on Skinny since his capture seemed to soften.

Ma wasn't given to easy words, but she had been different since the raid—unpredictable. It might be best to jump in before she gave in to his pleadings.

"Save your breath, Skinny. You filled your belly on ham hocks that rightfully belonged to us. I don't reckon Ma begrudged you the jar of alum pickles, but Horace is another matter. I'm not even going to mention Betsy."

"Never forget, Ebby, kindness costs nothing to those that give it," Ma said. "The problem is, kindness means different things to different folks. Now, Skinny there, thinks it be a kindness to ease those ropes a bit. We do that, and he slips away and goes back to his wicked deeds, some other poor soul pays for our kindness." She shifted her grip on the arm rests. "Kindness has to be measured, just like flour."

"Oh, ma'am, for a fact I've seen the error of my ways. You've a soft heart and gentle ways. I can tell by looking in those angel eyes of yours."

I couldn't help but snort at his greasy words. "Yeah, well, just don't show up with ticks hanging on you. You'll think different about her gentle ways."

"Fayetteville." Big Jolly panted as he trotted toward the rear of the procession.

The wagon crested the hill. Ahead the road descended gently into a valley cleared of much of its dense cover of trees. Scattered houses dotted the area. A thin column of smoke snaked from several chimneys and contributed to a veil of haze over the town.

Skinny yanked at the ropes again. "You know what those soldiers will do if they get their hands on me, don't you?"

I looked at Big Jolly and shrugged. "Reckon they'll give him a trial for thieving. Like as not, send him up to Cassville to prison."

"Trial!" Skinny burst out. "They aren't going to bother with any trial. Only ones got a license to steal from folks are soldiers. They call it re-qui-si-tion-in' supplies, even though everybody knows no farmer will ever get paid for lost cattle and such."

Several soldiers touched their hats as they trotted past and then reined their mounts around. "Hey, what do you have there?" one asked and nodded toward Skinny.

I peered ahead at the lead wagon. The old man hadn't wanted anyone to know about the bushwhacker. "Oh, just someone we got a complaint against. Where do we find out who's in charge here?"

"That would be Colonel Harrison. He's headquartered at Judge Tibbitts' house. It's a fair-size white house. Follow Dickson Street straight to the corner of College. It's not far."

The men continued to follow as if they had nothing better to do. Maybe they didn't. Brother Willy said there was plenty of time to be bored between fighting. One by one, others joined the procession down Dickson Street. Three boys, wrestling around on the ground outside the schoolhouse, abandoned their activity to follow alongside Skinny.

I hurried forward to Gordon Casey's wagon. "We got us quite a parade, sir. Colonel Harrison's at the judge's house. That must be it up yonder. I see lots of soldiers there."

"You let me do the talking when we get there, boy." He narrowed his eyes and added, "There will be those that will be for stringing him up and those that will be for letting him go. Can't tell by looking what a man's politics are. Keep a sharp watch."

Colonel Harrison leaned against a pillar on one side of the wide porch steps. He straightened and ran a hand through his dark hair as the wagons pulled to a halt in front of a large one-story building with tall windows running its length.

"Look at all those fine windows," I said as I helped Ma down from the wagon.

"'Tis an extravagance of glass, Ebby. Those that have money feel the need to display the fact." Ma tucked wisps of red hair back into a bun at the nape of her neck.

Skinny let out a long sigh and wiped sweat from his forehead with his bound hands. He straightened and smiled, his mouth a tight crease across his face. "It's been a pleasure, ma'am, to have made your acquaintance. I would take it as a compliment if you'd not forget old Skinny in your prayers."

It was disarming to have your enemy suddenly become polite, like maybe he thinks friendly words would make you forget his sins. "Why yes," I answered back, "I'll be sure to say a prayer for you, too."

Ma's hands rested on her hips. "Ebby, it's not Christian to begrudge a man your prayers." She turned to the bound prisoner. "Mister Skinny, it was in my heart to pray for you, even if you hadn't asked."

Skinny's smile spread from ear to ear.

Gordon Casey led the commanding officer through

the crowd. "Yes, sir! Must have been twenty of the ruffians. Come at us in the middle of the night. If it hadn't been for the boy standing guard, we'd have been murdered in our bedrolls."

I glanced at the twins. Twenty? They shrugged back.

"Murdered!" The word rustled through the throng like wind in the trees.

"Another blasted bushwhacker!" Several soldiers pushed forward to glare at Skinny.

"You know what we ought to do with him, don't you?" one man queried the others.

"Hang him!" several shouted their answer.

The colonel waved the crowd back. "Won't be any hanging until I get the facts. Twenty, you say?" The colonel glanced at Levi. "The middle of the night? You get a look at any of the others?"

"I did, sir." I spoke up. "A boy named Curly and I had us a good tussle. I didn't see him clear, but most likely one of the attackers was Shilo Riddle."

"Shilo?" The name echoed back and forth in the crowd.

"Shilo." The colonel's long beard hid the top two buttons on his uniform. Bits of gold brass sparkled between strains of the trimmed beard as he talked. "If you didn't see him, how can you be sure?"

"Because—" I touched the bruised side of my face "—I don't guess I'd forget who about kicked my brains out. Skinny and Curly were both with Shilo a couple of days before. They'd been to our place and was in possession of our cow and pig when I come up on them. That was the day before we lit out for Fayetteville."

The colonel took a deep breath. "Anybody killed?"

"Well, unless you count Horace, I guess not."

"Horace?"

"Our pig."

Laughter rippled through the soldiers and civilians gathered around the wagon.

Heat burned up the back of my neck. "I guarantee you, it wasn't funny at the time. They put about a pound of lead in him. Doesn't that seem excessive? On top of which, they threatened Ma when she was alone. All because my brothers are here in Fayetteville, in the Union army, A Company."

I looked around at the faces in the crowd. The levity of the moments before were vanishing. The telling of the event fueled a renewed sense of injustice. Unstoppable words poured out.

"Stole everything we had. They split Ma's mattress open and ran their horses through the feathers to scatter them, and if that wasn't enough, they carried off the ticking. Those boys scared Ma good, who never turned so much as a hungry critter away from our door."

The crowd sobered at the familiar tale. A rumbling of threats toward the prisoner rolled from the front to those in the back. "Ought to take care of him right here and now."

I pointed to Ma. "What kind of man threatens a little bitty woman?"

Ma, red hair fluttering about her face, looked straight at me. For once, she seemed at a loss for words.

The throng of onlookers glared at Skinny again and surged closer. "What are we waiting on?" someone yelled.

Still bound at the wrists, Skinny held his hands up, wagging one finger. "I never killed nobody. I swear it on my dead mother's grave."

"Everyone settle down. The military will take care of this fellow." Colonel Harrison motioned several soldiers forward to take charge of the bushwhacker. They led him through the jostling crowd, pushing back several men who tried to block their exit.

"Nobody! I never killed nobody! You hear me?" Skinny's voice rose above the loud grumbles. "Nobody!"

With a sigh, the colonel shook his head. "That's what they all say."

Chapter 12

Sunlight streamed through a pinprick in the canvas roof, boring into my forehead. Now that it was daylight, there seemed to be all manner of holes letting in shafts of light. No wonder the tent had been empty last night. Come a rainstorm, we'd have ourselves a regular Saturday-night bath.

Last night, it seemed a godsend to sleep with a roof over our heads. There's safety in numbers, and for the first time since leaving home, I slept free from the fear of rascals bent on mischief too terrible to contemplate.

Outside, a constant murmur of voices rose and fell. In the near distance, the thunk of an ax sounded. Several giggling youngsters walked past—girls, most likely on the way to the outhouse.

I pushed up on my elbows and looked across at the other cot, a quilt spread neatly over its length. Ma had already met the day. It was her way to watch the sunrise. She could forecast the day's temper from the first faint streaks it cast across the early morning sky.

The idea of rolling over and going back to sleep teased my brain. Soon, the air in the tent would be stale with the morning's warmth. With a sigh, I swung my legs off the cot and reached for my pants. My bare toes dug into the layer of sawdust on the dirt floor, stirring a reminder of the abundant trees we were blessed with in this part of Arkansas.

Outside, I stretched the kinks from my body. The aroma of bacon, corncakes, and coffee was just this side of heaven and sharpened the ache in my stomach.

Levi, sitting cross-legged on a blanket, looked at me and grunted. It was plain he thought I was a laggard.

The twins were nowhere in sight.

"You've come back from the land of dreams, have you, Ebby?" Ma, perched on the edge of her memory chair, smiled. "I knew the sun would turn you out soon enough. 'Tis a fine day, the warmest we've had yet." She leaned toward the campfire and pushed golden pancakes around in the bubbling skillet of grease with a wooden spatula. "I figured the smell of bacon and coffee would stir your bones."

"They did for a fact, Ma." I scanned the meadow, crowded with tents and wagons. Squatter's Field was filled with all sorts of humanity drawn out of the hills and huddled together for protection. "Where's the boys? Still sleeping?"

"They been up since daylight." Flames sputtered as Martha Standing Corn flung the last of her coffee into the campfire. The coals hissed and sent a spindly puff of gray smoke into the air. She gathered the corner of her apron into her hand to lift the blackened coffeepot, refilled her cup, and held it out. "Herded the animals out a piece while there's still dew on the grass. Forage been nibbled down to the roots around here."

"Oh." The cup warmed my palms. With Horace and Betsy gone, there'd been no need to rouse me. I sipped the steaming coffee, made bitter with the memory of the past week.

"I've a keen eye on the road, hoping to catch sight a familiar face." Ma shook her head and scooped cakes from the skillet. "Soldiers aplenty, but none belong to me."

She handed up a plate of corncakes with brown edges still sizzling beside curled strips of bacon. I shooed a stray dog away and squatted next to Levi to eat breakfast.

"Talked to a couple fellas last night," I said between warm bites. "Said I should go up to Judge Tibbett's house. That's the place where we let off Skinny. The officers use it for their headquarters, and someone is bound to know the boys' whereabouts. If they don't, I'll just go on over to A Company. They're camped north of there."

"Never knew there'd be so many lads all to one place." Ma rocked back, still searching the constant stream of soldiers traversing the roads. Most kept their eyes straight ahead. Several hallooed the old men milling about the scattered tents.

"Fella last night said might be five hundred soldiers stationed here in Fayetteville." Thick bites of bacon greased my mouth and throat. I swished a mouthful of coffee back and forth. Coffee grounds settled in the crevices of my teeth, and I went to sucking them out.

Three boys burst around the side of the tent, skidded on their heels to keep from colliding into Ma's rocking chair, and changed direction toward the wooden buildings that served as outhouses.

"Too many." Levi set his plate down and looked around at the field, so crowded that it stifled the stirring of any sort of breeze. Muddy trails crisscrossed around tents. Fresh-washed clothing hung limp on ropes strung between poles. "Too many people. Air hard to breathe."

He stood, the ends of his mouth drawn down, as he inhaled through his nose and expanded his chest. With a shake of his head, he tromped off between the tents toward the tree line.

"Levi thinks to take the twins and drive the livestock way back in the hills tomorrow." Martha sighed and ran her fingers through her long, dark hair, combing the tangles free. "Bushwhackers would get them on the farm, and the Union will get them if they stay here." She shrugged and gathered her hair into a ribbon at the back of her head. "Figure me and our goods will be safe enough with the wagon. Truth is Levi can't abide this much togetherness."

The news that the Jolly brothers were going off to the hills sobered me. That would leave me here with two talkie old ladies like I'm some kind of young'un. No livestock to tend, no field to plow. Nothing to do but sit like a bump on a log, growing older by the minute. The thought soured the corncakes in my stomach. The constant buzz of voices, children's laughter, and dogs yapping filled my ears with a growing roar until I couldn't hear myself think. It was like being stuck in the middle of a beehive.

I lit out as soon as respectable to find my brothers. A freckled-face boy was perched on the top step of Judge Tibbett's house. He didn't make any motion to move aside.

"You here to sign up?" he asked.

The question was like salt in a wound. I just looked at him.

"Because, if'n you are," the boy went on in a know-it-all voice, "the recruiter has been sent on an errand for Colonel Harrison. I was here first, so you just sit down where you are and wait your turn."

"Well, I'm not here to sign up." The admission pricked my heart. This smirky-mouth boy didn't look any bigger than a grasshopper with big ears, and he was there to join the army. I moved to the other side of the wide stairs. "Got business to tend to."

"That so? What kind of business?" The boy leaned back on his elbows and tilted his head. Oily hair, more red than brown, hung in matted locks over his forehead.

"None of your business. That's what kind of business."

"Well, if you aren't petticoat touchy." The boy puffed his cheeks, spreading out the generous sprinkling of freckles. "I was just making friendly conversation. There's nobody here but an orderly. He doesn't seem to know much about nothing. Since you seem so all-fired important, don't suppose you'd want to wait."

"As a matter of fact, I do suppose I want to wait." I climbed the four steps to the broad porch, a disagreeable smell growing more powerful the higher I went. The boy, with a grin spread so wide his lips disappeared, patted the porch.

"How come you're not going to sign up, like me?"

"I'm just not. I already got three brothers in the cavalry, right here. In fact, they were in the big battle when the Rebs thought they could lay hold of Fayetteville last year." Bragging on my brothers was small comfort when I couldn't be part of the army. "One of them was even wounded."

"That so? Well, then I suppose you know that bullet hole up there was when the Sesech tried to storm this very house." The boy turned and pointed to the large hole that splintered a panel chest-high in the whitewashed door. "Saw the whole battle from right over there, Pastor Baxter's house." His arm swept in a wide arc to a large house across the street. "Yep, fightin' was fierce." He leaned across the top step toward me like he was telling a big secret, emitting a rancid odor with each word. "Red-faced Rebels thick as ticks on a coon dog. I can tell you, they were mean looking fellas, too."

I scooted back, away from the smell about to sour my belly, which was full of corncakes. "What were you doing in the big middle of them? I mean, if they were over there, shooting over here, seems to me you were on the wrong side of the road." I looked hard at the boy. "Lots of folks fight on both sides, I hear tell."

"Well, I may be slow, but I'm not a Sesech if that's what you're saying." The boy sat up, arms across his chest, his know-it-all voice a whine now. "I was, um, I was delivering wood to the Baxter house. Yes, I remember now. That was what I was doing when those devils come swooping down so fast all I could do was crawl under the porch and hunker down, bullets flying thick as hornets."

"If you say so." I breathed easier now that the boy had retreated to his side of the step. "But if you think those Rebs are mean-looking fellas, you ought to come face to face with a bushwhacker."

The boy's eyes widened with a new respect. "You've seen a bushwhacker?"

"Sure as I'm sitting here. I saw Shilo Riddle, the very worst of them."

"Is he worse than old Buck Brown? Folks say Buck is an inhuman fiend."

"Well, if Buck is an inhuman fiend, then Shilo is brother to the devil. Look here." I touched the still tender spot on the side of my head. Since I hadn't been anywhere near a mirror the last couple of days, I trusted I still sported a glorious purple bruise. "He laid me low when I objected to his taking our livestock. Wonder he didn't just shoot me. Guess he was feeling generous."

"Why, looks like you took a pretty good whomp there. Did it bleed much?"

"About like a hog stuck with a pitchfork. I sure enough saw stars." For truth, my mood lightened with the telling, especially with such a willing listener. "You hear about the bushwhacker that got brought in yesterday afternoon?"

"The whole town heard about him." The boy narrowed his gaze. "Why?"

"That was my group brought him in."

"Well, shut my mouth before it draws flies! You don't say?"

"Yep. Him and about twenty others attacked us a day south of here. Pretty hard fighting, too. Drove them all off, except a fella named Skinny. We brought him along with us. Turned him over to Colonel Harrison right here on this very spot."

"I hear they're going to hang him. You ever see a hanging?"

I shook my head. I'd heard the same grumblings. For some reason, the notion caused an uneasy feeling in my stomach, like I'd swallowed a jar full of fireflies. It was true Skinny was a bushwhacker, but not the same sort of evil as Shilo Riddle. And like Ma said, Skinny was most likely going to hang for the company he kept, not because he had a hard heart.

The boy stretched a hand out. "My name is Tazewell, on account of being born in Tazewell County, Virginia. Tazewell Benton. Last name used to be York, on account of that's where Pappy came from. But Pappy changed it on account of liking Benton County, Arkansas better than York, England. Folks just call me Taz, for short."

I gripped the offered hand, glad for the change of subject. "Folks call me Ebby. Named after my pa, Ebenezer B. Fears. *My* pa was named after *his* pa. The B doesn't mean anything. Reckon my great-grandma just liked the sound of the second letter in the alphabet."

"Your last name is really Fears?" Tazewell snapped his mouth shut.

"As far as I know, it's never been anything else. I mean, no one has ever changed it on account of liking something better."

"Names are supposed to mean something. How you go about getting a name like Fears? Unless you come from a long line of cowards. That why you aren't signing up?" Tazewell's mouth went lipless again in an attempt to suppress a fit of laughter. The effort was unsuccessful and he hooted, "Might as well call you, Ebby a'scared. No, more like Ebby 'fraid 'o hisself."

"Stop it." Heat crawled up my neck and ears and darn near built to an inferno inside my head. My fingernails dug into my palms. "You take that back right now before I give you what for. I'm not afraid of nothing."

"Oh." Tazewell bugged his eyes in pretend fright. "I'm all atremble. I've been threatened by a coward what's too scared to sign up."

The rush that flooded my every muscle threatened to explode and leave me a shredded pile of flesh. I had to do something before that happened. I opened my mouth, meaning to issue another warning to the braggard sitting there all puffed up. Instead, my words got caught in my throat, and nothing came out but a growl.

I lunged across the step and drove my shoulder into Tazewell, forcing an involuntary stench-filled "*oomph*" from the boy. We rolled and bumped down the stairs and out into the yard.

My fist smacked into Tazewell's jaw. He was a freckle-face know-it-all with jackass ears. Shilo Riddle's sneering grin blurred my vision, and I went to swinging with all my strength. Damn bushwhackers, damn promises, damn war! A rough jerk to the back of my shirt nearly strangled me and brought me to my feet.

"What kind of trouble we got here?" A scowling sergeant reached down to pull Tazewell to his feet. "You fellows need to put that energy into fighting the enemy and not each other. What started this?"

It might have been pride, but for some reason, my tongue was glued to the roof of my mouth. I'd been teased about my name before. It was the taunt that I was afraid to join up that pushed me into hitting someone fully ten pounds lighter. Nothing more I wanted to do than fight the enemy, make their kind pay for the cruelty done Ma. I had been powerless to stop Shilo Riddle, but it was the promise to stay out of the war that was eating at my innards—making me grouchy as a man with a four-foot turd turned crosswise.

"Well?" The sergeant's frown seemed etched in

place.

Tazewell cupped his jaw in one hand and worked his chin as if to make sure it was still hinged to his face. "Aw, it's nothing but a bet over who could hit the hardest. Reckon Ebby Fears won on that score."

The sergeant released his hold and fixed a gaze on me like he was trying to see right through me to the truth of the matter. "That so?"

"Yes, sir. Reckon it was something like that." I looked at Tazewell still holding his jaw. Maybe jackass ears didn't feel so proud about poking fun at another man's name.

"If you two don't have business here, I suggest you carry your bets somewhere else." The sergeant put a hand on the stair railing and stopped. "Fears. You any kin to a Corporal Josiah Fears in A Company?"

"Yes, sir. That would be one of my older brothers."

"Good man, Josiah. Him and your brothers held a steady point when General Cabel threw his Rebs against the town. Those Fears boys put up a heck of a good fight."

"Thank you, sir." I swallowed back a tightness gathering in my throat. My tongue was about to overtake my brain, and I was powerless to stop it. "In fact, I wanted to ask that if I was to sign up, could I be put in A Company with my brothers?"

"Well now, I'm sure I could arrange that. Come on into headquarters. There's a bit of paperwork to signing up." The sergeant smiled and turned back to the stairs, ascending them with a light step.

Tazewell's wide grin wrinkled the corners of his amber eyes as he threw an arm around my shoulder, the injured jaw evidently forgotten. "Won't it be great signing up together?"

It might not be mannerly to speak of another man's smell, but my tongue was well loosened now. I waved the air between us. "What is that awful stink that follows you around, Taz?"

"Oh, I reckon you mean the garlic. Ma puts it in everything. Says it keeps a man stout." He followed me up the stairs. "I'm going to ask for A Company, too. Say, reckon we can be tent mates?"

Chapter 13

"Hey, you! Get out of the way."

I swirled at the command. A mountain of a man, one large flour sack balanced on each shoulder, glared at me from ten feet away. Sweat rolled down his forehead and glistened in dark bushy eyebrows.

"'Less you intend to camp in the middle of the road. In that case, I can walk right over you." The man huffed the threat from the side of his mouth and stood balanced on legs as sturdy as oak trees. "Move or not, take your pick."

"Sorry." I nodded toward a field busy with soldiers scurrying between a dozen rows of tents. "Just wondering how you find anyone in all that mess down there."

The soldier rolled his eyes, ignoring the question, and shifted the sacks slightly as he moved past. The ground fairly trembled with each heavy step.

"You know where I might find any of the Fears boys?"

"Do I look like the general's secretary?" The mountain kept moving. A fine white powder puffed from the sacks with the motion and settled on his sweaty shirt.

I matched my pace to the soldier. "I can see you got a heavy load there. You brought them all the way from headquarters? Must be 'most a half mile or so."

The soldier grunted.

"Doesn't the army have wagons? Seems to me it would be a sight easier to use a wagon."

"It'd be supper by the time them blatherskites got around to issuing a wagon." Without slowing his stride, he added, "Officers don't like supper late."

"Must be a hundred pounds you got there."

The man, biceps bulging beneath his shirt, veered from the road onto a wide path. This time, he didn't so much as grunt a reply.

Ma always remarked on how honey draws more flies than vinegar. Maybe an offer to help would make him more agreeable. Surely this fellow would know at least one of my brothers.

"You got the strength of a regular Sampson. I'd help you tote those heavy things, if you want. Most likely I couldn't go more than a few steps before I'd be driven into the ground, though. A regular Sampson, I think. Still, wouldn't one sack have been enough."

The mountain stopped moving, exhaled a great sigh, and swiveled around. "It's plain you're about as green as a crab apple, so I'll allow for the stupidity. Supply wagon rolled in from Springfield this morning, with but half its requisitions." His voice grew husky with the effort of speaking. "Doesn't take a Solomon to figure you better get while the gettin's good." He stiffened his back and resumed plodding toward some tents clustered under the only stand of trees in the meadow. "When those privates finish unloading at the armory, there won't be anything left but salt pork." He paused and muttered. "About time you learn, a man doesn't last long in this army if he doesn't look out for his business."

A mounted soldier paused to allow us to pass. "Hey, Edwards, I see a supply wagon made it through. Maybe biscuits will put the lieutenants in better humor."

Edwards grunted in response as the soldier spurred his horse and galloped on, without so much as a nod to me. I had no other choice than to continue following the unsociable mountain to the officers' mess in hope of finding a more helpful-minded fellow.

A breeze brought the stench of a long row of stables on the far side of the encampment. Conversation, accompanied by the ring of hammer and anvil, rose and fell in the air like so much buzzing of bees. Broad streets separated the orderly lines of tents that seemed to stretch forever. Finding the boys would be no easy task.

Edwards ducked under an awning that was stretched over several long tables and allowed one sack to begin a slow slide off his shoulder and down his arm. The sack settled on the ground with a thud. I reached to steady it on end, while the other load plopped beside it.

"Now then," Edwards said as he arched his back. "Who was it you were looking for? *Fears*, you say?"

"Yes, sir. Any of them. Willy, Josiah, Jim. A Company. They're my brothers."

"Let's see. Used to see Willy all the time when he was quartermastering for the regiment. Of course, that was before he got busted for that drinking business a few months back. Hear he's running the mail now." Edwards wrapped a white apron around his middle and let the back gate of the cook wagon down, exposing a wall of cubby holes and drawers. "Stay out of my way, and you can wait here for Jim. Most all those corporals come around hoping to get into the officers' mess at supper time."

"Thank you kindly." It would be a relief to see a familiar face, someone actually happy to see me. And Jim would be happy, I was sure.

Edwards held his hand up and turned his back, friendliness gone as abruptly as it had come. He set a huge bowl down with a bang, ripped open the top of one bag, and settled to the business of transferring cupfuls of flour to the bowl.

Shadows lengthened as the afternoon wore away. I went to pacing back and forth. What if Jim wasn't happy to see me? I slipped my hand in my pants pocket to finger a folded paper. A single sheet, yet it was heavy as a book—heavy with the responsibility it represented. It fair weighed my pants down. What had I done?

In time, the aroma of stew and biscuits wafted in the air, growing more powerful with the waning sun. Officers, in groups of twos and threes, descended on the mess tent from various directions. I kept a tight lookout.

No doubt about it. I'd recognize Jim's stride anywhere. There he was, fingers hooked in his belt, loping along with his friends.

"I figured if I hung around by the food, you'd come along soon enough."

"Ebby?" Jim stopped. "Why, boys, it's my little brother." A grin lifted the ends of his droopy mustache. He grabbed me up in a bear hug, then held me at arm's length. "I swear, you grew a foot since Christmas." His eyebrows furrowed. "Nothing's happened to Ma, has it? What are you doing here? You're supposed to be taking care of the farm."

"Yes and no, something happened to Ma. She's pretty much back to normal, though, after those bushwhackers hit our place. We…"

"Bushwhackers?" Jim's voice rose.

"Not just any bushwhacker, neither. It was that black-hearted Shilo Riddle and his boys. Stole Betsy and Horace. Just about wrecked the place. Didn't have much choice. Had to pack up what was left. Ma's over at Squatter's Field."

"Those cowardly devils coming down on a widow woman. What do you mean, she's back to normal?"

"Mostly scared. They threatened her. Hung the chickens up by the feet. Headless! In the doorway, too. Made an awful mess to look on."

Jim's gray eyes darkened. "C'mon. Willy's back in my tent. Come in from Little Rock today. We better get him."

He snatched several biscuits from a pan and hurried toward the far row of tents, talking over his shoulder as he went. "He got in at noon. Rode all night with orders for the general. Josiah's still up at Springfield, I think."

For a short man, Jim had a quick stride. He was slow to rile, but once his dander was up, he could chew nails. I hurried to keep up.

Jim slung a tent flap back over the top, barely stopping as he did. "Get up, Ebby's here." He crossed to a cot and shook a form curled into a ball. "Brought Ma up from the farm. Come on, Willy, get up."

"Huh?" Willy mumbled and unfolded his body, one long bare leg dropping over the edge of the cot. "What you talking about?" Both arms reached up in a lazy stretch. "I haven't slept out, yet."

"Ebby's here."

"Ebby?" Willy, thick black hair ruffled, pushed up on his elbows and squinted toward the entrance. "What's going on?"

Being the oldest and with our pa long dead, Willy considered himself the head of the family. He wore his authority like a badge, second only to Ma. He had risen easily in the ranks, most likely because he was used to taking charge of things. Getting busted for drinking on duty a year ago had gone hard on his ego.

"What're you doing here, Ebby?" Willy sat up and frowned.

"Shilo Riddle made a visit to the place. Stole every last crumb. Betsy and Horace, too. Busted things up. Took Ma's mattress out, split it, and scattered all the feathers. No telling how long it will take to get enough feathers for another mattress."

Both brothers sat on the cot, mouths set in tight lines, fists clenched. Anger was building in them. I could see it.

"Worst part, they threatened Ma. Said they'd be back. Killed the chickens and left them hanging in the doorway dripping blood everywhere."

Willy leaned forward. "You let them do that to Ma?"

"I wasn't there to stop it. And I been regretting the fact ever since."

"You weren't there?" Willy's voice held a menace to it. "Where were you?"

There it was. The one question I had been dreading.

"I, well, I was out fishing. Trying to catch us some supper. Can't hurry fish. And you know how Ma likes them big brownies lazing around those big pools over to the natural dam." I hurried on, hoping to gloss over the fact that I wasn't home.

"Then, me and Big Jolly got in a race. Ran right into Shilo and his boys herding Betsy and Horace down the road, pretty as you please. I tried to get them back. Really, I did. But all I got was a boot to the head for my efforts."

I pushed my hair back to show the wound. Maybe that would buy a tad of sympathy from the boys.

Jim frowned as he stood, took hold of my chin, and tilted my head to peer at the cut in the dim light. A slight "*tut, tut*," was all the sympathy offered.

Willy reached for his clothes draped over a camp chair. "You were out fishing. Fishing and racing like always. Fishing and racing." He stabbed one leg into his pants. "Of all the irresponsible…"

"Now, Willy, you can't say any more than I already said to myself. I've been eating myself out ever since it happened. You're mad with the telling of the facts. I've been madder with the seeing of the lowdown deed. Ma's here. She's all right. Got her settled over at Squatter's Field. We came in with Levi Standing Corn and his family."

I took a deep breath. Might as well get it all out. "And I signed up this afternoon." I patted my pants pocket to make sure the folded agreement was still there, still weighing my pants down. "I aim to do my share of fighting for the cause. It's only right I do my part, now I'm here."

"Signed up!" Willy shouted loud enough to be heard on the other side of camp.

I cringed. Anger and yelling seemed to go hand-in-hand with my brother. If you couldn't see he was mad, you'd sure enough hear it.

Jim held his hand up. "The boy isn't deaf. It was bound to happen sooner or later."

Willy stood, both hands on his hips, and bent forward. "Who told you, you could sign up?"

"No one. But I don't aim to wait any longer. I signed up, and that's that."

"That's that, is it? That's that!" Willy drove fisted hands into his shirt sleeves and paced, buttoning his shirt, all the while glaring at me.

Willy was like Ma—able to melt a man to a puddle of lard with nothing more than a stare. Usually, they both had their own way. I squared my shoulders and stood tall as I could. It wasn't going to happen this time.

"Well." William stopped pacing. "The good Lord gave Ma four sons. Reckon it is a blessing he give most of us an ample helping of common sense." He folded his arms. "Being the last in line, it appears you've been slighted some in that regard."

Chapter 14

Squatter's Field was alive with the activity of displaced families. Women gathered around campfires in the process of preparing supper—mostly beans and fatback by the aroma that wafted from the bubbling pots.

A pack of young boys chased toward us, shooting at each other with carved wooden guns. Several dogs snarled and snapped at their heels.

"Bang! Bang! Take that you ol' guerriller," the oldest boy shouted at his companions before disappearing around a tent.

"Noisy young'uns," muttered Willy. "Nothing but a bother."

I breathed a sigh of relief as I led the way through the encampment. The mile-long walk from the cavalry camp down Telegraph Road, past headquarters and the college and the few businesses still operating, seemed to have tamed William's anger to a tolerable level. At least, now, he was only mumbling to himself.

Gordon Casey's voice rose above the children's laughter as we neared his wagon. Several men, weather-beaten and bent, lounged in the shade of a canvas awning. The old man sat on a straight-back chair in the midst of them like a king regaling his subjects with past glories. By now, there wasn't anyone in the settlement that hadn't heard the story of Skinny's capture at least a half a dozen times.

"There he is now," Casey's voice reverberated in the air. "Ebby, let out another war whoop like you done when them fiends come swooping down on us innocent civilians in the dark of night. We'd have been killed in our sleep without that boy."

I'd not told Willy and Jim about the ambush on the way to Fayetteville. I grinned at my brothers, who, for a change, seemed in awe of me.

"Aw, Mr. Casey," I yelled back and waved. "Better not. Might scare the ladies and curdle the buttermilk." The old men hooted and slapped their knees.

"War whoop?" Jim asked.

"Yep. A damn good one, too, even if I do say so myself." I pointed toward our tent. "Wait 'til Ma sees you both."

Ma, red hair reflecting the orange rays of the setting sun, bent over a steaming kettle and lifted a ladle to check the pot's contents. She straightened when she saw us three boys, dropped the ladle back into the pot, and ran toward us. The biggest smile ever, crossed her face, and she held both arms out like a mother chick gathering her brood.

Jim reached Ma first, folding her into a hug that wrapped all the way around her small body. "I swear, you're still the prettiest woman in these parts, Ma."

She pushed back to arm's length, looking him up and down. "Aye, and I'm glad to see no rebel bullet has silenced such a gift of the blarney." She touched Jim's elbow. "You haven't been hurt? And 'tis only the truth I want to hear. Don't lie to me, for I can smell…"

"A lie as well as a fart," Jim chanted with her and laughed. "I know better than to try to fool you, Ma." He shrugged. "I'm fine."

Willy stepped between them and lifted Ma from the ground, swirling her around. She threw her head back and laughed in her sweet lilting voice. It was as fine a music as any. It had been silent too long.

"Aw, don't worry about Jim. He's too tough to hurt much," Willy said. "It's me you got to worry about." He sat her back on her feet. "I swear, all these town girls about wear me thin, all the time chasing after me, batting their eyes and such."

"Ah, Willy, me lad," Ma said and shook her head. "A handsome face such as this, with your clear blue eyes, be a curse. You'll have to run faster than the lasses, or you'll be caught for sure." He bent his tall frame to receive her caress as she ran a hand down his cheek.

"Ebby said you're all right after the fright of Shilo Riddle." Willy grabbed her hand and held it. "Are you sure you aren't hurt any?" He scowled at the bruises that discolored her wrists.

"The hurt is gone, now. 'Tis this Irish blood won't let the wrong done me go, though." Ma's mouth tightened, and she slipped free of his embrace to settle her fists on her hips. "You know the hooligans took Betsy and Horace?"

Willy nodded. "Betsy was your special pet, Ma. Star-blessed like she was and all. Maybe we'll find her yet." He shot an accusing glance over at me.

"Even the wicked have hungry mouths. They'll not choke on ill-gotten food like an honest man. I fear my Betsy has come to a sad end like Horace." She pushed at a lock of hair that took on the waning sun's glow. "All my sit-abouts smashed, too. The mattress your pa

118

and me shared—ripped to shreds, feathers scattered to the four winds. Shilo Riddle is brother to the devil to do such a thing. Surely the man is bereft of a mother. You know how many chickens I plucked to fill that mattress?"

I looked at my brothers, and we all nodded. We knew. She had told us often enough. Five hundred and seventy-six chickens, maybe more, because not every feather was fit to be used.

Ma paused and peered past them, her brows drawn into a frown. "Where's Josiah? He's not hurt again, is he, and you think to spare me the news?"

"No," the boys chorused.

"He's just on a detail to guard a wagon train up to Springfield and back," Jim said. "In a couple days, you'll look up, and he'll be sa-shay-in' your way."

Ma took a deep breath and smiled again as she looked William and Jim up and down. "I wish your father could have seen what fine lads you grew up to be." She clasped her hands together in delight. "Handsome in your uniforms. My heart skips a beat at the sight. The Lord forgive me for the pride stirred in these old bones."

"Well." Willy straightened, the joy of the reunion dismissed. "Might be I have a different opinion about one of your boys. You could've been killed, Ma, all alone like you were. Ebby was supposed to be taking care of the farm, not gone off racing and fishing."

"Willy, I been taking care of the farm." Irritation set my teeth on edge. Willy was always finding fault. "The horses got carried off by Buck Brown's gang months ago. And I still got the south field planted with no help from anybody but my own back. Had to loan the Ewings the plow since those guerrillas broke up all the old man's equipment when he refused to give them forage. Farming isn't an easy chore these days like you seem to think."

"I never said it was. Just seems to me it's not so hard to stay close to home."

"No need of setting your temper at Ebby." Ma wagged a finger. "Shilo Riddle deserves your ire, Willy. In truth, I thank the Lord the lad weren't at home. He seems to think there is something he would've done to prevent the outrage, though I'm hard pressed to know what it'd be. 'Tis naught a household hereabouts that hasn't felt the sting of hooligans such as Shilo Riddle and Buck Brown and Tuck Smith and, oh!" She swatted the air. "I can't even name them all."

A tall, thin woman, hair pulled into a severe bun, nodded as she passed through the campsite. Ma smiled back and rolled her eyes toward the woman. "That's Helda Smidt. Her people are Hessians, ye know. That Confederate devil, General Hindman, conscripted her two boys right out from under her table when she didn't have any vittles for him to steal. Said he weren't going away empty-handed. Hasn't heard from her boys in months."

Ma settled in her rocker after a quick glance at the kettle. "I count it a blessing Ebby was gone. Besides, the lad proved himself right enough when he had the chance. You've heard of the bushwhacker we brought in?"

For the first time since finding my brothers, I felt an ease work its way into my soul with that warm glance from Ma. It was her way to confer a blessing with little more than a smile.

"Bushwhacker?" Willy and Jim both echoed the word.

Willy softened his stance. "You didn't say anything about capturing a bushwhacker."

"You didn't give me a chance, what with you indulging yourself in a good case of mad. Besides," I answered, "it isn't in my nature to brag, like some I know."

Martha brought several straight-backed chairs from her wagon. "Happened night before last when we camped on the way here."

"Your brother was standing guard." Martha motioned for the boys to sit. "Some of Shilo Riddle's boys hoped to catch us in our sleep, but Ebby, here, fouled their plans. Before it was all over, we had us a captive."

Willy and Jim settled themselves onto the chairs. For once, my older brothers were at a loss for words. I crouched down on my heels, ready to make the best of the opportunity.

"I was squatted up in a big old hickory about like an owl, wishing I could see in the dark. Black, it was black as pitch. I knew something was out in the brush. I could feel it, creeping up my spine like a creepy crawler. All I had was Levi's bear claw for a weapon." I held one hand up, fingers splayed apart. "It belonged to his grandpa. I was wishing I had a gun, but that thing was second best, I tell you. A right grand weapon." I spread my thumb and forefinger wide. "Those claws were this long. Rip a man's face right off."

"Damn!" Jim whistled. "Well, go on."

"Then I saw them. Like ghosts rising up out of the dark. One fellow was making for the mule right below me and must've been three, four others creeping up on the wagons. Me, with no gun. Just this here bear claw." I paused, held my arm up and curved my fingers out again. Best to let the suspense build. I'd learned that from Little Jolly.

It took a spell to tell the whole story. I could tell Willy and Jim were right impressed with me, for once. The best part had nothing to do with me though. My sides hurt from laughing by the time I finished telling about Skinny's thievery.

"A whole jar?" William shook his head and reached for a plate.

"I didn't know anyone could eat a whole jar and live," Jim said, wiping tears from his eyes.

"Don't think he thought he was going to live. He had the miseries all the way here." I clasped my arms across my stomach, bent over, and shuffled about in tiny steps, knees tight together. "Ohhh," I moaned, "I never been this sick before. Ohhhh."

"Ma's pickles will do that to a fellow," Jim said between renewed fits of laughter.

"Serves him right," Ma said and spooned beans onto a plate.

Ma doesn't waste sympathy on stupidity, and eating a whole jar of alum pickles was about as stupid as one could get.

"Hope to never see such a sight again," I said and reached for the offered dish. Steam lifted from the hot beans. "Ma was all the time saying, 'Don't take your eyes off the hooligan.' Eewwww, the man's got the whitest butt I ever did see. Not that it has anything to do with Ma's pickles, but I hear he's likely to be hanged."

"Colonel Harrison is a fair man—" Willy scraped a

spoon around his plate "—but some of those bushwhackers aren't only Southern-leaning anymore. They're plain stinking mean outlaws that go around terrorizing folks in the name of the South. Reckon the colonel thinks to make examples of the like of that ruffian you brought in. And if hanging is what it takes, then I say hang him." He blew on the spoon of beans. "You won't believe some of the things we hear about the mischief these fellows do."

Jim set his plate down. "Truth is, me and Willy and Josiah have been talking on how maybe it's time you come in. Look around." He gestured at the crowded meadow. "Pretty soon, nobody is going to be left on his farm. Too dangerous. Some of these folks were starving when they got here. All their food stolen. Womenfolk strapping on a harness, trying to pull a plow."

I could hardly believe my ears. "You mean, after all the mad you been heaping on me, you were thinking of bringing Ma to town all along?"

Willy lolled a mouthful of beans around and nodded. "Of course, I was afraid as soon as you got to Fayetteville you'd do something foolish, like you did, Ebby. Don't know as I can do anything about it, either."

"Foolish?" Ma lowered the long ladle back into the kettle. "What's he talking about, Ebby?"

Chapter 15

Food bunched up halfway down my throat. It might as well have been a hot coal I was trying to swallow for the pain it caused. I should have known Willy would blurt out about signing up before I could prepare Ma for the fact. Charred wood crackled and fell apart in the smoldering fire, sending spirals of bright ash into the air.

"Ma, I was meaning to tell you as soon as you got your visit with the boys out. Reckon now is as good a time as any." I studied Ma, sitting upright, frozen in place, her eyes burning big holes in me. I could feel my courage ooze out those holes.

"I know I promised you, but sometimes a promise isn't meant to be kept. I'd feel mighty small, not doing my part in this war. Like I'm only half a man."

"Well, aren't you?" Willy muttered, just loud enough to be heard.

Ma slumped back in her memory chair. "You signed your name, didn't you?" Her face paled, framed by curls that seemed to have gone limp, like there was no life left in them. She covered her eyes with her hands and exhaled a sigh, barely audible against the crackle of the campfire.

"Yes, ma'am. This afternoon." The admission slipped out easy once Ma broke the stare that bound me to her like glue. I glanced at my brothers. For once,

Willy sat quiet. Didn't look up, as if intent on studying the dirt under his fingernails. Jim picked at a frayed hole in the knee of his pale blue trousers.

"It appears the water's about gone, Catherine." Martha stirred from her spot beside the campfire and reached for a bucket. "Believe I'll fetch more. Levi and the boys ought to be coming in from the woods soon." She paused and rested a sympathetic hand on Ma's shoulder.

The gesture annoyed me. It was as if both women acted like I was a dead man. What was wrong with them? Ma didn't take on so when the boys signed up two years past. I took a deep breath. Apologies usually softened an admission of guilt. The trick was to make it sincere.

"I'm sorry, Ma. I never aimed to disquiet you any. Never aimed to break my promise, either. And I swear it wasn't my intention to sign up when I went looking for the boys this morning."

"Like it weren't your intention to forget the salt and go fishing instead?" Ma asked, only it wasn't a question meant to be answered. Ma wouldn't be softened easily this time.

"This is different. You're right as rain. I should have known better, and I've already fret a heap over that. But I feel cowardly and small seeing all those fellows working hard, including my own brothers, knowing they're out fighting to secure the country."

"You're but a boy, Ebby. This fighting is mean work, fit only for those that know the tricks of grown men."

"No, Ma. Lots of boys my age are wearing the blue. I hear as how there's this young'un back East, not but ten or twelve, and he's serving with the Union army. How? How could I not sign up?"

Ma pushed the ground with the toe of her foot and started the memory chair to rocking. It was a hopeful sign that she was adjusting to the idea.

"How could you not sign up?" she repeated and leveled her gaze at me. "You could have sat on your hands. Or since the urge to sign your name was so strong, you could have come to me to be freed of the promise. The only thing a man has control over in this life is his word."

Ma was right, and when she was right, she could melt you to a puddle of lard with one stare. Sweat rolled down my back, puddling in my waist band.

"No denying I should have come to you first," I said. "For some reason, a feeling came over me. It was powerful as a roaring lion, and I didn't hear anything else but that loud roar."

"I reckon," Ma said, "as how that roar was the sound of canons seeking to devour you."

"Ma?" Willy broke the tension. "You want me to see what I can do about it? Back when I was quarter-mastering, I made a heap of friends. Maybe I can get him shuck of the signing."

"Willy, I don't want shuck of the signing." I shook my head, trying to keep my voice level. "Why do you always think you're in charge of everyone?"

"Because someone in this family has to take the reins." Willy puffed up, eyes intense. "Being the oldest, reckon I drew that lot." His voice rose. "Families got to pull together. We had an agreement on who was going to take care of Ma and the farm, and you broke it."

"I didn't do any agreeing. I just got told, like I had

no say in the affair."

Jim raised a hand, palm down, and patted the air, as if to tamp Willy's angry words to the ground. "Things change, Willy, you know that."

The effort to control the retort I could feel building caused a throb to the sore side of my head. "You saying I shouldn't have brought Ma here?" I swept an arm around at the crowded meadow. "We should have stayed at home? That's what you're saying? I should have left Ma where Shilo Riddle could get at her after he hung dead chickens up on the porch?"

The throb became a sledge hammer. "Or maybe you're saying I was afraid of Shilo, and that I skedaddled with Ma before he came back."

Willy jumped to his feet. "Don't be telling me what I'm saying 'cause I didn't say nothing of the sort. I know no brother of mine to be a coward. I'm not faulting you for coming to Fayetteville. In truth, it was the smart thing to do, and I'm a mite surprised you got here in one piece, what with the countryside crawling with bushwhackers like ticks on a dog." He folded his arms across his chest. "You're trying to di-vert the fact you signed up onto another thing altogether."

"I'm not doing any such thing."

Jim rose from his seat with a groan. "Just like old times, isn't it, Ma? The two of them gnawing on each other." He pushed Willy back into a chair. "Ebby, you know Willy doesn't like it when plans get tangled, is all. He's like an old mother hen worrying about her brood. Since the day you were born, he felt responsible for you, like a pa would."

Three older brothers, all feeling like they had a right to boss me, and a Ma that nigh on to smothered me to death. I knew I was luckier than a lot of boys, but sometimes the burden of keeping everyone happy was kin to juggling balls in the air. Every once in a while, one was bound to fall. I forced a steady breath, willing the sledge hammer banging away in my head to stop.

"Well, Ma." Willy's voice was back to normal. "You want me to see what I can do over at headquarters to get him out of this mess."

"No." Ma drew the word out and stopped rocking. She sat and stared up at the darkening sky, like she was trying to see invisible stars. "Even if he didn't mean it to be, I reckon I knew, deep down, Ebby's promise was made on the air. I knew, sooner or later, he would slip away. I confess to wanting to keep him young and out of harm's way for my own selfish reasons. But you can't hold back time any more than you can a flooding river."

The color returned to her cheeks as she glanced at each of us. "It's in a man's blood to rile back, and I reckon, deep down, I wouldn't have wanted him easy tempered. It would be a lie of his Irish blood. The wrong was mine in forcing the promise."

She looked down at her hands, twisting one inside the other. "I weren't able to keep your pa to home, either. He went off to fight, hoping to earn his pay in land. I confess to not wanting him to go fight those Mexicanos clear the other side of Texas. When the letter came, I knew before Othella read it to me, you pa had gone on to his heavenly reward. At first, I was right angry with him, going off and dying like that in a foreign country. Leaving me alone with four young'uns."

It was a surprise to learn Ma had been mad at our

father. By the look on Willy and Jim's faces, the surprise was mutual. I couldn't remember Ma remarking on the subject before.

"I think, maybe, I wondered if it was your pa's name that was unlucky," she continued, still worrying her fingers together. "Just having a middle initial and all. Why that 'B' could stand for anything. A body ought not to leave something like that to the spirits to decide. They're all around us, you know." She hugged her arms to her body.

Ma was a firm believer in the spirits. Any mischief not seen by her own eyes, she attributed to them, like when a plate cracked for no reason, or milk clabbered in two days instead of the usual three.

"Still," she continued, "burdened with grief, it seemed right to name you after your dead pa. Aw, well, it was a waste of energy staying mad. I loved him too much."

To learn you carried an unlucky name was a sobering thought, and I didn't much believe it was so. But my brothers did. They sat, mouths open, staring at me like I was Mr. Ewing's two-headed calf. Now that was unlucky.

Ma broke the silence. "Life is hard enough without carrying an unlucky name." She sighed and bit at her lower lip. "But once his name was written on your soul, I could nay change it when I pondered the matter. I fret I've done you harm with the deed. 'Tis the real reason I forced the promise, I reckon."

Ma rocked forward, hands on her knees. "This time the fighting is down on our ears, right here to home. Sometimes I think to take up arms myself, to fight for the land he died for." She motioned for me to sit in front of her and ran fingers down the side of my face. Wrinkles blossomed from the outer corners of her green eyes, and she smiled.

"You go on with your soldiering. Make me proud, Ebby. Make me proud like your brothers have."

Relief banished the ache in my head. "I will, Ma. I will. And don't go worrying yourself. My name hasn't been unlucky so far."

Willy snorted and leaned back in his chair. "You not saying that kick to the side of your head was lucky, are you?"

"Willy." Ma leveled her gaze at him. "I expect you to keep an eye on your brother."

"What?" Willy groaned.

"Maybe you could take Ebby's shoes away," Jim said and smiled. He resumed pulling threads from the hole in his pants. "He won't be in such an all-fire hurry to go racing off every chance he gets."

"Well—" Willy drew himself up in his chair "—you want me to watch over him, then he best do what I tell him. I don't aim to be coddling him like some baby."

"Oh, I didn't expect you would," Ma said and started her memory chair to rocking again. "Ebby will listen with both ears open, won't you?"

I knew perfectly well the statement wasn't a question as much as it was a command. I'd best agree if I knew what was good for me.

"I look forward to the benefit of all your expert soldiering, big brother. In fact, I'm dang well hanging on your every word."

Willy folded his arms. It was a stance he took when building up to a lecture. And since he tended to like the sound of his voice, the lecture could take a day and a half, unless something interrupted him.

"First off, Ebby, you listen well to your captain. Remember the captain is the boss, and if he tells you to muck the stalls, then that's what you do. If he tells you to dig a latrine ditch, then that's what you do. No tomfoolery. Me and Josiah and Jim are in this army, too. I don't want you doing anything to embarrass the family. So, think first, and don't do anything stupid."

"You mean, doing something stupid like you did, Willy?" I got to my feet, ready to run. "Let's see, like maybe getting drunk on duty and losing your stripes?"

Willy's chair thumped backward as he sprang from it. I bounded away, sure in my ability to outrun my slow-footed brother.

Yes, it was like old times, being back with the boys.

Chapter 16

The awareness of morning came slow, like the fog that creeps over the land covering the rocks and bushes. Only it came in the reverse, rolling back and exposing life little by little. The smell of frying corncakes outside the tent flaps, the buzz of an insect, the dull ache in my bladder that begged for relief—all tugged me from bed.

I sat up to find Little Jolly sitting cross-legged on Ma's cot. "Morning. You been here long?"

"Not long. Mother send me. You sleep good. I wait." Little Jolly stood and stretched. "We go today. Take animals up along grapevine ridge. Plenty grass, water good. Stay there." He tilted his head, a smile lifting the side of his mouth. "You go with soldiers now. We not see each other for long time, I think."

I slipped my arms into my shirt and worked the buttons closed. "Aw, sure we will. I'll be seeing my ma, and you'll come down off the mountain to see yours." I reached for my overalls which were draped across a small trunk. "Didn't your pa say he'd be on the hunt, fetch meat back when he could? It isn't going to be easy, what with all the game scared from these parts, but if anyone can tease a rabbit out of his hidey-hole, your pa can."

Little Jolly nodded. Long black hair fell forward as he cast his head down and studied his bare feet, one sturdy and well made, the other twisted. "Long time ago, before first man, when animals were friends, brother bear had long tail. He could not wag tail to chase away biting insects. He too fat. He sat with sad face and looked at useless tail and wished to be rid of it."

"Is this story going to take a while?" I was feeling the discomfort of too much coffee the night before. "Because if it is…"

With a grin, Little Jolly continued as if he had not heard the question. "Brother wolf asks why big friend sad." He lowered his voice to a deep rumble. "Useless tail catch in thorns of blackberry bush and drags along ground. I wish for tail to be gone."

Returning to a normal voice, Little Jolly opened his eyes wide and threw his hands up. "This surprise wolf, who had no tail, and much admire bear's tail. 'Give me your tail,' wolf told bear. 'I do not eat blackberries.' Bear thought this good idea. Him let wolf bite tail off close to rump. Wolf happy with new tail and prance around with tail curled over back. Bear happy, too. Waddle to blackberry bush and fill belly."

"Well, now I don't catch the drift of that story at all." It was a puzzle, like most Indian stories turned out to be.

Little Jolly held one finger up. "Next day, brother bear sat with sad face. Wolf come along, waving tail back and forth. See friend and ask why so sad. Bear said, 'I miss tail. Before, I know tail always there. Now, I am lonely.' To this day, bear and wolf see each other sometimes. Bear still misses tail that was always there before wolf bite it off."

"Yeah, I'll miss you, too. But you could have just told me, instead of making me about to water my pants."

I pushed through the tent flap, out into the bustle of the camp. Ma held a long stick that was hung with strips of bacon over the fire and lifted it up and down out of the flame's reach. Rivulets of grease fed the blaze. Martha flipped hotcakes from the skillet onto a plate. Levi looked up at the boys, tossed the last of the coffee from his cup, and grunted as he stood.

"Don't fret about me, Levi," Martha said. She straightened from her work and glanced over her shoulder at their wagon, a canvas stretched over upright poles fitted along each side, to form a shelter. "You and the boys keep out of reach of those bushwhackers, is all I got to say." She held out a cloth with its corners lifted and tied together on top. Grease blossomed in dark spots, advertising the fact that corncakes were bundled inside.

Levi paused in front of his wife as if to say something. Instead, he grunted again, took the food, and walked toward the woods where his animals were hidden. Leather pouches, slung over his shoulders, bounced with each step. Little Jolly followed, his limp all the more noticeable next to the long strides of his father.

Ma moved to put an arm around Martha, in the same ageless fashion that women often did when words of comfort seem hollow. "May the sun warm your face, Levi, and the wind guide your steps homeward again," she called after the two figures. Only Little Jolly turned and waved.

Big Jolly didn't make an effort to rise from the campfire.

I squatted next to him and watched as he sucked

bacon grease from his fingers. "You going, too?"

"Soon." Big Jolly nodded, releasing a loud belch. "Spirit of grandfather's grandfather say you make good warrior, Ebby. You not bring dishonor to bear claw. But spirit of old uncle say you poor fisherman. Say you need fish charm more than Big Jolly." He stretched one leg, to allow his hand to slide into his pants pocket, and pulled out a handful of items—a small ball of sinew strips, several smooth, round game-stones, a broken piece of pumice, and an arrowhead as large as a man's thumb. He lifted the arrowhead from the assortment with greasy fingers and held it out.

There was nothing special looking about the charm—gray stone with edges chipped to a dull sharpness and a hole drilled in the notched end. Cracks zigzagged from the hole, making it useless as a weapon. Strung through the hole dangled a worn strip of rawhide threaded with small glass trade beads.

"You're giving me your true-enough fish charm?" I couldn't believe it. A real live Indian charm. Somehow, I couldn't touch it. Shaking my head, I said, "I can't take it. Wouldn't be right."

Big Jolly's mouth dropped open. "Why? You bet salt against fish charm."

"Sure. That's different. I'd have earned it then. Since Shilo interrupted that fine race, wouldn't be right to take it."

Big Jolly ran his thumb back and forth against the surface of the arrowhead. "You earn," he said without looking up. "When Shilo threaten brother, my blood ran hot. I ready fight. You save brother with words, not fists. You trade salt for brother."

"Aw, Shilo would have taken that salt, even if I

hadn't told Little Jolly to give it to him." My bladder couldn't wait much longer. I backed toward the outhouses.

Big Jolly bounded to his feet and shoved the charm into my hand. "Take. I win back sometime." He gave a quick nod to his mother and trotted out into the meadow.

The arrowhead filled the palm of my hand. I wadded the beaded leather around it and shoved it into my pocket. With such a charm, the fish would be bound to jump into my arms.

I took off on a run for the latrines, hollering out to him, "I hope you know, you don't have much chance of winning this back in any race against me."

Without turning around, Big Jolly threw his arm up in a wave and disappeared into the trees. Already, I missed my friends.

"Ebby?" Ma held out a plate of cakes when I returned. She arched one eyebrow. "You bet my hard-earned salt for a fish charm?"

"Oh! Well now, Ma, you know there wasn't much chance of me losing any race. That salt wasn't in any danger, until Shilo and his gang came along."

"Um-hum." Ma slid the bacon from the stick onto the plate. "So you say." She swatted the stick against the side of my pant leg hard enough to sting. "And if you'd lost my salt to a bet, there'd be the devil to pay."

Gordon Casey burst around the side of the tent, yelling as he came, "Come on! Hurry! Hurry!"

"Why, Mr. Casey, what be the problem?" Ma asked.

"A hanging." He panted and bent, hands on his knees, to catch his breath. "Over to the headquarters.

Skinny's luck has run out. I came to fetch you folks."

"Hanging?" I almost choked on the word, what with a mouth full of corncakes.

"Merciful heavens," Ma breathed.

"Right now?" Martha asked. "The sun hasn't been up an hour, yet."

"Yep." The old man nodded, straightened, and took hold of Ma's hand, pulling her toward the road. "Skinny's re-quest. Said he wanted to say his regrets to Mrs. Fears." He called to several old men who were busy with their morning ritual of yawning and stretching. "Come on if you want to see that bushwhacker stretched."

Ma pulled her hand free. "By the saints, I nay wish to see a man take his last breath in such a vile way. Even if he is a scalawag."

"Ma," I said, spitting bits of corncake and taking her elbow. "He asked for you."

"You wouldn't deny a dying man his last request, would you?" Casey asked.

"Well, merciful heavens," Ma repeated, allowing herself to be hurried down the road. She looked back at Martha who shook her head at the entreaty to join them.

Curious townsfolk swelled the group into a small crowd as we hurried along College Avenue to old Missouri Road. Ma protested and twisted her apron hem the whole way.

The whitewash on Judge Tibbett's house gleamed in the morning sun. Several soldiers, loitering on the broad porch, looked up at our approach.

"Here she comes," one of them yelled through the open door. He bounded down the steps, motioning for us to follow him around back to the open field behind the house.

A gigantic sweet gum tree, old as the hills, stood like a sentry in the center of the unplowed field. Bunches of star-shaped leaves furred the thick branches that twisted and crossed each other. A rope, dangling over a high branch, stirred slightly in the breeze.

Ma stopped abruptly at the sight. Small groups of citizens stood in huddles around the tree and looked our way. A dozen soldiers hurried into a line, straightening their coats in the process. The back door of the house slammed as a captain walked out and down the steps.

"Attention!" His voice bellowed in the sudden stillness that his appearance caused. Ringed in by wooded hills, the word seemed to hang in the air as if it had nowhere to go.

The soldiers drew up stiff, the stock of their rifles snug in their palms, barrels resting on their shoulders. The crowd, except for an occasional cough or whisper, and the rustle of those maneuvering for a better view, grew solemn, expectant.

I held my breath. I was about to see a dead man. Ma leaned against me. She was shivering, even though we'd broke out in a sweat with the hurry. I put my hand in hers.

The captain retraced his steps to the back door and held it open. Skinny, tall and lanky, ducked as he walked out, flanked by a soldier on either side. His hands were bound behind him, but he stepped briskly, not halting as one might expect from a man going to his final reward. Skinny stood for a moment at the top of the stairs, his face shaved smooth, long hair slicked back, and shirt tucked in.

Several young women oohed. Confederate

sympathizers I guessed and glanced back over my shoulder at them. What do they see in Skinny, all dandied up like he is? Most likely, he wants to look his best in his coffin, is all.

One dabbed at her eyes with a handkerchief and sighed. "Poor man."

Skinny stared out at the hills, the soldiers, the crowd, and finally the tree.

If he hoped Shilo Riddle would rescue him, he would be disappointed. Squads of cavalry were posted at various intervals along the ring of hills. The bushwhackers were bold and brash, but not stupid. Fayetteville had its number of citizens with tenderness for the Southern cause. One of them would have certainly warned Shilo against attack.

"Here he comes," rippled through the onlookers. I felt the press of those behind us stretching for a better view. "Don't go wasting tears on that bushwhacker," someone hissed.

With a grin as wide as a river, Skinny strode across the lawn and stopped in front of Ma. "I aim to thank you, ma'am, for coming. I do take a fancy to women with red hair. If my eyes are doomed to eternal darkness soon, let them take the memory of your glory along."

The girls behind us tittered and giggled. For once, Ma was tongue-tied, which, in itself, seemed as strange as watching a man walk to his death. Ma wasn't often at a loss for words.

"I was a dead man soon as those soldiers put hands on me," Skinny continued. "Weren't your fault, I know, even if you had such opportunity to free me as you did. Still, I wish to apologize for the wrong done you and yours." He looked past Ma to the girls behind her. His smile increased. "Will you forgive me?" he asked bringing his attention back to Ma and bowed slightly.

"Why…why," Ma stuttered. "I'd nay send a man to his eternal rest with a troubled mind. Of course, I forgive thee for thy thieving ways. 'Tis the Christian thing to do."

As soon as the words were out of Ma's mouth, the captain nudged Skinny forward. He glanced back over his shoulder at her, the smile fading, eyes fastened on her face as if imprinting it forever on their surface. He turned forward toward the tree, never missing a step.

A soldier carrying a wooden box marched a few feet in front of him. He set the box below the rope.

Casey bent and hissed in Ma's ear. "Skinny didn't ask *me* for forgiveness."

"What?"

"Scared my woman and the little ones half out of their wits," he grumbled, scratching through his beard and casting a one-eyed squint at Skinny. "Intended bodily harm on all us honest citizens. It's a wonder we aren't rotting in our graves right now."

Behind them, the girls' giggles transformed into sniffles which grew louder with each step Skinny took closer to the hanging tree.

"Didn't ask my forgiveness, neither," I said, trying to ignore the blubbering. I'd half a mind to turn around and tell those silly creatures just what all Skinny was guilty of. Instead, I stared at the procession, my eyes glued to the hanging, not wanting to miss a thing.

Skinny paused at the box. One girl abandoned her attempt to stifle her sobs and wailed openly.

"Go on. Get it over with," Gordon Casey called.

Several in the crowd echoed his sentiments, the somberness of the occasion broken. Hatred for the war and what it had done to their lives sounded in their voices. "Hang that Sesech!"

"Skinny has done wrong," Ma said. She gripped my hand so tight I thought blood would squirt out the ends of my fingers. With a glare at old man Casey, she forced her way back through the crowd, dragging me with her away from the hanging. "We don't have to take glee in his end."

I wanted to watch clear to the end, but there was no use in arguing with Ma. Her long skirt flared with each purposeful step taken around headquarters house and down toward the road. Ma was never one for glorying in another's misfortune.

I slipped my free hand into my pocket and fingered the arrowhead. The sun wasn't even high yet. I'd seen my two best friends slip away into the shadows of the woodland. They would travel far into the hills, taking shelter in ravines and caves, trying to be invisible to friend and foe—trying to preserve what remained of their livestock.

I'd seen Skinny walk to his death and do a good job of it, too. It was hard to hate such a man. A chorus of voices rose and carried down the hill and we knew—knew without seeing—that it was all over for Skinny.

"Wonder why it was so important to be forgiven for stealing your pickles?" I turned back toward the hanging. It was a useless effort. The house hid what was happening in the field. "He sure enough slicked up for his last day on earth, didn't he?"

"A man worries, first, on his legacy, and then, on his soul when he faces the everlasting, Ebby." Ma lifted her apron hem to her eye and sniffed. "All those onlookers will remember how he went to his end, proud and strutting, and little enough on his evil doings. Mind you now, Skinny didn't hang for stealing my pickles. 'Tis a shame, but it was the company he kept put him at the end of that rope."

Chapter 17

"That's all?" I looked down at the few articles of clothing that were folded and piled on a table in front of me. "Don't I get a weapon?"

"Yeah, how we supposed to do soldiering without a gun?" Tazewell reached for his pile of Union-issue clothing and pulled a pale-blue pair of trousers from the stack. He held them up to his waist and looked down at the bottom of the pant legs resting on the floor. "Aw, toad spit. They're too long. Don't you have another pair a tad shorter?"

The supply clerk didn't look up from his log book. "They are all the same size, private." He continued making entries." Take 'um or leave 'um."

"Look here, Ebby." Tazewell held the pants up. "You reckon yours are any shorter?"

I backed away from the stench of garlic that floated my way. "Gee, Taz, didn't you hear the man? They are all the same size." I raised my voice and leaned over the table. "Excuse me, sir, what about a weapon?"

The clerk flipped the cover of his book closed with a thud. "See those two Whitneys over there?" He pointed to two muzzle-loading rifles propped against the wall, both missing their wooden stocks. "That's all I got right now. And they won't be fit for service until the gunsmith picks them up. Some bucketheads don't know which end of their rifle to fight with."

"What's the matter, Ebby? You oversleep and get here too late to get yourself a rifle?"

I spun around at the sound of my brother's voice. Willy leaned against the open door-frame. Shafts of sunlight poured into the supply room around his lanky form, leaving his features in shadow.

"No one told me what time to be here, Willy." It was just like my brother to deliver up a slight every chance he got.

Willy ignored the response and nodded at the clerk. "Morning Chester. When's that wagon train from Springfield due in? Any rifles coming down on it?"

"Morning to you, too." Chester smiled back. "The supplies are due in, maybe tomorrow. Don't know for sure. The telegraph is down again. Guess you heard, they caught a couple of Sesech women up on a pole a couple of days ago, trying to cut the lines." He whooped. "Most outlandish thing I ever heard—women climbing poles! The Rebels have got women out doing their dirty work now."

Willy tucked both thumbs into the waistband of his pants and crossed to the table, shaking his head. "Doesn't that beat all. What will those fools be up to next?" He brought a heavy hand down on my shoulder. "Chester, this here is my little brother. Name's Ebby. Going to bring the war to a close, all by himself."

Chester nodded. "Aren't they all."

"Now, Willy, I never said any such thing." It was a struggle to pull free of his grasp.

"Oh, no. Ebby won't be getting all the glory." Tazewell puffed his chest out. "I aim to be elbow-to-elbow with him. You old codgers can just run on home. We'll get this mess straightened out."

"Shoo-ee!" Willy grimaced and fanned the air. "You eat the back end out of a skunk, fella?"

"Nah, that's just the glorious per-fume of garlic." A wide grin split Tazewell's face until all you could see were his teeth, crooked as a rail fence. "Keeps a man stout," he boasted, holding up a bulging cloth sack. "Got plenty to share here."

"Willy," I said, "this here is my friend, Tazewell Benton. Signed up same time as me."

"Benton?" William narrowed his eyes as he studied the boy. "Didn't we pick us up a couple of Bentons trying to raid the last wagon train?"

"Could be." Tazewell shrugged. "Bentons are as plentiful as ticks on a dog. Some aren't too bright, if you know what I mean. I aim to bring glory to the family name." He made a show of refolding his pants and placing them on top of the pile.

The clerk turned to a bin in the row of shelving behind him. "Willy, I got an Arkadelphia, here, picked up by one of the boys." He laid a battered rifle on the table. "It hasn't been checked over, so I hesitate to issue it, but since this is your little brother, and if you want to do the checking, I could let him have it."

I reached for the weapon. It was ill-used for certain. The wooden stock suffered a hairline crack clear back to the iron butt plate. A strip of rawhide secured the widest part of the stock, and the tip of the trigger was missing. It would be a might unhandy to use, all right, but it was a gun and would do until something better came along.

Willy slapped a hand on my arm and pushed the rifle back toward Chester with the other. "No, thanks just the same. Not going to have him using a

Confederate gun. Might be unlucky." He nodded toward the stack of clothing. "Get your issue, Ebby. Better find out what your captain means to do with you."

"Willy, I'm not too proud to use an Arkadelphia," I protested as Willy hustled me out the door. The late morning sun near blinded me, and I stumbled down the steps.

"That so? In case you don't know, the metal's inferior in those rifles. They aren't any better than shotguns as far as hitting anything."

"How's a man supposed to soldier without a weapon?" Irritation simmered in the back of my brain, with Willy all the time tellin' me how the cow ate the cabbage. "What am I supposed to do when bullets start flying my way? Spit on them?"

Willy stopped, hands on his hips. "Why don't you try outrunning them? As I hear tell, there's nothing you can't outrun."

Tazewell trotted up, brandishing the rifle. "Chester, back there, let me have it, seeing as how I'm a friend and all. I'll get it fixed up good as new."

The simmer roiled to a full boil, and I near exploded. "Now see there, Willy. I could have had that rifle myself except for you interfering."

"You could have." Willy glanced at Tazewell who balanced his stack of clothing in one arm and the Arkadelphia in the other, beaming so wide his smile was lipless again. "Except I don't give a lick if he gets his face blown off. Something happen to you, and Ma would skin my hide and hang it out to dry."

I hugged my bundle close and tromped after Willy. That was the thing about being the youngest in the family—no one forgets the fact even when he gets grown and takes on a man's duty. Plumb foolishness being in the cavalry without a weapon. If I got shot dead because I didn't have a gun, it would serve Willy right. It was high time someone else got taken to task by Ma.

"Captain Pollard," Willy called to an officer crossing the parade field. "Morning," he continued when the man turned and waited for our approach. "I want to introduce a recruit to you. This is my little brother, Ebby. Going to make a fine soldier."

Pollard shifted a stack of papers to one arm. He pushed his kepi hat to the back of his head and made a thorough job of scratching through an abundance of curly black hair. "Kind of young isn't he, Willy?"

"A mite. But he can read and write pretty fair."

"Reading and writing won't help much in a fight." He walked around me, looking me up and down like I was a prize heifer or something.

"Well." Pollard stopped in front of us, settled his hat back over the top of his head, and shrugged. "Does he know the countryside?"

"Like the back of his hand. Born and raised just south of here. Knows every hill and fishing stream between here and Fort Smith."

"Good. What I need is scouts. Reckon he can do that?"

"Yes, sir," I spoke up, before Willy could answer for me. "But I'll need a weapon. The quartermaster didn't have any to issue out."

"Don't have any horse to assign you, either, kid. You'll just have to make do."

"That's all right, cap'n," Willy said, a smile lifting

one corner of his mouth. "Ebby's got the fastest legs this side of the Mississippi. He won't need a horse."

The captain allowed a grin to flit across his face at the shared joke and flipped a thumb at Tazewell. "Who's this? Another brother?"

"No. That kid's no relation. But you better keep upwind of him, else you might grow faint. He could take out a whole company just by breathing on it."

"Tazewell Benton at the ready, sir." Taz stepped close, bringing his own distinct aroma with him. "Your worries are over with me and Ebby here." He attempted a salute, brandishing the rifle in the same hand and banging it into his forehead. "Aw, dang," he muttered, closing his eyes in a grimace.

Pollard took his hat off and slapped it against his leg with a laugh that filled the parade ground.

Willy joined the merriment and shook his head. "What'd I tell you, Ebby? Looks like them Arkadelphias are dangerous in more than one way."

Wiping his nose along his shirt sleeve, the captain sucked in a lungful of air. "Aw, mercy, where do these boys come from? Reckon I might as well make Taz, here, a scout, too." He resettled his hat and nodded toward the rows of tents lining the parade ground. "You boys find an unoccupied space down Company A's street. Be back here straight-up noon."

The captain turned and walked toward the officers' quarters.

When the captain was a respectable distance away, I aimed to give Willy a piece of my mind. "Willy, did you make the rounds this morning and tell the quartermaster not to give me a gun? And since I'm at it, why would you tell them not to give me a horse, either?"

Without waiting for a reply, I continued while the anger was fresh and boiling over. "What could it hurt to let me have a horse? How am I supposed to get along and do any soldiering? Why didn't you just tell them to strip me naked?"

"You flatter me to think I have that much influence, Ebby," Willy shot back. "So, you can unruffle your feathers. Supplies are rarer than hens' teeth west of the Mississippi. Doesn't matter if we are talking food, guns, saddles, or horses. Lots of fellows are making do, and you're no better than them. You just make sure to do what the captain tells you."

Willy leaned over to me and said under his breath, "And mind who you're friends with. Understand?" He turned and trotted after the captain with nary a backward glance over his shoulder.

I stared after my know-it-all brother. Who I was friends with didn't seem like it should be much of a worry. No gun, no horse—now that was a worry. What kind of army was this, anyway? I turned and stomped in the direction of the tents.

"Wait!" Tazewell called, taking long strides to keep up. "You're not mad because I got the only gun left, are you? Because if you are, that's not a problem. We'll share it."

"Now how is a man supposed to share a gun? You shoot a bullet, and then hand it to me. Doesn't seem like that makes much sense. You keep that busted-up old Arkadelphia. Willy says they're not safe, anyway."

"Aw, I've seen lots of these rifles. They're all right."

Large wedge tents lined either side of a wide lane.

Articles of clothing hung to dry on lines stretched between the shelters. Campfires smoldered with blackened coffeepots nestled in the coals.

I peered into the open tent flaps, looking for a vacant cot. Not only was there no horse, no gun, but there appeared to be no shelter, either. Several soldiers, hunkered down on their heels in front of a campfire, nodded to us as we passed.

"Hey." Tazewell squatted in front of the last tent. "This one appears to be empty. Guess we got us a home." Still talking, he duck-walked into the interior. "Dang, it's a dandy. Just some little bitty holes. Don't take any mind of the mold. That doesn't hurt anything. Pretty near perfect. What do you say, Ebby?"

"I say we haven't got any choice in the matter." I bent to look through the open flaps. "We signed up with some kind of pitiful army." I deposited my clothing on a cot. "This thing isn't too sturdy. How about yours?"

"Naw, mine isn't either. Most likely I'll just keep my stuff on it. I like to sleep on the ground anyway. How about we celebrate?"

"Celebrate? How we going to celebrate?"

"Simple." Tazewell lifted the garlic sack.

"I'm not munching any garlic bulbs."

"Just you wait." Tazewell opened the top of the sack, withdrew two brown eggs, and held them up between his forefingers and thumbs.

"Where'd you get these? I haven't had eggs since Ma's chickens were killed."

"Oh, around," Tazewell answered, depositing the eggs in my palms. He pulled open his knapsack and withdrew a small iron skillet. "How you like your eggs?"

"With the eye up."
Maybe things were going to be all right, after all.

Chapter 18

Dozens of flies, shiny green and big as pecans, clustered on the fresh mound of horse droppings. In a frenzy, they lifted and resettled, climbing over each other like pigs at a trough.

"Supper's over," I muttered and pushed a wide shovel under the mound, lifting and depositing the mess in an already full wheelbarrow. The flies followed along, their incessant buzz raised to an ear-splitting level.

"Missed some horse apples over there."

I turned around to find Willy standing in the entrance of the horse stall. "See?" he continued. "Right over there in the corner. Got to get them all. Don't want a half-done job."

"You did this on purpose, didn't you?" The mucking shovel had almost grown to my hand. Just the sight of my brother, standing there all smug-like, made me think of what else I might do with that shovel.

"What?" William shrugged his shoulders and threw both hands up.

"You told Captain Pollard to keep me mucking out stalls." It was just like my brother to do such a thing, showing he was still the boss. "I didn't join up to be spending my time in a barn. Once I get me a gun, I've got as much right as you to hunt down Rebs. Nobody knows this part of the country better than me."

Willy folded his arms across his chest and let out a long sigh. "Ebby, lots more to soldiering than riding around the countryside, shooting at Sesech and bushwhackers. They call us cavalry, but we've never had enough horses. And what horses we got are pretty near used up. Keeping them healthy is as important as shouldering a rifle."

He flicked a thumb toward several horses on the other side of the barn. "Those bays over there need a couple days' rest, but they're not going to get it. When the patrol comes in, you can bet some of their mounts will be in sad shape. There's nothing those riders are going to appreciate more than a good cup of coffee and a clean stall to rub down their nags before they turn them out in the corral. You didn't think being a soldier meant prancing around in your uniform with pretty girls swooning at your feet, did you?"

Flies buzzed around my head, and I let loose my frustration on the pesky critters, slapping them to perdition. Willy pointed toward the corner of the stall until I scooped the missed dung onto the blade.

"No, I didn't think any such thing," I said, balancing the shovel in mid-air. "And I'm not stupid about horses."

"Didn't think you were." Willy leaned against a post, his eyes daring me to action. "Just thought you ought to get the same talk I got when I was mucking stalls."

"Yeah?"

"Yeah!"

I thought better of what I was tempted to do. Instead, I heaved the shovel toward the wheelbarrow. A horde of flies loudly protested being disturbed, circling up, around, and back down.

"Well, now you give me the talk." I wiped my face along my sleeve again and just about gagged on the smell of my own sweat. "Don't reckon you know when I'll get something else to do besides this here work."

"Matter of fact, I do. Looks like you'll be sent out in the morning. You and Tazewell."

"Tomorrow? Why, it's about time. Where they sending us?"

"Got word a wagon train will be starting down from Cassville the day after next. Colonel Harrison wants to know the whereabouts of Buck Brown's bushwhackers. The captain seems willing to give you a chance to show him if you'd make a good scout." Willy looked around. Besides the snorting of two horses and the buzz of flies, the large barn was quiet. "Where's Tazewell?"

"Haven't seen him since breakfast. Got the luck of the Irish, he does." I leaned the shovel against the barn wall, gripped the barrow handlebars, and muscled it past William. "Hasn't ever been on barn-mucking duty."

"Lucky, huh? Just what do you know about him?"

"Not much. Right funny fellow, I can tell you. He's got something like thirteen brothers and sisters and a passel of uncles. Thirteen! Ma says that's an unlucky number, you know."

"Ma says lots of things are unlucky. Where's Tazewell from?"

"From all around. Virginia, mostly." I guided the wheelbarrow into the next stall. "His family doesn't seem to live in one place for long."

"Virginia, huh? There's something about him I

don't cotton to. You watch yourself around him."

"Aw, he's all right once you get used to how he smells. Eats them garlic bulbs like they're fried pork rinds."

Willy straightened and turned toward the barn entrance. "Something about him smells, and I'm not talking about the garlic." He paused before stepping into the sunlight and looked back, a wide smile creasing his face. "Ma's been a mite worried about you. I'll tell her you're keeping busy with important work. In fact, the Union can't do without your services."

He wagged a finger at me like he was talking to some small child. "Best turn in early tonight. You'll be out before dawn. I expect you to do the family name proud. By the way, same time you'll be heading north, a detachment will be heading to Van Buren to guard a supply of corn coming up from the south. That means there aren't any extra horses, so you'll be afoot. Of course, I told the captain you were nearly as fast as most of the poor nags we got, so that fact wouldn't matter none to you."

No gun. No horse. Uniforms that didn't fit. What kind of sorry army did the Union have in Arkansas anyway? I was still fuming on the matter that night when Willy paid me another visit in my tent.

"Cinch your backpack up tight," he said and sat down on my cot. "Else the metal will rattle and announce the fact you're out in the bushes." He looked around. "Where's your friend?"

"Don't know for sure." I threaded a strap through the buckle and made a show of pulling it tight just for Willy's sake. "Taz said he thought he'd go twist the tiger's tail."

Willy frowned and took on his know-it-all voice. "He'll have a hard time finding a game that will let him in without any money in his pocket."

"Oh, Taz ought to find someone willing to play a game or two of faro. He has a whole handful of coins and a wad of paper shinplasters, to boot."

"Where'd a fella like him get money like that?"

I shrugged because I'd wondered the same thing, too. "We were just talking about going on the scout tomorrow and how I was proud of the opportunity to foul Buck Brown's plans to rob the Cassville wagon train, when all of a sudden Taz decides to go hunt up a game. I told him we had to get up early, but he went anyway."

Willy's jaw went to working, which meant he was thinking—probably thinking about what else he could order me to do.

"What is it, big brother? I suppose you want to save me from myself, or maybe you got more advice you just can't wait to tell me?"

Willy stopped exercising his jaw and folded his arms across his chest. "Advice? About the only advice I haven't told you yet is to never climb a fence leaning toward you and never kiss a girl leaning away from you." Lines deepened in his forehead as he leveled his gaze.

"What I came to tell you isn't advice. It's a fact. A scout came in an hour ago. Shilo Riddle has joined up with the likes of Buck Brown. There's four or five hundred men threatening the road through Benton County all the way north to Missouri. Tomorrow, the woods will be crawling with Confederates and the like."

Chapter 19

My toes were plumb gleeful, wiggling about in new brogans. I was lucky enough to be near the supply tent when the clerk handed them out a day or two back. There was no right nor left to the things, but my feet would soon settle that score. I bowed the laces on the boots, stood, and stomped the dirt floor. Yes, they'd do.

Light from the stub of a tallow candle flickered against the tent's interior, casting shadows over Tazewell's empty bed. Darn fool! Must have been up all night playing faro. Should have gone and dragged him out of wherever he was.

I bent down to gather my equipment, and my eyes near popped out of my head. Tazewell's belongings stored under his cot yesterday were gone—canteen, haversack, knapsack, cartridge box, even his old Arkadelphia rifle.

"If that don't beat all!" The words popped right out of my mouth, though the only thing sharing my tent, at the moment, was a fat ol' wooly worm crawling up the center pole. "That big-eared, loud-mouthed back-end-of-a-donkey thought to make himself look good. Leave me sleeping whilst he appears to be Johnny-on-the-spot." I grabbed my gear, snuffed out the candle, and bolted from the tent.

The night air was cool, a pleasant respite from what would be a sweltering day once the sun fixed itself high in the sky. A chorus of snorts and snores testified to sleeping soldiers in the rows of tents. I took out on a run toward Captain Pollard's.

Five hundred bushwhackers roamed the miles of valleys and ridges between Fayetteville and Cassville, and I wasn't about to let Tazewell outshine me. I was woods-savvy and a fair tracker. I'd do all right. Still, the unease in my stomach had grown since I first sat up in bed.

Captain Pollard's lighted tent radiated a warm welcome. I stood a moment, looked down to check everything was buttoned that should be buttoned, then cleared my throat to announce my presence.

"Don't just stand out there hem-hawing around," the captain's voice boomed from behind the closed flaps. "Identify yourself, man."

"It's Private Fears, sir." I swallowed. My stomach seemed tied up tighter than a hangman's knot. "Reporting for scout duty."

"Enter, private."

A lantern hung from the center pole ridge of the tent, throwing a golden glow on the interior. The captain sat on a camp stool behind a small table. He wiggled two fingers to motion me in. Next to him, Willy, grinning like a possum, sat with both elbows resting on a map spread open before them.

"Morning, sir." I shifted my glance over to my brother. "Willy. Didn't know you would be here."

"You didn't think I was going to let you go off without a musket, did you?" Willy lifted a Springfield from the ground and laid it across the map, balancing the almost five-foot length on the table. "She's seen a lot of action, but she's sound." He ran his hand along the blued barrel. "It's got a new hammer and barrel bands. Ought to give you good service unless you go around using her like a club."

"It's mine?"

"Uh-huh." Willy ran both hands under the rifle and lifted it, as if testing its balance. "It is, unless you don't want it."

"Oh, no. I'm pleased as punch to shoulder such a prize."

"Good." Willy held the Springfield forward like he was presenting it to old Abe Lincoln himself.

I took the rifle. It was, indeed, fine looking. A few scratches on the butt. Nothing that couldn't be rubbed smooth. Both the rear and front sights still in place. I cradled it in my arms. Yes, a fine-looking weapon.

"Ebby! Quit mooning over that rifle. I said we haven't seen hide nor hair of Tazewell. Didn't he come with you?"

"Oh, Tazewell?" The captain and Willy both frowned at me "You mean he hasn't been here already?" The notion surprised me. Maybe I'd been wrong about Tazewell tying to outshine me. I turned toward the entrance, half expecting to see the boy's freckled face grinning back. Where in thunder was he?

"Could be he stopped off at the latrines. I reckon he'll be along soon enough."

The captain snorted. "Can't wait all day. You boys need to get up early enough to take care of the necessaries before you report for duty." He pointed a grimy finger at the map. "Here's where I suspect Buck Brown's main camp will be. Plenty of water, grass along this valley. Caves back in here, too." He ran his finger along the Wire Road from Fayetteville to the

159

Missouri border, and then tapped a spot to the east of the road. "Or, here. Heard reports of campfires scattered around here."

He looked up. "Don't get in any fights, even if there's only one or two men. The point of being a scout is not to let the enemy know you're about. It won't do any good for you to find them if you don't make it back to inform us of their location. Numbers, weapons, horses, wagons, provisions—no matter how insignificant you think the information, we want to know what you see. Understand?"

Captain Pollard sat back and fished in his shirt pocket for the stub of a cigar. He stuck it in the corner of his mouth. I could tell he was considering whether a raw recruit was up to the mission or not.

I swallowed the lump in my throat. "Yes, sir. Don't get in any fight. Just get back with what I see."

"Humph. Good, good. Since you're afoot, don't go any farther than you can return to camp in a day or two. A couple scouts left yesterday to join up with the wagon train. When the soldiers riding night duty get back in with their horses, several more scouts will leave out. They will go north to the border and up into Missouri, toward Cassville. You don't cross the border. Draw rations for four or five nights. Now, you better rustle up that partner of yours and be gone before the sun is up."

"Yes, sir."

Willy slapped both hands on the table and pushed up. "If you're finished with me, captain, I'll take my leave now and go with Ebby over to the mess tent."

"Very well. These dispatches should be complete in an hour or two. I'll need you to get them on down to

Fort Smith in a hurry."

Once outside, Willy clapped me on the back and held out a black pouch that was suspended on a leather strap. "I reckon you ought to have a cartridge box to go along with that Springfield."

"Thanks, Willy. I was afraid, when the captain found out I didn't have a weapon, he'd send me back to mucking stalls." I slung the pouch over my shoulder, along with my canteen and haversack.

Willy cleared his throat and led the way to the mess tent. I could tell another lecture was coming on. "If you're not careful and get yourself captured, you'll wish you were back to mucking out stalls. That'd seem welcome duty to looking down the wrong end of a barrel. I'm not sure I did you any favor rustling up that Springfield. Might make you braver than you ought to be."

I kept my mouth shut and unloaded my gear on a table. Just when I thought we were on even terms, my brother always seemed to belittle me in some manner. It was as annoying as a wart on my nose.

Except for two other soldiers eating at a far table, the mess tent was empty. Willy nodded to the two men as he went for our food and returned with tin plates of steaming corn mush, bacon, and biscuits. He plopped them on the table and motioned for me to sit opposite.

"Notice you got your new brogans on."

"Yes, sir." I waved steam off my plate. "Didn't have any beeswax to work into them and soften them up. Reckon you're going to tell me it was a mistake to wear them."

"No, appears you already know that. I was going to tell you, if those things get wet, don't take them off to let them dry."

"Wear wet boots?"

Willy nodded as he poured sorghum onto the plate and stirred. "Toes will curl plumb up without your foot to keep them flat while they're drying out." He lifted a spoon of steaming corn mush into his mouth and wallowed the hot bite from side to side before swallowing. "Whooo!" He sucked air between clenched teeth. "This'll burn the hair off your tongue. Eat up. Likely the last decent meal you'll have before you get back."

Large drips of sorghum ran down the can onto the table. William swiped at the thick puddle of dark liquid and sucked his fingers. "Probably best you don't start any fires. And, if you do, use dry oak or sycamore wood. It doesn't smoke as bad as some."

I stirred my plate of mush to release the heat. My stomach pulled into knots again as I listened to my brother speechify. No fire? Reckon Willy thinks dried beans don't need cooking.

"There's not much chance that it'll rain, but if it does, look on it as a blessing. Rain covers a lot of sounds. Sentries tend to pull in. They don't figure anybody will be crazy enough to be out sneaking around. Even when the rain stops, tents and duds have got to be dried out." William shoveled another bite into his mouth and swallowed. "Stick to the creeks. A big camp has got to be near water." He paused, spoon mid-air. "Then again, maybe they'll be camped in groups of no more than twenty-five or fifty in order to have enough forage for their horses. Whatever, in this heat, they will want more than a canteen of water."

The warm mush slid down my throat, easing the

tightness in my stomach. Food always was a sure-fire cure for most anything that ailed a person, and I was thankful that at this moment it appeared to have captured my brother's full attention.

"Keep that canteen full," William ordered, breaking the silence. "Even if it's half full, you come across a clear stream, fill it to the brim." He pointed toward the canteen resting on the table. "Another thing! Wrap that chain holding the cork with a scrap of fabric so it won't clank. Leaves crunching or a branch cracking could be an animal prowling around. Something clanking can't be anything else but a two-legged critter."

My mind went to churning with all the things I needed to remember. Even though I knew I didn't have a handkerchief, I patted my pockets for one—anything I could use to silence the sound of metal.

"Here," Willy huffed and handed me his handkerchief. "Should have told you last night not to wear your uniform today."

"Why?"

"Think about it, Ebby. There's no mistaking you for a Union boy with that uniform on. Wearing ordinary clothes, you might talk yourself out of a tight spot. Make 'em believe you're just minding your own business, out for a hunt or something."

"Well, my other pants had holes in both knees. Besides, I know how to keep my head down. I have no intention of getting caught."

"No one does." Willy broke his biscuit into pieces and spooned sorghum over them. He stabbed a bite and swirled patterns through the pool of heavy molasses. "In case you haven't noticed, that fool Tazewell Benton isn't out of the shitter yet."

"I noticed." I glanced toward the entrance. In fact, the boy's absence was proving to be a real obstacle to digestion. If Taz was sick with the runs, he should have sent someone over with a message.

"I aimed for him to hear some of this." William shook his head. "Not much telling what kind of scout he is, so you tell him what I told you. And tell that idiot to keep his voice down, not go blabbering at the top of his lungs. Plenty men have died for lack of brains in this fight."

His spoon clattered as he dropped it in the empty plate. "I'd sure feel a heap better if I was going with you on your first time out." He frowned and bit his lip. "But seems Captain Pollard has a satchel full of dispatches I'm to take to Fort Smith soon as they're ready."

He leveled his gaze, blue eyes intense. A shiny lock of black hair escaped his combed-back style to rest on his forehead. "I'd loan you my horse, Ebby, if I could. But out there, sometimes it's best to be afoot. Just don't go taking any darn-fool chances."

"Why, would you miss me if I got myself taken prisoner or killed?"

"Maybe." Willy straightened, and for a moment, I thought I saw a sure-fire smile. "About like I'd miss a boil on my butt." He pushed away from the table and stood. "What are you lollygagging here for? You got rations to draw. Day's getting away." He took out his watch, looked at it, and tucked it back into his pocket. His voice took his normal big-brother tone. "One last thing. Don't go shaming the Fears name, Ebby."

"I haven't got plans to do any such thing. And

settle your mind. You don't need to worry about me. Remember you said so yourself. I can outrun most anything, even a bullet."

"Hmm…" Willy stood for a moment, thumbs worrying the edges of his suspenders. "Well, I suppose I was a mite angered when I remarked on that fact. Mostly, I was just funning you about all that running business. Everybody knows the devil rides those Rebel bullets." This time there was no mistaking the smile he allowed to cross his face as he turned to leave. "If you get yourself hurt, it's the scolding I'll get from Ma I'm worried about."

Willy was a mystery. Mean-tempered and bossy one minute, bordering on nice the next. One thing for sure, there wasn't anything easy about being the youngest in the family.

Wooden boxes lined up behind the serving table held paper twists in one-day measures of salt, sugar, and coffee beans. I tucked five of each in the bottom of my sack, while cook dipped two cups of dried beans from a large barrel into a sack. Dried apples, ground cornmeal, hardtack crackers, and a dozen rashers of fried bacon completed my draw. I'd eat okay as long as I had the opportunity to cook.

I settled the haversack on my back with the canteen and cartridge box over my shoulder. The Springfield rested in the bend of my arm, just like it belonged there. For the first time since joining up, I felt like a sure-enough soldier. An honest-to-goodness soldier in the Union Army.

And I wasn't waiting another minute for Tazewell Benton.

Chapter 20

The rugged line of trees that ringed the camp's broad meadow looked dark and foreboding against the gray-tinged sky. Another thirty minutes and the sun would be fully over the horizon. I paused before stepping out onto the road to glance back at the tents, many of them aglow with a soft yellow light, lit from within by lanterns. A scattering of men shuffled toward the row of latrines.

If Tazewell had fallen in one of those pits, that was his affair. And if he'd stayed up all night gambling, that was his affair, too. Something didn't feel right about either one of those possibilities. An irritation worked at the back of my mind, like a chigger bite that couldn't be scratched.

The captain said to be on our way before the sun was up. If I jogged the short hike up to College Avenue, there might be a chance to see Ma on the way out of town.

"Well, howdy-do! I thought you'd never come along. Did you oversleep or something?"

I couldn't believe it. Tazewell, head propped on his haversack, lanky body stretched out on a patch of clover, grinned up at me, looking like a frog that had just swallowed a fly.

"Where you been?" I tore into him. "And don't tell me you took out early this morning." I settled the butt of the Springfield on the ground and rested both hands over the end of the barrel. The boy looked perfectly fine, not like someone who might have spent time in the latrines. "I know you never slept in your cot last night. I never mentioned the fact to the captain, but I ought to have."

"I can see you're not one to have the wool pulled over your eyes." Tazewell made a show of rolling the hem of his too-long army pants, stood, and shouldered his equipment. "It's not gentlemanly, but if you're going to make a mountain out of a molehill, I reckon I got to admit the fact I slipped away to see my girl."

Something else I couldn't believe. The skinny, freckle-faced, big-eared galoot standing before me had a sweetheart. He'd never mentioned the fact, and it seemed that was one of those things a man would share with his tent mate.

"You expect me to believe you got someone sweet on you?" I shouldered my rifle and started walking.

Eyes wide, Tazewell slapped his hand over his heart and fell into step. "Ah, now you've done hurt my feelings. I don't exactly have to slip up on the dipper to get a drink, you know. I have my charms."

"I've never seen any girl around here talk to you, much less moon after you. And with important scouting duty on us this morning, why would you go sneaking off in the middle of the night?"

"To tell you the Lord's truth, I didn't think on it until I was headed back to the tent after the card game last night. It came on me how dangerous this mission was. Well, I got to mooning over Flory Ann and how we've never done more than hold hands." Tazewell danced a few steps ahead and turned to face me.

Walking backward, he lifted his chin. "I trotted myself back over the ridge to her house and throwed myself on her mercy. I told her how it's not right for a man to go off fighting, maybe getting himself killed, and never even been kissed by a pretty girl."

"You're not going to tell me some girl fell for that sorry line?"

"Yep." Tazewell stopped in the middle of the road forcing me to stop, too. "She leaned onto me and wrapped her arms around my neck and sugared me good." He pulled himself up tall, a broad grin pulling his lips thin. "A great big ol' slobbery smooch that reached clean down and curled my toes. It was the kind of kiss that'll put ruinous thoughts in a man's head."

"Tarnation!" I jerked my hat off and slapped it to the ground. "Now I know you for a big old liar, Taz. Not any girl is going to brave that garlic breath of yours unless she's got a head cold and can't smell nothing." I pushed Tazewell out of the way, retrieved my hat, and broke into a lope down the road. One thing I can't abide is a liar and a braggart.

"Uh, that's the gosh honest t-truth." Tazewell panted as he trotted along. When he didn't get a response, he huffed to keep up the pace, muttering between breaths.

Our boots thudded against the hard-packed road. Leather trappings banging against our thighs set up a real ruckus. The assortment of wagons and tents in the refugee settlement loomed ahead, and I slowed my pace.

Did I have time to see Ma? Pink fingers of light streaked the lower horizon. Captain Pollard said to be out of town before daybreak. Of course, if Ma ever found out I'd passed so close and not stopped, I'd pay dearly for the omission. I stepped off the road. Of the two, Ma was certainly the most fearsome.

"Hey, where you getting to? Not likely to be any bushwhackers holed up in there," Tazewell said, his voice carrying in the early morning stillness.

"Shush," I hissed. Darn fool might as well announce to the whole world what we were up to. "Go on. I'll catch up." I turned toward the encampment. "Going to see someone. Won't be long."

"You aim to see your sweetheart? Get you a big ol' kiss, too."

"Just because you got your mind in the stars don't mean I do. Like I said, I'll catch up." I glanced back at Tazewell bent over, hands on his knees, catching his breath and staring after me. It was troubling. Somehow, I couldn't bring myself to admit to seeing Ma and not some girl who would swoon over me.

Several old men meandered around the jumble of tents or stirred ashes in campfires in an attempt to bring a flame to life. Light spilled through the entrance to our tent. Ma was up with the dawn just like I knew she would be. Wasn't any day going to catch her by surprise, she always said.

"Ma? It's me, come to see you." I leaned the Springfield against a wooden box and settled my equipment on the ground.

"Ebby?"

A work-roughed hand pushed back the tent flap, and Ma filled the narrow entrance. Lantern light from the interior haloed an abundance of red hair that fell loose about her shoulders. Her apron hung untied. Bare feet peeked from her long gray skirt.

"Saints be praised. My young'un come to see me."

I bent to allow her to hug tight on me. She kissed my cheek. "It's plumb good to see you, Ma, but I'm not a young'un in case you haven't already noticed the fact."

"Ah, lad, you get ten feet tall, you'll always be my young'un. Now, don't you look handsome in your uniform." Ma pulled her apron tight and tied it behind her back as she looked me up and down, approval evident in a broad smile.

"I've a bit of coffee beans left." She lifted a blackened coffeepot from atop a flat rock next to the campfire.

"No, Ma. I don't have time for such as coffee." I looked around to check for nearby people and lowered my voice. "I'm on my way north. Just stopped to say goodbye."

"North?" Her smile faded. "They sending you out already?"

"Not far, Ma. Only be gone a few days. Scouting. But don't go telling anyone."

"I knew it." She sank into her rocker and balanced the coffeepot on her knees, unmindful of the black smudge it left on her apron. "I knew it. It was a fearful sign."

"What are you talking about, Ma?"

"There." She pointed to a splattering of dried coffee grounds next to the campfire. "The sign of the cross, like a tombstone, it be." She hugged herself as if suddenly cold. "I felt the chill of the graveyard when I emptied the coffeepot last night and saw it."

I studied the discarded grounds, and if I squinted at them a certain way, I guess the spot resembled something like a cross. "I don't know, Ma. Can't say it looks for certain like a cross."

Ma drew up, green eyes pale, frightened, the joy of our meeting robbed by her certainty of the bad omen. "Be you blind? It is as plain as the nose on your face."

"Ah now, calm yourself, Ma." I studied the spot again. Once Ma got an idea in her head, it would take a swirly windstorm to dislodge it. "Seems to me it's your imagination." I ran the toe of my new boot through the grounds scattering them into the dirt.

"No!" Ma cried, leaping from the rocker and sending the coffeepot tumbling. "No. You've desecrated the sign. Oh." She buried her face in her hands and wailed. "And with an unlucky name you're carrying. Now, there's sure to be a death!"

Chapter 21

It felt good to be out in the deep woods again. The earthy aroma of decaying leaves among the thick timber was a welcome change from the odor of camp, ripe with cooking pots, unwashed bodies, and rows of outhouses. I shrugged out of my backpack and sank to the comfort of a spongy bed of ferns and moss. My feet ached with a fierceness that strained my natural civility.

"Blasted new shoes about rubbed me free a layer of skin," I said, pulling at the laces of one brogan. "Tramped all over creation and haven't seen hide nor hair of nobody. Makes you wonder if this report of five hundred bushwhackers hereabouts is a fish tale."

Tazewell was busy assembling a pile of leaves into a mattress, and I couldn't help but remark on his certainty that this was a good hiding place. "I thought you said, if those scoundrels were to be hiding anywhere, it would be down in this holler. We must have walked twenty miles."

Tazewell spread his blanket over the leaves and settled down with his hands behind his head. "We've walked thirty miles and not a lick shorter. Why Boone Holler's twenty-five miles long all by itself. I sure enough could've sworn they'd be here, with that creek meandering through it."

"Boone Holler is too narrow. That creek isn't but a trickle and shrubs too thick for a camp. You should've thought about that. Why, you'd have men spread out all along these twenty miles." I glanced at Tazewell. He yawned and crossed his feet at the ankles, a picture of contentment.

"Well, best not get too comfortable. What say we climb the ridge? Maybe we can catch sight of smoke rising above the tree tops."

"What say we just make camp?" Tazewell raised to his elbows. "I'm tuckered, not to mention the little fact that I could eat an oinker in one sitting. Getting shaky, what with you not taking a noon break—always pushing. Brain doesn't think right if it gets starved too long."

I studied my discarded brogan, the newness worn off after a day's tramp. Hunger had been an unwelcome companion, along with aching feet, for the hot afternoon. Maybe Taz was right. Get a fresh start in the morning.

"Tell you the truth, my belly is in a bit of rebellion, too. Might as well get a fire going. Use that old hickory branch." I pointed to a bare limb, several long dead leaves still stubbornly attached. "It's hardwood. Won't make much smoke. Trees so thick in here, don't have to worry about a bit of smoke announcing our presence. My beans have been soaking all day." I shook my canteen eliciting a dull rattle inside. "Won't take long to cook. You soak your beans?"

"Beans?" Tazewell broke twigs from the branch and threw them into a pile. "I don't have any beans."

"Don't have beans?" I couldn't believe it. "Didn't you draw any rations? Suppose to draw enough for four, five days."

"Nope."

"What'd you think to be eating? Or are you going to tell me you expect to live on garlic bulbs."

"Nope. You can eat those beans and hard wormy crackers the army hands out if you want. I brought my own vittles."

"Your own? Like what, and where'd you get it?"

"Oh, about a dozen hard-boiled eggs and fried chicken, corn pone, some salt pork, a measure of dried peas, and garlic, of course. Ma's not content unless she's cooking up a mess of greens and fried chicken. When she found her baby boy was going on a scout, well, she just wouldn't let me go until she provisioned me proper. Said all army food is good for is binding a fella's innards up tighter than a sausage." Tazewell wiped his hands on his pant legs. "Now, what you got?"

"Dried beans, dried apples, a few rashers of bacon, hardtack, salt, pepper. A little cornmeal. Oh, and coffee."

"Coffee? Hooeee! Reckon we can make a deal. You share your coffee. I'll share my vittles."

"You got fried chicken? Honest to goodness fried chicken? Tarnation! Ma and me haven't had chicken in weeks. Not since Shilo killed our Dominickers. Yeah! It's a deal. Get that fire going." I unloaded my backpack, pulling a small container from the bottom. "We'll use my pail for the cooking and yours for the coffee." I emptied my canteen. The soaked navy beans slid into the pail with a series of plops. In no time, I'd tied the coffee beans up in a handkerchief, pounded them good, and emptied the pieces into Tazewell's water pot.

Waves of heat rose from the flames flickering among the jumble of hickory limbs, and set supper to

174

cooking. Satisfied, I scooted back and leaned against a tree trunk. It was a few degrees cooler down in the holler, but the absence of so much as a puff of wind made the air heavy and sticky.

Tazewell squatted, arms circling his legs, and stared at the pail of bubbling coffee. "Howdy-do! Look! It's about the right color," he said and glanced up, a grin spreading across his face. "Give me your cup. What say I give you a chicken leg? We can have us a feast while those beans cook."

Steam curled from the pail as Tazewell, fingers wrapped against the heat of the metal, divided the brew between the two cups. He refilled the pail with water over the used coffee grounds and settled it back on the coals.

"Really, Ebby, there is nothing better than hot coffee to settle what ails a fellow. Pa has been brewing chicory 'n' wheat berries, but it's a poor substitute for real coffee." He settled back and held the cup under his nose, inhaling the aroma.

"You never said just exactly whereabouts your folks live." I'd puzzled on the question before, and now seemed a good time to ask.

"Here lately, we got us a place on Clabber Creek, north of Fayetteville." Tazewell pursed his lips to the cup rim and took a sip. "Mmm. Of course, before that, we were up at Rattlesnake Holler, then over to Gobbler's Knob. Lived in Missouri a bit. Virginia, too. Where do you live?"

"Lived all of my life on a farm down around Cedarville. Had to leave on account of bushwhackers. Your folks sure move around a lot."

"Pa says he doesn't like to wear out his welcome.

Says he wanted each of his boys born in someplace different so he can name them for the county they were born in."

I gnawed the chicken leg down to the bone, every bite, pure goodness. "How many boys you got in the family?"

"There's ten, last time I counted. Yes, sir, each one of us named for a different county." Tazewell clicked off names on his fingers. "The oldest is Franklin. Ma and Pa lived in North Carolina, at the time. Then Warren and Guilford. But Pa said there were too many Quakers, all the time religionifyin' there, so he moved to Kentucky, because Pa heard Pike was a fine county, so Pike's the fourth." He closed his hand and stared at his fist a minute. "Pike's my least favorite brother. He's mad-dog mean. Pa says it's 'cause he was born in Kentucky."

At the mention of Pike, a frown worked its way across Tazewell's face, drawing his brows down and his lips tight. He rubbed his hands together, as if banishing the memory, and started anew, ticking off another round of names.

"That's when the folks moved across the border to Logan County, Virginia. After Logan, they moved over to Greenbrier. Let's see, then Monroe and Mercer and Giles come along." He smiled, brandishing a mouth full of crooked teeth. "And, finally me. I'm the last."

"Jehosephat! Never heard of folks moving so much."

Tazewell chewed his bottom lip, his expression unreadable. Finally, he smiled again. "Moving isn't so bad. Kinda in the habit now. Pa likes Benton County so good, he changed our last name to Benton. That's about the fourth time he's done that." Tazewell reached for the pail of coffee and filled our cups again. "You ought to change that last name of yours, you know."

"Change my name? Now don't start that again." I swirled the last few swallows of coffee around in the cup trying to make the grounds settle into a cross. "I'm not ashamed of my name."

"In case you never noticed, people poke fun of your name."

"Not more than once, they don't." Surely Tazewell hadn't forgotten the thrashing delivered when he slighted the Fears' name. Strange, people changing their names like they changed their unmentionables.

"True." Tazewell nodded as if suddenly remembering the confrontation. "Guess if your pa likes the name, there's not much you can do about it."

"I haven't got a pa. He died before I was born, down in Mexico, in the war." I fished a bean out of the pot and blew on it. "I got three older brothers, and they more than make up for a pa. All the time bossing me around." I tested the bean with my front teeth. "These are done. Empty your pail, and I'll share."

Tazewell tossed coffee grounds next to the campfire and held out his pail. "You think three brothers be a bother, you ought to try nine. Still, it'd be funny not having a pa around."

"Well, not having a pa makes you special-like." I took a pinch of pepper from the paper twist and sifted it over my beans, ignoring the temptation to peek at the discarded coffee grounds. "For instance, I can cure babies of thrush mouth."

"Anybody else tell me that, Ebby, I'd say he was blowing wind."

"Why, I've done it lots of times. Mothers all the time bringing their little babies over to the house, sometimes in the middle of the night, just so as I could breathe in their mouth and cure them. It's just one of those things the Lord gives to those that haven't ever looked on their pa.

"Come spring, I got to do all the planting in Ma's garden patches. I hold the seeds in my mouth until they're good and wet, then plant them. When I doctor up corn like that, it breaks ground two weeks earlier than undoctored corn. Same with peas and such. My mouth runs plumb dry sometimes." I scraped the spoon along the bottom of the pail, chasing the last of the beans. "On occasion, being special 'cause my pa died before I was born is a real bother. Ma says it's a duty, and that specialness will turn against me if I get selfish about it."

Tazewell squinted, as if seeing me in a new way.

Right then, a new thought took root. Special people didn't have unlucky names. Ma ought to know that.

I took up the Springfield and ran my hand down the barrel, feeling the tiny nicks in the metal. Several targets—a couple of squirrels and a rabbit—had crossed our path earlier. Any other time, I would have taken aim, tested the pull of the weapon. Even though the woods seemed empty, it'd be foolish to risk the noise and alert the camp of bushwhackers that was bound to be out here somewhere. I heard Willy's cautioning voice in my ear every time the temptation presented itself.

"You haven't so much as let that rifle out of your sight, even took it to the bushes with you," Tazewell complained. "How come you never let me take a gander at it? What do you think I'll do to it? Why you being such a stingy-gut?"

I settled the Springfield across my legs. I'd resisted handing over the weapon all day, a sense I couldn't explain kept my fist tight around the barrel.

"Ah." I shrugged, hoping to put him off. "Might put one of those hexes on it. Big Jolly said it's not good to pass around a weapon. Weakens the spirit that lives in it."

Snorting, Tazewell settled down on his blanket. "Stupid Indian nonsense you're spouting." He turned his back and muttered loud enough to be heard. "You're just being selfish. Don't want me to have a look at it, is all."

No, it wasn't that. There was a different reason, one I didn't understand, a feeling that followed me all day and raised the hair on the back of my neck.

The whir of night crickets grew loud as evening settled. A golden glow, cast by the campfire, threw the surrounding woods into deep shadows. With the darkness, I felt a tiredness creep into my bones—a tiredness born more of the constant vigil, rather than the distance traveled.

An entire day, and there'd been no sign of a living soul, not even a farmer or hunter, no matter which direction we'd taken. Downright spooky, unless you consider most folks had abandoned their farms, leaving the whole countryside a wilderness. Tomorrow, I planned to hike over to Little Coon Creek and follow it, regardless of whether Tazewell agreed to the plan.

I dug a handful of dirt to sprinkle over the embers. No use risking leaves drifting into the campfire and sending up a column of smoke. The scattering of coffee grounds tossed earlier by Tazewell drew my eye. I didn't want to look, didn't want to see something ominous written in the dirt, but the pull was irresistible.

"Hey, Taz," I whispered, "does that look like a cross to you?"

Chapter 22

I crouched in the shade of a stand of sycamores lining Little Coon Creek and swatted a swirling cloud of summer gnats. They seemed drawn to my face, darting up my nose at every opportunity. Tazewell squatted beside me, chewing on a clove of garlic like old men do when they nurse a wad of tobacco in their cheeks. The boy was undisturbed by the tiny insects. Must be that almighty awful stench.

"Give me one of them," I whispered and pointed to the bulb of garlic Tazewell rolled about his palm in boredom.

"All right," he whispered back and pulled a fat section away from the bulb and picked the tissue-thin skin off with the tip of his pocketknife blade. He held the clove between his thumb and forefinger. "Ma says it's a sure-fire cure for what ails you. Besides which, it will keep you stout and strong."

"I just want to keep those bugs out of my face."

Tazewell leaned over, his breath announcing his closeness. "How long we going to sit here? I got moss growing up my backside now."

I shuddered as I bit into the crunchy clove, releasing the garlic's sharp tang. Fresh hoofprints were dug into the soft dirt. Three horses had watered at the creek not long before. Despite the heat, water still pooled in some of the tracks.

"Until I'm sure there aren't any stragglers coming up from behind..." The inside of my mouth began to burn, and I plumb lost my ability to speak the second time my teeth ground into the garlic pulp. The clove wrapped around my jaw teeth, as if glued in place, and I worked to dislodge it with my tongue. Spit filled my mouth, carrying the strong taste to the back of my throat and finally, into my nasal passages. I gulped a mouthful of air, gnats, and all, and accidentally swallowed the chewed lump.

Tears erupted and rolled down my cheeks as I struggled to hold back my breakfast of hard biscuits and bacon. Potent fumes rolled up from my stomach. I exhaled, sure that, if I had a Lucifer stick in my fingers, it would ignite. I buried my face in the crook of my arm to suppress a fit of coughing.

"Lord Almighty, Taz, how do you stand chewing that stuff?" I managed to croak. I took a big swig from my canteen. Water, laced with the tinge of metal, chased the fumes back where they came from and diluted the bitter flavor that coated my mouth.

"Ah," Tazewell drawled, his cheek bulging, "reckon it's just one of them acquired tastes. Been chewing the stuff since I was a young'un. Ma said it's a measure of a man what can take it on raw. There's those that can't, you know." He spit bits of spent garlic to the ground and grinned as he bounced the remainder of the bulb in his palm. "Not supposed to swallow it, you know."

"How come you never told me that?"

"You didn't ask"

"Tarnation. A body puts something in his mouth, he figures it's all right to swallow. I didn't aim to swallow it on purpose."

"Aw, won't hurt you any." Tazewell frowned. "Oh, say, you not seized up, are you? Because if you are, swallow another two or three cloves, and they'll clean your innards in no time."

"I'm in firm control of my bowels, thank you." I gripped my stomach because, at that moment I wasn't quite sure of the fact. Saliva pooled under my tongue in response to the lingering taste. It was enough to give a man new respect for Ma's alum pickles as a sure-enough cure for constipation.

"Don't look like anyone's around." By now my canteen was empty. I peered through a screen of tall switchgrass at the sparkling stream a few feet away. Overhead, birds swooped and dipped between branches. The trill of cicadas swept along the treetops in a continuous chorus. "And I aim to get me some water."

Little Coon Creek splashed over rocks and pebbles, a half-foot deep in hollowed-out places. In another month, it would be barely a trickle. I lowered my canteen into the creek and watched bubbles rise, as water filled the container.

"Hey, Taz. You notice this?" I pointed upstream. "Another rider came along down the middle of the water. Get down close, you see the marks still in the gravel. Water hasn't smoothed them out yet. This fellow met up with those three who come out of the woods back yonder."

"Hmm. Could be hunters meeting up."

"Don't know. Something strange about it." I belched another round of hellfire and brimstone. "I want one of those boiled eggs you got stored in your pack. Got to eat something that'll sop up this awful taste in my mouth." I gathered several small sycamore branches and held them out. "Tie these up in your bedroll. We got lucky last night with plenty of hardwood. Might not be any like this where we make camp tonight. Don't want to advertise our whereabouts with a lot of smoke. Got a feeling, maybe we're getting close."

"I was thinking," Tazewell said as he harnessed the sticks in with his blanket. "Why don't we follow the creek upstream where those tracks come from? There's a big meadow that'd make a good place to camp about six miles away. Been there hunting for deer. Bushwhackers might be camped in such a place."

"I been there, too. It's more like ten miles." I shaded my eyes to check the sun's position. "These tracks are the first we've seen since leaving camp yesterday. They're fresh, and they pick up over on the other side. See where the ground is torn up?" I pointed to the far bank. "It'd be dark before we could get back here if the meadow doesn't prove out." I finished knotting the leather thongs that held the scavenged firewood. "I say we follow the tracks, see where they're going, instead of where they been."

"What if those tracks aren't anything but farmers out hunting?"

"What if they're bushwhackers?"

"If they are, aren't more than a few. I thought we were supposed to find the main camp—four or five hundred men, you said."

"We are. Ever think those riders might be scouts for Buck Brown or Shilo Riddle, heading in to the big camp? And all we got to do is follow them."

"Nah, like I said, they're likely farmers, out for a

hunt. Those horses weren't trotting. Tracks aren't deep enough. Men heading in for camp, where there's sure to be hot grub, most likely don't amble along, casual-like."

I just looked at Tazewell, standing, arms crossed, jaws slowly working the ever-present cud in his cheek. Must be that garlic juice had pickled his brain. It doesn't make sense to go ten miles on a *maybe* when you got a sure thing right in front of your eyes.

"I'm following the tracks. Only got an hour left before it'll be too dark. We don't turn up any sign of the main camp this way, we can check out that meadow tomorrow. Now, you can come along with me, or you can strike out down that-a-way on your own."

Indecision was written, plain as day, on Tazewell's face. His amber eyes were dark, darting first downstream and then off into the woods and back. The tip of his tongue pushed through the gap in his front teeth like he was plugging a hole in his mouth. It was a habit he engaged in whenever he was thinking, which wasn't often since he seldom quit talking.

"Always has to be your way, doesn't it?" Tazewell's Arkadelphia leaned against a tree trunk. He reached for it and fingered the sight at the end of the barrel for a moment. With a sigh, he swung it over his shoulder. "We'll go your way for a bit."

"Good." I held my hand out, palm up. "I believe we got us a deal. Coffee again tonight for a share of your vittles. I'll take my egg now, please."

"You'll be sorry you didn't listen to me." Tazewell dug into a heavy cloth bag which sagged at his waist and pulled out a large brown egg. He slammed the egg into my hand, turned, and splashed across the creek, unmindful of the water that sloshed over his boot-tops.

I tried to avoid the deepest holes, but water still managed to soak through my shoe leather and socks. Tazewell waited on the other side, balancing his rifle across his shoulders.

"You've been obstinate ever since we stopped at that squatter's camp back in town. What's the matter?" he asked. "Didn't your girl give you a goodbye kiss, like mine did?"

"Oh, I got a goodbye kiss, all right." I thought it best to keep Ma's premonition to myself. Some people might not understand seeing signs in coffee grounds. "Now, get out of my way." I pushed past Tazewell, scanning the ground while peeling away bits of eggshell. "Some of us are gentlemen and don't go around rooster proud over fletching a kiss off some empty-headed little ol' girl."

"Flory isn't a little ol' girl. She's full grown—straining the buttons on her frock, if you know what I mean. And it seems to me, most women are a mite empty-headed."

I ignored the chatter behind me and sank my teeth into the soft egg. If anything was my favorite food, it was an egg. Nothing I liked better than eggs, no matter which manner they was cooked—eye up, green onion scrambled, boiled solid, or pickled.

"Most times, eggs are plenty scarce. I meant to ask you last night. How is it you're never at a loss for them, Taz?"

"Oh, Ma has her ways. She'd consider it a hanging offense anybody touch her chickens. Wait up a minute. Got me a problem." He squatted to one knee, reworking the laces on one brogan, changed knees, and picked at the knot in the other boot.

I shifted from one foot to the other. A standing man was a sure invite to gallinippers, and sure enough, one stung my neck. Darn bloodsuckers. The bushes and underbrush were alive with them this close to the water.

Tazewell spit into his hand and rubbed his neck and face. "Garlic spit. A little garlic spit and I'm never bothered with mosquitoes. You need another clove?"

"No! I'd rather be eaten alive by those critters than munch another one of those stinky things, and that's a fact."

"I got plenty of spit for both us." He cupped his hands and with a loud hack spit into them. "I might not be able to doctor seeds, but I can keep bugs away."

"Thanks for offering to share." I shook my head. "Believe I'll decline your generosity. Come on. We've wasted enough time."

I bent to the task of following the hoofprints showing through the creeping foliage. Dense vines covered the narrow trail in places, leaving only a pile of horse droppings or occasional broken branch to show the way. Oak, hickory, and spindly hackberry trees, their branches interlocked, blocked waning sunlight, and threw the forest into deep shadows.

"Might as well make camp, Taz. Liable to miss something in the dark, maybe go off the wrong way. We can pick up the trail in the morning."

"We should have gone on upstream," Tazewell grumbled as he dropped his equipment on the ground and kicked several rocks into a pile for ringing a campfire.

"Maybe." Deep down in my bones I knew I was correct. Somehow, it didn't seem right to be going away from the direction of the tracks. Still, if I was wrong, it'd be hard admitting the fact. I squatted and arranged the dried sycamore branches inside the circle of stones.

"I'll get some of these coffee beans broke up. How about we put some of my bacon in your dried peas? We can make a dandy soup." I glanced at Tazewell, who only grunted his agreement and dug in his haversack for a pail.

Before long, the hearty aroma of coffee rode gentle puffs of air. Tazewell stared into the simmering pail, his empty cup dangling from one finger. He chewed the ever-present pulp of garlic with a deliberate purpose, his normal chatter absent.

No doubt about it, Tazewell was piqued over the direction we were going. I cleared my throat to get his attention. "I pondered the matter a lot, Taz. We're heading northwest, away from the Wire Road. If I was hiding a big camp of men, it wouldn't be close to a well-used road. Like as not, they'd be discovered."

Tazewell divided the coffee between the two containers. He paused, amber eyes almost golden, as he stretched to hand back the cup. "You sure you want to get that close to a camp of bloodthirsty guerillas and Rebel bushwhackers?"

"Well, I don't aim to walk right in and shake hands." I blew across the rim of my cup. "I get me a gander at them, and skedaddle out of there, quick as a rabbit."

"Quick as a rabbit?" Tazewell slurped his coffee and sat back.

"Sure, I'm a pretty fair runner." I wiggled my toes inside the damp brogans. They had molded to my feet, the stiffness which marked them as new, broken down, making the leather almost a part of me. "Don't know anybody can beat me in a race."

Tazewell didn't answer. Instead, he turned his attention to the pea soup and ate in silence.

The boy was a puzzle all right. Normally such bold-faced bragging would elicit a response. Without my companion's constant chatter, the woodland sounds grew loud—fiddler crickets and water frogs, tree locusts and the hoot of a distant owl, all stirred together in a nighttime chorus. Beneath the music, an annoyance, like an uneven hum, rose and fell.

"You hear something?" I asked, peering at Tazewell through heat waves rising from the simmering campfire.

"Nope, nothing but crawly critters," Tazewell answered without looking up.

"Well, I'm tuckered out. Kick dirt over those coals when you're ready to bed down, Taz." I shifted to get comfortable, wishing I could take my wet shoes off and allow my feet to breathe.

The bushwhackers were out there. I could feel it, feel it settle over me like the dew that was already settling out of the night air. I closed my eyes and hugged the Springfield up to my body, the odor of oiled metal strong in my nostrils. Tomorrow, we'd find the bushwhackers' camp and be on our way back to Fayetteville with the information. Maybe then, Willy would quit treating me like a child.

"Time to shake out of those blankets." Sharp and quarrelsome, the husky voice broke the early morning quiet. "Haven't got all day."

I struggled to sit up and blink my eyes awake. A

lanky man, face shadowed by a week-old beard, sat astride a buckskin horse. Clouds of smoke wafting from the campfire ebbed and flared, alternately revealing and obscuring the rider's features. There was no mistaking the rifle cradled in the bend of his arm, with its long barrel resting on the saddle horn and pointing straight at me.

Chapter 23

"Morning, little brother." the rider nodded to Tazewell, who sat leaning against a tree, looking as if he'd swallowed his cud of garlic. "Thought Pike told you to keep the scouts clear of the camp."

Within seconds, the sting of smoking leaves smothered me, filling my throat and nose, watering my eyes. My heart jumped to my throat. Evil stared down on me, and I was caught like a rabbit in a trap. The Springfield lay beside me, heavy and unwieldy. Still, my fingers slid down and sought the trigger. Madness to try a defense, yet the urge was powerful.

"Wouldn't try nothing, if I was you." The rider shifted the rifle butt to his shoulder. "It'd be plumb foolish for a fellow to think he could get off a shot when he got a bullet aimed right at him." He smiled, then, and it was pure soul-shaking. "Of course, I haven't seen too many Union boys with a lick of sense." Motioning with the gun's barrel, he raised his voice. "Get over there, Taz. Get that Springfield. Pike isn't going to like you letting someone get within a couple miles of the camp."

Tazewell spat a wad of chewed garlic onto the ground and stood. "Morning, Monroe. You know anything brother Pike does like?" He walked around the campfire, his Arkadelphia laid casually in his arm, and squatted next to me. "No o-fense, Ebby. You just wouldn't listen to reason. I told you we should have gone on down to that meadow."

I stared hard into Tazewell's freckled face, searching for the signs of treachery I should have seen. The realization was a punch in the belly—disappearing from work duty, lagging behind, quarreling about the direction we were going, food most people couldn't get—all indications something wasn't right. I'd just been too dumb to see what Willy must have suspected. At that moment, I wasn't sure who I hated most—me or Tazewell.

"Listen to reason?" My head felt tight and big as a washtub, ready to explode with the anger building inside. "You mean listen to your lies. You piled leaves on that fire, so your Sesech kinfolk would find us, didn't you?" I steadied my voice. "Why didn't you just shoot me whilst I slept?"

"Aww, we shared vittles, coffee together, Ebby. We've been friends, tent mates. You're not a bad sort." Tazewell exhaled a loud sigh. "Truth is, it don't seem the polite thing to do, shoot somebody whilst they sleep."

"Not polite?" I thrust my face close to Tazewell's and looked him straight in the eyes. I was so riled, not even the stench of garlic repelled me. "So, you get someone else to do your dirty work, is that it?"

"Enough palaver! This isn't a tea party," Monroe growled. "Shilo sent me over to check out the smoke before I had breakfast." He narrowed his eyes, and his words took on a certain menace. "And I aim to get back before it's all gone. If I have to get down off this nag and get that rifle myself, I won't think kindly of the extra work you put me to."

"Keep your drawers on, Monroe. I've had me a powerful covet on this Springfield." Tazewell ran his hand over the wooden stock and reached for the barrel.

I still had several fingers hooked in the trigger guard and couldn't let go.

"Come on, now. Give it up." Tazewell rolled his eyes toward his brother as he tugged on the rifle. "I might not want to shoot you, but Monroe, here, would as soon put a hole in you as to worry about getting you back to camp."

"Take it, then." An insult formed in my mouth and rolled out before I could think better of it. "I should have known, if it smells like a skunk, it probably is a lowdown, rotten, miserable skunk!"

A slight frown flashed across Tazewell's face. He shrugged. "I've been called worse. Now, reckon you better gather your stuff." He stood and hooked the Springfield under his arm. "Hey, Monroe, what was brother Guilford fixing for breakfast? I'm a mite hungry, myself."

"Usual, I reckon. Gruel and biscuits. Couple of the boys brought in some smoked hams from over in the territory yesterday." Monroe lifted his hat with two fingers and scrubbed at his scalp, resettling the hat over large ears, proof positive of a Benton trait. He continued to chase the itch by running his fingers through his thick beard and scratching under his chin. "Getting hard to find grub hereabouts these days. Farmers all cleared out. Brother Greenbrier came in last night with a deer."

His ritual complete, Monroe stretched and motioned me down the trail with the end of his rifle. "Get moving. Reckon Pike'll want to have a word with you before the feasting commences."

I slung my haversack across my back and grabbed up my blanket. Even with wisps of ground fog still settled in low spots, the trail obscured in shadows yesterday evening, was easy to follow in daylight. Meadow larks calling and blue jays quarreling replaced the chirrup of night crickets.

Tazewell led the way, the barrels of both guns resting on his shoulders and staring back at me like two dead eyes—a sure-enough taunt of my stupidity. Plans of escape flitted in and out of my mind. The hair on the top of my head prickled. With Monroe on horseback behind me, rifle trained at my back, I was trapped. At least I still had one weapon—Curly's knife—tucked in the bottom of my haversack.

I could smell the camp long before I heard it. The odor of wood smoke and hundreds of horses and men, faint at first, grew stronger with each step. A mile! If I'd pushed on another mile before making camp, I would have realized how close I'd come to my intended mission.

The whicker of horses and hum of voices, punctuated by the occasional clatter of pans and ring of an ax, announced the camp minutes before we emerged from the thick forest. A broad clearing, bounded on one side by the rugged face of a steep limestone hill, stretched the length of several cornfields. Ribbons of water oozed from a dozen cracks in the limestone and flowed into a large pool that sparkled in the morning sun. A cave, cut into the base of the hill, gaped like a toothless yawn.

The sight sucked the breath right out of me. Thin columns of smoke from dozens of campsites snaked upward. Wagons, tents, and lean-tos dotted the meadow in haphazard array. Everywhere, men crawled from their shelters to stretch and go about morning chores, squatting beside their fires and tending to breakfast, leading groups of horses to water. It was magnificent. The perfect place to hide—a broad clearing, ringed by a forest of ancient oaks and white gum, hawthorns and hickories, with plenty of water.

The horse snorted and I felt a splatter of mucus on the back of my neck. Pushed from behind, I stumbled down the slope and into the open. Hair bristled along my arms and the top of my head as men glanced up, unsmiling—making me feel like Daniel in the lions' den as I moved deeper into their midst.

Flies swirled around a deer carcass strung up on a pole supported by crossed timbers. A man, hands bloody and holding a large knife, stopped his work on the carcass to watch us pass.

"Morning, Taz," the fellow called. "Pike won't like you bringing an outsider in." He threw a handful of entrails to several dogs. They bounded onto the offering and took off, dragging the long intestines behind them.

"Morning, Greenbrier," Tazewell answered. "How about telling me something Pike does like?"

"Oh, corn liquor, cigars, a good fight, Ma's fried chicken, and a pretty woman. That ought to cover it." Greenbrier let out a laugh that rippled across the field causing the attention of half the camp to turn our way. "He's up there with Shilo and Buck right now." He pointed toward the cave with the knife. "Make sure he's finished breakfast before you go busting in."

Monroe reined his horse, dismounted, and ground-tied the animal. "We brought in a couple scouts last night." He nodded to two uniformed men, sitting with hands tied together under their legs. "We're getting us quite a collection. Union folk are almost thick as ticks on a hound dog."

I stared at the men as we passed, searching my memory for recognition of them. Glum-faced, they stared back. Calvary, by the insignia. Maybe I'd seen one of the men around camp. I couldn't be sure.

I leaned into the short climb to the cave, following the trail sprouting with bright green ferns that stirred with my passing. Water streamed from a large fissure and pooled at the back of the cave. Smoke blackened the roof, attesting to its use over a number of years. Indians, most likely. With the exception of the inhabitants, it was a beautiful place.

Three weather-beaten men sat at a rough wooden table and looked up at our approach. Tin coffee cups held down corners of a map.

"Well," one man said, pushing his battered gray hat back off his forehead, "what we got here?" He spit a stream of tobacco on the ground, stained a dark brown with previous such hits.

Shilo Riddle! A chill went up my back. I caught the gasp that rolled up with last night's supper in my throat. Maybe Shilo wouldn't recognize me. It'd been close to a month since the bushwhacker and his boys made the raid on Ma's farm.

Tazewell stepped forward. "Morning, Shilo." He tilted his head toward another man with tidy good looks, curly brown hair, thick mustache. "Buck." Then he nodded to the third man at the table, red hair, big ears, a cigar clamped in his mouth. "Morning, Pike."

I would have known the fella for a Benton without

introduction. He looked like an older Tazewell. Age hadn't improved the family characteristics, just deepened the wrinkles and darkened the freckles.

"This here is Ebby Fears from down around Cedarville. He's my tent mate back at the Union camp."

I felt my heart sink and hazarded a glance at Shilo, who'd stopped working the wad of tobacco in his mouth and sat forward, eyes as black and lifeless as two lumps of coal. If there was any hope I wouldn't be recognized, it was gone now.

"Fears. If that's not a peculiar name." Pike spoke out of the side of his mouth, the cigar fluttering up and down with his speech. He stopped to puff on it, creating a brilliant glow on the tip; then, he removed it and, with mouth pursed, blew the smoke upward. "It needs changing, if you ask me."

A flicker of anger heated the chill I'd felt moments before. I knew better, but the retort wouldn't stay put in my head. "Only reason I can figure a man would shuck his name is if it wasn't honorable, so I reckon I'll keep what I was born with."

"I already commented on the shortcomings of his name, Pike." Tazewell shook his head, as if appalled at my lack of good sense. "You can question him if you want. But I can save you the time. I know everything he does, which is three groups of scouts have been sent out, hunting your whereabouts because a supply train is on its way down from Cassville. Looks like you already captured a passel of the scouts back there."

"These boys are afoot, Pike." Monroe snorted. "Sent them out without any mounts. Pitiful, don't ya think?"

Pike pushed away from the table and stood. "Yeah,

pitiful." He removed the cigar from his mouth, flipped the ashes, and settled it in the crevice behind his ear. The corners of his mouth snaked up into a smile as he walked toward us. "Thought I told you to keep clear of the camp, unless you heard something we needed to know."

"You told me, Pike. Only you didn't tell Ebby, here. He doesn't know you like I do. Seems he figured to sneak up and have himself a look-see, then skedaddle back to Fayetteville. I couldn't shake the notion out of him."

As if he were talking to a child, Pike spread his hands out. "Well, then, why didn't you just shoot him and be done with it?"

"Aww, Pike. We shared coffee. I couldn't shoot a man I shared coffee with."

Quick as a flash, Pike boxed Tazewell across the side of the head and bellowed. "Unless you want to share his coffin, I say you start thinking about doing as I say."

The action was so unexpected that I stumbled backward. Rough laughter echoed in the cave.

Tazewell brushed the side of his face with his hand, pushing back a strand of red hair. Without flinching, he lifted his chin. "Well, now, I didn't want to deprive you of the honor, Pike, knowing how you like to use that Sharps of yours."

"Fears," Shilo slammed both hands down on the table, causing everyone to jump. "I see you didn't think about what I said, did you? Went and joined up. Can't say that was a smart thing to do."

I shuddered at the memory of the gravelly voice, took a deep breath, and stood as tall as I could. It wouldn't do to look cowardly. Willy always said to stare trouble in the face. Only, it's hard to look a man in the eye that has designs on killing you.

"Answer me, boy. You think that was a smart thing to do?"

My voice failed me. I sucked my lower lip between my teeth to quell the quiver taking root.

"Cat got his tongue, I reckon." Shilo narrowed his eyes. "No, you don't have to answer that. A man doesn't like to admit he's dumb. What you do have to answer is, anything else Taz forgot to tell us? Like when that wagon train was expected to hit the Missouri border? Or how many men Colonel Harrison plans on sending out to escort those supplies down to Fayetteville?"

I shoved fists into my pocket, searching for something to say—anything to throw them off the track and thwart an attack on the wagon train. I'd never mastered the art of lying or even bending the truth. Ma had always seen right through such attempts, and, most likely, Shilo Riddle would, too. Then, there was Tazewell, who'd for sure know the right of the matter.

"You hear the man talking?" Pike questioned as the silence stretched. He retrieved his cigar from its perch in the bend of his ear and rolled it back and forth between his thumb and forefinger, the lit end flaring from orange to red with the motion.

"Ebby might have gone deaf, but I haven't." Tazewell stepped up to face Shilo, Pike's handprint still bright red on his cheek. "There is nothing I forgot to tell anybody. Colonel Harrison doesn't hardly talk to lowly scouts. All we were told was get out, scout around, and bring back information."

He turned to Pike. "But Ebby's got something I know you'll like." He jerked my haversack off my back and tossed it on the table. "He was issued a five-day ration of coffee. Might be enough left for a couple pots in there."

The mention of coffee sweetened Pike's mood. Even Shilo turned his attention to the haversack as Pike unbuckled the strap. Upended, the contents tumbled out onto the table—paper twists, the poke of coffee beans, crumbles of bacon wrapped in grease-soaked paper, a pair of socks, tin cup, plate, small pail, fork, and Curly's knife.

My shoulders sagged, the wind sucked right out of my lungs. If I was going to escape, it would have to be without the help of a weapon.

"Lookit here." Shilo reached for the knife and ran his finger over the crude *C* carved in the handle. "I believe this is Curly's knife. He's been bellyaching about losing this old relic for nigh on to a month." He wiped the stain of tobacco juice from the corner of his mouth. "I'll send Curly around. Reckon he'll want to thank you for taking such good care of it."

A rumble of helloes echoed across the meadow and reached the cave. When I turned with the others, to watch six riders trot through the encampment, my heart near jumped into my throat. Two of the men, hands tied to their saddle horns, wore Union uniforms.

"Damn!" Tazewell grinned and turned to his brother. "Looks like every one of those scouts Harrison sent out from Fayetteville have found us! Only trouble is, we found them first! I told you, Union boys can't do anything right."

Chapter 24

I pulled my knees to my chest and hunkered down, barely daring to breathe, lest a sob break loose and shame me. The anger that fueled my strength in front of two of Arkansas' most fearsome bushwhackers, Shilo Riddle and Buck Brown, abandoned me as soon as I sat down with the other captives.

As if in cahoots with the bushwhackers to make me miserable, the July sun blazed a slow path across the midday sky. Mouth and throat dry as cotton, I shifted about in the Union army's wool pants. Sweat soaked me good. I closed my eyes and rested my forehead on my knees. That was easier than enduring the curious stares of the swarm of outlaws in constant motion about the camp. But I couldn't plug up my ears.

"If it's not another batch of Yankee lovers," a voice taunted.

"Yeah! About all those fellows are good for is target practice. Understand they aren't even good eating."

Judging by the laughter that followed, those fools must have thought that was the funniest joke ever told. It seemed an eternity until they tired of poking fun at us Union boys and moved away.

"Hey kid," hissed a man beside me. "Don't let those horses' hinnies get to you. Nothing they like better than scaring the wits out of young'uns."

I raised my head to study the soldier. A floppy hat shaded the man's eyes, and a beard, as shaggy and thick as a bear's coat, hid his mouth. Ma would have said he needed a good scrubbing. His manner seemed kindly, though. And right now, kind words were in short supply.

"Aw, I'm not scared of them." Maybe saying it out loud would make it so. "Reckon those rumors about five hundred men gathering up were true." The man just grunted. I guess he thought I was remarking on the obvious.

Groups of men rode in and out of the surrounding woods. Some reported to their leaders in the cave. Others stopped and engaged in conversation along the way. Men squatted around campsites, eating or cleaning their equipment, their conversation a constant hum.

"Y'all scouting out from Fayetteville?" I asked, hopeful they weren't. Maybe they were couriers, plucked off the trail between stations.

"Yep," the bearded man said. "I'm Amos Johnson." He nodded to his partner, who didn't bother to look up but sat with his chin planted on his chest. "Me and Uley struck out on a scout from Fayetteville yesterday."

"Yesterday?" A third man wiggled around to face them, his broad face moist with beads of sweat. Blond fuzz sprouted from his chin. "Name's Franz. Me 'n' Fat Shorty, ve come two days from Fayetteville. Captain tell us, scout north of border."

"Well, that does it." I ran my tongue over my lips to wet them. "Me and my miserable, good-for-nothing, snake-in-the-grass partner lit out day before yesterday, too. Captain said he was going to send out three groups of scouts. Unless he sent out more than I know about, guess that's all of us. That wagon train doesn't have a chance."

"Miserable, good-for-nothing partner?" Amos cocked his head. "Who would that be?"

"You forgot snake-in-the-grass. And that would be Tazewell Benton." The name left a bitter taste as it rolled off my tongue. "The fella bent over those maps up there with Shilo Riddle and Buck Brown is Pike Benton, and he's kin to Taz. It shames me to know I was bunked up with a traitor."

"Bunked up? He's a Union man?"

"No, he's a Sesech in a Union uniform. Been spying on the camp. I reckon that's how you men got picked off. Taz probably passed the word, and they were waiting for you to come along. He offered me up like a turkey on a platter."

Amos's partner looked up, a pale-faced man with squinty eyes. "They're going to kill us."

"Shut up, Uley," Amos said. "Maybe not. Buck Brown's been known to be reasonable on occasion."

"I was afeared all these outlaw hoodlums decide to band together, they'd be a frightful lot," Uley said. "I heard they put a man's eyes out just for looking on them. Going to kill us. Wait and see." He stole a quick look around the camp and ducked his head again. "Oh, no! Here they come. Don't look on them."

Uley's prophecy unnerved me for sure, but I was drawn to see who my attacker was and hazarded a glance. Tazewell, a wide grin spread across his face, ambled toward the group, dipper in one hand and bucket in the other. Water sloshed over the sides with each step. It was an awful waste of water for a thirsty man to look on.

"Well, boys, this here is the traitor I been telling you about. My tent mate…" Insults crowded my brain and I had to clench my teeth together to keep them from pouring out. I was dry enough to accept water from the devil himself, and it wasn't likely the devil would tolerate a good cussing out.

Tazewell sat the bucket on the ground and squatted next to it. "Ah, now Ebby, you don't have to give me that scornful look you got pasted on your face. We've done shared grub and good times. Plenty of laughs, I can tell you." He lowered the dipper and allowed it to fill with water. "You got yourself to blame for the fix you're in. If you'd listened to me, we'd be down to Round Rock Meadow and out of harm's way right now. Your stubbornness got me and you, both, in a heap of trouble. Pike wasn't much happy with me. I count it mostly your fault."

"Why Taz, you…" The words exploded in my mouth. and I couldn't get them out they were so tangled. I fought to control my rage and the insults tripping over each other.

"Oh, you don't have to thank me." Tazewell held the dipper to my lips. Cool water dribbled down my chin and neck. It washed over my tongue and down the back of my throat, drowning all the hateful words stored up there. I leaned into the dipper, sucking in huge mouthfuls and swallowing as fast as I could, lest the offer be taken away.

When my belly was full, and I couldn't have soaked up another drop, I was grateful. Grateful to the devil, if that was the case. But I couldn't give a proper thanks, not out loud, not to a Sesech. Instead, I caught my breath and nodded to Tazewell.

"Reckon you can give the boys a drink, too? We are near stewed in our own juices, sitting out in this sun."

Tazewell leaned back on his heels and narrowed his eyes to study the other captive men. "Don't know them. Those boys aren't anything to me. Just Union pukes. Pike says don't give quarter to your enemy."

"Sure, you know them." I searched my memory for the introductions made minutes before. "That right there is Amos and Uley. Over there is Franz and Fat Shorty. They're scouts, just like you and me."

"Aw, now you done it. Why'd you have to go and name them? I'd as soon not know their handles." Tazewell clamped his lips so tight that they disappeared and his nose flared.

"Don't know a man's name, they can't ever come back to haunt you," he muttered. With a quick glance up toward the men still huddled over the table in the cave, he stood and lowered the dipper into the pail, allowing it to fill to the brim. Moving to each man, he sloshed water into their open mouths.

Even Uley looked up long enough to get a drink. He kept one eye closed and the other barely open, as if that would protect him from certain death.

Tazewell tossed the remaining water from the bucket. The ground drank its share, leaving a dark spot in the dirt. He stabbed the toe of his shoe into the dampness, pushing the dirt into clumps. Then he just stood there, not saying anything.

It wasn't like Taz to be at a loss for words. If he was waiting for thanks for a mouthful of water, he'd be waiting until we met in the hereafter. It wasn't but a minute before I was sorry for the thought and a shiver raced up my back.

Tazewell took a few steps backward and stopped. "Still think you should have changed that last name of yours, Ebby. It doesn't fit you." He turned and walked, bucket swinging, toward his brother, Greenbrier, who was still stripping flesh from the fly-covered deer carcass.

Amos, water glistening in his heavy beard, nodded toward the retreating figure. "Thanks for what you done. My tongue was dry as beef jerky." He grunted and shifted his position. "Don't mind me asking, why would he think you should have changed your last name? What is it?"

"Fears. Ebby Fears. Taz thinks a name marks a man." I studied Tazewell, his frame even thinner, lankier at a distance. "Maybe if you're a Benton, it does."

"Fears? You any kin to the Fears brothers?"

"Reckon so, seeing as how we are the only Fears in this part of the county. There's Willy and Josiah and Jim. They're my older brothers."

"Good men." The corners of Amos's eyes crinkled in a smile that was lost in his beard. "Fought elbow-to-elbow with them when Gen'ral Cabell thought his Sesech boys could take Fayetteville last year. Guess we taught them Rebs a lesson. Sent them scurrying back south with their tails between their legs."

"*Ja*, I vas there, too," Franz said. "It vas a rude avakening we got that morning, I can tell you."

"Gun shots are always a rude avakening," Fat Shorty added. He looked out at the enemy encampment. "Even if they be nothing but them worthless

Arkadelphias. Guess they can kill a man as good as any other, if the shooter gets lucky."

Uley shivered. "They're going to kill us, I know it." He kept his head bowed.

Amos snorted and shoved a shoulder into the bound man. "Uley, I'm gonna kill you myself if you don't shut up." He turned to me, his voice softer now, like we were old buddies. "Lots of men got wounded in that fight. Your brother, Josiah, I think it was, took a bullet."

"Yes, sir. Josiah doesn't talk too much about it seeing as how the bullet's still in his arm. Says talking on it calls the spirit of the bullet to account. He isn't so sure the devil got shook off it."

"Vell, it vas a fearful fight. *Ja*, took us by surprise it did." Franz shook his head. "One minute vas rolled up, peaceful as could be, next minute, the captain shouting, ordering us to grab our guns. Night barely letting go so's the sun could come up. *Ja*, a hell of a rude avakening, I tell you."

"Aw, Franz, I been shook out of bed lots of times," Amos said. "That isn't so bad as hunkering down behind nothing more than hedge bushes and peering out at the whole side of East Mountain crawling with hundreds of Rebs. Enough to make a man mess his breeches when they started that charge up out of the ravine, yowling like wildcats, bullets flying everywhere. They were on horseback, and most of us didn't even have the sleep out of our eyes, yet."

The men exchanged glances and nodded in solemn recollection of the battle. Uley rested his chin on his knees and released a deep sigh. "It was those two big guns from hell I remember. Sitting high up on the hill, raining bloody shells down on us, roaring and ripping everything in sight. Couldn't do nothing. Couldn't do nothing at all." His voice quivered. "Just curl up and pray."

"Uley, you didn't run away." Amos spoke in his friendly voice. "Plenty men did. Some kept running almost fifty miles to Cassville."

"I couldn't." Uley's answer was barely audible. "My legs were worthless. All I could do was listen to the cries of hurt men and the unearthly hollers of those banshees and the big guns up on the hill."

I shifted my body away from Uley. Bravery is a fragile thing, and I didn't want what little I had to slip away.

"You see the man that shot my brother?" I was anxious to change the subject.

"See him? Hell, we could smell him, he was so close. That artillery blasted away most of the hedge, didn't have a lick of cover. Those Sesech captured the Baxter house, and it give them all kinds of puffed-up courage. They come swarming toward us like bees out of a hive." Amos looked over at Franz as if to confirm his memory. "Then your brothers, Josiah and Willy and Jim, raised up on one knee and went to shooting with their Starr carbines. Damn good rifles. Mowed down a half-dozen men. This tall Texan—and I knowed it was a Texan 'cause he wore this big sombrero—well, he just kept coming." He shook his head. "Josiah got hit and spun around slicker'n a button."

"Damn." I shook my head. "A Texan done it."

"That isn't the half of it. Willy went wild. Guess he thought Josiah was dead. He went to yelling, not even aiming, just shooting. Pretty soon, that Texan had enough and limped back to the Baxter House. Wasn't long after that, Lieutenant Robb led a couple companies up the hill and silenced the big guns."

"*Ja.*" Franz nodded. "Those Rebs pulled out and left us lick our vounds. Sun veren't even high vhen it vas all over. About all that raid done vas get a bunch of men killed."

"Well, it did that for sure." Fat Shorty leaned forward and grinned, exposing a smile that was missing two teeth. "Besides causing us to miss breakfast that morning."

"Would you listen to that?" Amos fumed. "Shorty, don't you ever think of anything except feeding your face?"

"Purty girls," Fat Shorty exclaimed, as if surprised there was anything else in the world to think about.

In that instant, the recounting of the battle was over. Uley stayed hunched over, head down, while Amos and Franz badgered Fat Shorty over his single-mindedness.

I gazed off at the trees, upper leaves brilliant, as the sun bounced off their surface in its glide west across the sky. The cliff threw shadows across us and the meadow, relieving some of the discomfort of sitting trussed up like Christmas turkeys.

When pressed about it, Willy had been reluctant to talk of the battle. Still, I had to admit, my brothers had done the family name proud.

"Hey, Amos, you think a name can be unlucky?" I asked.

"Unlucky? You mean, like a name has got a hex on it or something?"

"Hex?" Fat Shorty leaned forward to see around

Amos. "I heard tell of an Indian shaman putting a hex on another man that was sweet-talking his wife."

"No, not a hex," I protested. "Just a name that is unlucky."

"Never thought much about such a thing," Amos said, shaking his head, "but I suppose…"

"Right now? You want me to do it right now?" A gruff voice brought our conversation to an abrupt halt. I turned to watch Pike, Monroe, and a group of men stroll toward us. At their center, Shilo sat astride a large roan like some sort of grand general surveying his troops.

Pike stopped, hands resting on the holstered guns at his hips, cigar perched in the corner of his mouth. "Of course right now," he said out of the other corner. "Don't see any sense in waiting. We'll be leaving at midnight to be at Butcher's Bend by daybreak."

Monroe snorted and spit. He wiped his arm across his mouth. "Where you want to take them?"

"Up yonder. The other side of the ridge. I aim to eat my supper in peace without any vultures circling overhead."

Chapter 25

Vultures?

The word exploded in my mind, nearly blinding me. Vultures! I tried to gain my breath but couldn't. For an awful minute, I thought I'd choke on my own fright and save the bushwhackers the trouble of shooting me.

Then I heard it—Uley's high wail, pleading like a little girl about to be thrashed.

"Nooo, you don't have to kill us! No, you don't! You don't." He held his bound hands over his head. "I haven't looked on nobody. Nobody. For the sake of the Almighty, please!"

Uley's voice quivered with terror—the same terror I felt—it nauseated me to hear it naked, stripped of any cloak of bravery, no matter how thin. I swallowed back my own urge to beseech mercy. What good would it do? Bushwhackers, hearts hard as stone and driven by hate, have no pity, no soul of kindness left in them.

Although it was useless to struggle, my hands refused to listen to my brain and fought the confines of the hemp rope binding my wrists. I warmed to the effort and focused my attention on the ropes, forcing back tears that threatened to humiliate me.

"Get them up! Get them out of here!" Pike commanded, shoving one of his men forward. "Soon as it's over, we can get on with our eats."

From atop the roan, Shilo's voice boomed, "Listen

up, boys. Tomorrow, we'll bring them Fed'rals to their knees." He stood in the stirrups and pumped a fist into the air, as if to gain support among the onlookers for the coming battle. "We'll learn them to leave our kinfolk alone. Learn them we're free men that don't want their kind around here, telling us what to do. Telling us how to run our own affairs. Tomorrow, we'll learn them good." He fairly screeched his rallying call, "Tomorrow, we win!"

Cheers erupted, radiating through the knots of men squatting at their fires, and carried down the valley to far-off campsites. The surrounding hillsides captured their glee and rolled it back and forth until it pounded in my ears.

I twisted my wrists, trying to do the impossible—stretch the rope enough to slip my hands free. Bits of flesh peeled away under the scrape of the rough hemp, searing me with pain, the pain of not wanting to die. Deep down, I knew it was useless, but I couldn't stop. Even if I accomplished the impossible, my feet were bound, too.

"Time be better spent praying to the Almighty."

Startled, I jerked away as someone grabbed the rope tethering my hands to my feet. A straw-headed boy, aged by three long scars down the side of his face, peered back at me. Curly!

"You're not going to be getting away this time," he continued and pulled an ancient knife from his belt. "Reckon you got lucky that day on the road. Shilo must've been feeling generous he didn't shoot you right then and there." He laid the blade against the length of rope and began to saw back and forth. The action brought fresh pain to my raw flesh and the return of my voice.

"You're looking mighty good, Curly. Believe those scars made an improvement on your appearance." The taunt slipped out before I could think better of it.

Curly stopped for a moment, shrugged, and allowed a flicker of a smile. "Yeah. The girls seem to think so. No balm better than a girl's healing kisses. I shudder to think what might happen if I was to get more than these tiny scratches."

"Well, if you hadn't run like a scared jackrabbit, I could've put a matching set on the other side of your pitiful face."

"Aw, something like that would drive those silly girls love-crazy. Cause me to plumb wear out my manhood."

The knife severed the rope with a jerk, and my back was instantly grateful to be free of being bound hand-to-foot. Curly had matched me, taunt for taunt. Despite the fact my hands and feet were still tied, the release sent a flicker of hope.

"It was an old Indian bear claw, what done that to you."

Curly stopped working on the twist of rope binding my ankles together and looked up, brows raised above large brown eyes. "Bear claw? If that isn't a sight." He touched the welt of scars with his fingertips and shook his head. "I wondered. That night was the first time Shilo sent me out." He resumed sawing with the dull knife until the ropes fell away. "I wasn't much good at thieving, then. Doing better here lately."

"What about killing?" I stared hard at Curly, hoping to force the boy to look back at me. It was always harder to pull the trigger on a deer looking straight at you. "Got the hang of killing, here lately?"

Curly didn't answer. Head down, he leaned back on his heels, turning the old knife around and around in his hands. It was the same weapon he'd flashed that dark night, weeks past, when he'd tried to steal Levi Standing Corn's mules. That was a lifetime ago— before the war made a soldier of one and a bushwhacker of the other.

Monroe and Pike finished releasing the feet of the bound prisoners. Pike jerked Uley off the ground and forced him to stand, prompting a wail from the frightened man.

"I'm getting up. I'm getting up," Franz said as he struggled to rise before Pike could manhandle him. "All you got to do is ask."

"Ask, is it?" Pike walked around Franz, looking him up and down. "Well, I'm asking you to step out of that uniform."

He turned to his brother, Logan, "Release the Swede long enough to get that outfit off him. He isn't going to need it, and it seems Shilo's got a need for a uniform."

"Vhat for you want my uniform?" Franz asked as his hands were untied.

"You're not going to need it," Logan muttered, fumbling with the brass buttons on the coat to hurry the undressing process along, despite Franz's objections.

Curly looked at me and shrugged, still turning the knife in his hands.

"Doesn't seem sporting to kill a man whilst he still be tied," I said and held out my still bound hands. "I'm not even sure a man can get to heaven, if he can't make a proper prayer, hands put together in supplication to the Lord."

"Get that boy on his feet," Pike commanded as he led his horse past us.

Eyes moist, Curly straightened. "There is a long ways between thieving and killing, and I haven't been down that road. Yet." With a quick glance around, he put the blade to the underside of the rope wound around my hands and severed several strands of hemp.

The rope loosened but didn't fall away. I nodded to Curly. A little more work and I might wiggle free. I struggled to my feet and stomped to work the blood back into my toes.

Shilo pranced his big roan close and peered down, frown lines wrinkling his leathery face. "Never did make it back to the Widow Fears for that chicken dinner, did I?" He grinned, tobacco stains outlining his teeth. "But I haven't forgot the fact."

Amos pushed forward, thick beard bristling. "He's just a kid. Hasn't been in the cavalry more than a month. Let him go."

"The boy had his chance." Shilo leaned forward, elbow on the saddle horn, his glare deliberate, slicing through a man's soul like a sword. "Play a man's game, pay a man's price." With that, he jerked the reins and yelled. "Get them pigs out of my camp! They're stinking up the place!" He urged the roan into a trot through the valley, pumping his fist in the air again. "Tomorrow, boys. We got business, tomorrow."

All down the line, hoots and yells answered his proclamation.

Uley's knees gave way, and he staggered into Pike.

Amos swung around, hands still bound, to steady his friend. "Come on, Uley. We're going to march up that mountain like the soldiers we are. That's an order."

Uley took several faltering steps. Then he lifted his chin and started forward, Amos at his side. The others shuffled into place behind them.

Several bushwhackers ambled forward to follow the procession toward the base of the ridge. Others averted their eyes to what was happening, intent on stirring a fire to life or whittling a stick.

My mind refused to count the names of men that had disappeared in the last couple of years, leaving only rumors of their fate. Ma's reading of the coffee grounds was right. Now my name would float around eternity, not finding a resting place anywhere. Ma would grieve herself to a shadow.

I grabbed hold of a bush to help steady my climb along the rocks. A throb that had begun in my neck surged forward, threatening to push tears, dammed behind my eyes, out through the cracks. I bit my lip. It's not right when folks don't know what happened to their loved ones.

I glanced back down at the encampment, over to the skeleton-bare carcass of the deer. Looking small and insignificant, Tazewell stood, watching us climb.

The thought come to me right then, and I couldn't shake it out. "My name is Ebenezer B. Fears," I yelled.

Activity in the valley ceased as men stopped what they were doing and shaded their eyes to stare. A flock of birds burst from a nearby tree.

"I'd take it as a Christian act," I continued at the top of my voice and pointed down at Tazewell, "if somebody would tell my Ma what happened to me."

The words swirled in eddies of wind, rippling off the ridge and traveling down the valley.

Chapter 26

I shifted my weight to my heels on the narrow mountain path. My shouted words hung in space to become faint echoes dying away and lost to the rustle of branches in the wind. I would not be one of those poor souls wandering around without a final end. How can it be final if your loved ones don't know about it? Even my own pa, dead and buried in Mexico, had finality—written right on a piece of paper by the government and sent through the mail to Ma.

"Don't forget!" I yelled, "It's Ebenezer B. Fears you're killing." I strained to focus on the figure of Tazewell, standing poker-straight next to the deer carcass. Even at a distance, I could imagine the boy's golden eyes, deep and intense, and the splash of freckles across his face. No doubt about it, blessed with ears the size of elephants, Taz would have to hear what I was yelling. Heck, I could smell the potent stench of garlic from here.

"And Amos Johnson," a powerful voice on the trail above me called out. "It's Amos Johnson you be leading to the slaughter."

"*Ja*, Franz Larson of Uniontown, you remember that name."

"Fat Shorty," the plump man next to me bellowed, "Everyone in Fort Smith knows me."

"Uley," the voice, timid and wavering at first,

gained strength with the next breath. "Tell them Uley Faudree went to his death like a soldier."

The names came, one after another, rolling over each other, determined not to be forgotten.

A shotgun blast obliterated the echoes. The roar filled the valley, crashing against the mountain sides, using up all the air. I ducked, rocks shifting under my feet. Ahead of me, Fat Shorty struggled, grasping at a spindly shrub with his bound hands to keep from sliding back down the path.

"You Yankee scum think you're at a tea party or something?" Smoke trailed from Pike's gun as he shouldered it, a scowl creasing his face. His horse whickered, its bridle hardware clinking as it shook its head in agitation. "Or maybe you think they care who the Sam Hill you are? Keep moving on up that path because I'd as soon drop you right here and save myself the climb." He motioned with his gun and called to the man guarding the prisoners in front. "Monroe, you keep them moving up there. I guarantee I'm not going to like it, we miss the big feast."

The moment of defiance vanished with the acrid smell of gunpowder. One by one, we all stood and put one cautious foot in front of the other on the climb toward the top of the ridge. The hooves of Pike's horse struck against the rocks with a hollow ring.

"Waste of ammunition, if you ask me," another red-headed Benton brother muttered as he followed on foot behind the horse. "Ought to just leave them tied up tight. If the sun don't get them, something hungry will be along soon enough. A lot of trouble, you ask me."

"Now see there, Logan, that's why you won't never amount to nothing. Don't ever leave an enemy behind that's still breathing." Pike grunted as he kneed his horse into the effort of the climb. "Besides, we'll have all the ammunition we need after we hit that supply train tomorrow. Shilo's got plans to send Tazewell and Greenbrier, wearing that foreign fellow's uniform, toward Cassville. They'll meet up with the wagons and tell the officers they haven't laid eyes on any bushwhackers." His laugh rumbled out, deep and dreadful. "Going to tell them the road is clear plumb to Fayetteville. We'll just sit and wait for them at Butcher's Bend. Dumb fools won't suspect a thing."

The chill of fear settled in my spine again. Josiah, still sporting a rebel bullet in his arm, would most likely be bouncing along on a wagon seat, a sure target for attackers.

I choked back the bitter taste of bile that rose with each step closer to the top of the ridge and searched my brain for a prayer. Mouth, dry as cotton, stuck the words together so they wouldn't slip out. Not that it would matter if I could manage to unjumble the words into a prayer. Ma always counseled that God doesn't make any bargains. He either stays calamity, or He doesn't.

It wasn't a bargain that I wanted anyway. It was a clap of thunder to strike my enemies deaf and dumb, or a bolt of lightning to set them afire, or a heavy rain to blind them. Or, at the very least, I wanted a gun in my hands. I looked up at the sky, tinged with the setting sun, beautiful in its blend of reds and golds and oranges. Not a single rain cloud graced the vast heavens.

With the end of the climb a few steps higher, a terrible dread settled over me, like the time I'd been wading over in Lee's Creek when a water moccasin slithered out from the washed-out roots of a scrub oak and circled my legs. Paralysis seized me up then, just like now. I waited for the bite that would poison my blood and leave me puffed up like a horny toad and waiting for death.

"Get a move on, kid," Pike growled. "I aim to get this over with in short order."

I straightened. The snake moved on after a frog and left me frozen to the spot. It took the span of five deep breaths to get the strength to move again. I sucked in, forced my foot up, and stepped onto the level top of the mountain. Knee-high grass, sun-bleached to a pale yellow, swayed in the breeze that swept along the ridge. Scattered clumps of rabbit bush and cheerful spirals of goldenrod, Queen Anne's lace, and butterfly weed rose above the grass. A line of trees, maybe a half-mile distant, marked the descent on the other side.

Franz stood a few feet away with bound hands crossed at his abdomen, attempting to hide the fact that he was clad only in his undergarments. Monroe dismounted and, gun pointed, motioned to each man to line up. Amos, head high, bearded-chin jutting out, rested a bound hand on Uley's shoulder. Both walked to stand next to Franz.

Fat Shorty stopped, bent with hands on his knees, and huffed for breath. He looked back over his shoulder, bushy brows drawn over his brown eyes.

"Kid," he whispered, "shooting starts, get behind me." He straightened and took a deep breath, pulling the buttons on his uniform taut across his ample chest and stomach. "Reckon I'll make mighty good cover. Just hit the ground, lay still, and don't breathe none."

"Hey, you," Monroe snorted. "Get on over there with the others." Directing their path with the gun barrel, he added, "You, too, boy. Get in line."

Get in line.

The command, heavy with menace, cut through me like a knife. Tiny flying insects whirred up out of the thick grass as I forced one foot in front of the other. Ahead of me, Fat Shorty and Franz trudged toward Amos and Uley, who were trampling a narrow trail through the weeds and horse grass. Monroe plowed his own path, just off to the side of the procession, and out of reach of anyone who might make a try for his rifle.

Ma's prediction from reading the coffee grounds throbbed through my head. I'd scoffed at her prophecy of death. I should have known better than to run my boot through the sign of the cross left by the discarded grounds. She believed the sign, and that should have been enough. A careless act put a worry in Ma's heart and sealed my fate, and I wasn't sure which caused me the most pain.

I glanced behind to see Pike's horse scramble onto level ground and prance with evident pleasure to be free of the climb. Logan scurried alongside and grabbed hold of the bridle.

"I still don't see why you didn't make Taz come up here instead of me," Logan complained to his brother. "He's the one got that nice Springfield he took off the kid. He gave me this lousy Arkadelphia." He turned the rifle over in his hands. "I swear the thing's held together with spit. Likely fall apart with the first shot."

"Now, Logan." Pike stabbed the unlit cigar at his brother. "Since you done commented on the fact, I'd think it'd come to you that we don't want to be wasting any more ammunition on these boys than necessary. You know how Taz gets wound up. There's no sense to the boy. Besides, that little fart says how he didn't think he could shoot someone he shared coffee with. I'll have to break him of that notion. Now, you just hold that Arkadelphia steady. It's not like you'll be hitting a moving target. Let's get this over."

Pike dismounted and called to Monroe. "That's far enough. Just line them pukes up right there."

Fat Shorty shuffled into place. Beads of sweat gathered across his broad forehead, and he swiped the sleeve of his arm over his face. He leaned toward me and muttered, "Remember what I said."

Pike dropped the reins to allow the horse to graze. He ran his hand through his copper-red hair and retrieved a half-smoked cigar from above his ear.

I always thought red hair to be a sign of specialness. There weren't many people blessed like Ma with such finery. On the Bentons, the feature took on an ominous hue, as if colored by the devil himself.

An unearthly whine raised the hair on my neck. I didn't want to look on a fellow soldier in his misery, but my vision was drawn from the three men readying their guns to peer past Fat Shorty's bulk at Uley—lost in his own death song.

Amos, with his hands still bound, struggled to hold his friend upright. "It'll be over soon enough, Uley. No shame in being scared. Just stand up, man."

Eyes closed, Uley lifted his head, lower lip quivering, high-pitched wail growing stronger as he rocked back and forth. "I'm killed!" he cried. "Lord have mercy, I'm killed!"

"Shut that confounded noise up!" Pike screamed

and jammed the cigar back into the crevice between his ear and head.

Logan lifted the battered rifle to his shoulder and backed up.

"Where the hell you going?" Pike glared at his brother and motioned him forward again.

"I got clean clothes on if you haven't noticed. I don't aim to get any splatters on me." He motioned the Arkadelphia at the line of men. "You just say when, and I'll shut that caterwauling up."

"No," Monroe snorted, "let me have the pleasure." He snugged his Springfield into his shoulder and bent his head to sight down the long barrel.

Uley's wails became screeches.

My knees weakened. I struggled to breathe. My head seemed full—full of grief and remorse and rage. It forced tears into my eyes, making the three figures in front of me blur.

Blue fire seared my vision, and the roar of guns jarred the panic right out of me—cleared my head. Or maybe it was that I couldn't hear Uley anymore that allowed me to remember Willy's teasing stuck in the back of my mind—the teasing that had taunted me when I signed up.

Ol' Ebby can outrun a bullet.

Willy had said it just like outrunning a bullet was something done every day.

Logan let out a howl and dropped the Arkadelphia. "Damnation! Damnation! That confounded rifle done blinded me!" He grimaced and opened both eyes wide as if to let more daylight into his brain. Black powder masked his face, and he looked, for all the world, a raccoon, a fact that would have been funny had the

Arkadelphia not been pointed in my direction a minute earlier.

Without a note of sympathy, Pike waved a cloud of smoke away and fumed, "If you aren't just about useless, Logan. We got four men still standing. Monroe, looks like we got to do it all, just like always."

"You lily-livered cowards!" Amos roared as he stood over Uley's slumped body. "Doesn't take guts to shoot a man with his hands tied. You murdering thugs are going to pay."

Pike's jaw went ridged, his small eyes narrowed to mere slits. "Maybe, maybe not," he said in a steely voice. "But one thing's sure. I'm not going to die today, like you." Rifle hammers ratcheted back, the sound loud and deadly.

It's now or never, I thought, the metallic echo ringing in my ears. It's now or never before they pull the trigger again. Diving into the tall grass, I scurried behind a scrubby rabbit bush.

My mind screamed—*outrun the bullets!*

Chapter 27

The terrible roar of gunfire pulsed outward, grabbed hold of me, and held me crouched in a tight ball. But the capture was only for an instant, until the desire to live proved stronger than the fear of dying, and infused a powerful strength into my legs. My thighs tightened as I rose from the hard-packed ground and pushed off with the toe of my boot.

I didn't look back to see if the others still stood, if my escape had been noticed, if guns were trained on me even now. I didn't look back because I didn't want to know. I didn't want to know if Franz or Amos or Fat Shorty, who thought to shield me with his own big body, lay sprawled out like Uley.

Two more shots followed, and I felt a split in the very air I breathed. Just ahead of me, the tall snowy white crown of a Queen Anne's flower exploded. Willy's taunt, "Outrun the bullets!" screamed in my mind, and I pushed harder, lifting my knees and hitting the ground solid with my boots.

Outrun the bullets!

Tough blades of tall meadow grass and stick-tights grabbed at my pants, as if to slow my passage. I kept my eyes on the ragged line of scrub oaks and cedar bent by the constant wind that blew across the top of the mountain ridge. If I could make the trees, I'd at least have cover.

"Get him!" Pike screamed. "Get him! Get him, blast it!"

Another round of rifle fire and the dull thud of bullets as they plowed into the ground, kicking up small fountains of dirt, drowned any more of the bushwhacker's commands.

A cloud of grasshoppers whirred out of the grass, and I ducked my head, mouth clamped shut. Too late, I caught a glimpse of a rabbit's mound. My foot slammed down, breaking through the crust, and I tumbled like a shot pup.

I gathered my feet beneath me and chanced a look back at the bushwhackers. Logan, face smudged with gunpowder, and Monroe brandished their weapons in the air and pointed while they jumped up and down. Pike's horse danced circles, unwilling to let his rider mount.

Fools! Fools thought they shot me. I kept still, burying my head in the weeds, hoping they'd not come to check and go on back down the mountain. Bushwhackers were ne'er-do-wells, lazy whelps, not good for a plow. Most likely not want to bother to see if I'm killed.

I willed myself to stay where I was, peeking through the weeds, until I saw Pike hook a foot in the stirrup and swing into the saddle. Then I froze up solid. No doubt, I could best Logan and Monroe, or most any other man, in a foot race, but a horse? I'd never considered outrunning a horse.

Sweat and panic blurred my vision. I ran the sleeve of my arm across my eyes and glanced back at the trees to consider the distance left to run. From where I was crouched, a man could down a turkey poking about

226

along the tree line's fringe.

It would be a hard run if Pike took up the chase. And Pike wasn't a man to leave a little matter like an escaped prisoner to chance. Or was he? He seemed in a powerful mind to partake in the feast down below. It was a sliver of hope, and I turned toward the bushwhackers, toward the spot I'd stood waiting for a bullet only minutes before.

Pike took off his hat, swung it at Logan, and cursed. The words were indistinguishable, but I knew it was a curse, because no man with such a face full of hate could have been asking polite-like. Pike flapped his hat against the horse's flank, and it bolted forward, right toward where I hunkered down in the weeds.

My legs pushed up, and I stood, fist raised in the air. Then, I turned and bolted straight for the trees. This time, the race was for more than a sack of salt. It was for my life.

Chapter 28

Knee-high meadow grass rippled across the mountain ridge and blurred into a golden sea. It threatened to suck me down and pull my legs out from under me. The twisting vines of meadow creeper, reaching out to trip me, would hardly slow Pike's large roan.

I didn't dare glance back to see if my pursuer's horse struggled. I didn't have to. The dull clink of the horse's metal trappings grew louder, until I was sure I could feel the roan's labored breathing on my neck.

Keep your eyes on the tree, I told myself, willing strength to my legs, feeling the pull in my thighs, the jar of the ground against my heels. Just ahead, the blackened skeleton of a thin hackberry seemed to grow, to fatten, its spidery limbs reaching out to become the spirit tree.

Ragged gasps of air filled my lungs and roared in my ears. My arms pumped back and forth, drawing me to the meadow's edge. I ducked under a charred branch and pushed myself deeper into the tangled tree line.

The roan's whinny drew me to chance a look over my shoulder. I stumbled against a fallen tree trunk, its girth as big as a cow, and sank down on it.

It was hard to breathe, and I swiped my eyes dry. Pike's horse balked at tearing into the tangle of trees and shrubs. Maybe I was safe. Maybe the bushwhackers wouldn't want to take the energy to continue the chase into the forest. After all, I was afoot. How big a threat to their ambush could I be?

In a rage, Pike dismounted. Halfway across the meadow, Logan and Monroe waded through the tall grass, swinging the butt end of their rifles like scythes. Bits of foliage flew into the air with swarms of insects.

Pike turned his ire their way. "What you waiting for? Run, blast it! Get him!"

He settled the stock of his rifle between his feet and reached into the cartridge pouch at his waist.

Twenty seconds. I had twenty seconds before Pike had the rifle loaded and trained on my back. I bounded up and jumped the large trunk. The thought of a hole boring through my body gave me all the energy in the world. This time, it wasn't a whisper in my ear, it was a scream.

Outrun the bullets!

I tore my way through dense undergrowth, descending the north side of the mountain on the edges of my feet. I didn't stop until a barricade of decaying trees blocked my path. Layers of upended trunks, dangling roots, and broken branches deposited by the floodwaters of rain storms were stacked haphazardly in a five-foot tall mound.

A collection of boulders nestled to one side of the blockage looked none too stable. I paused, wondering which side would be easier to scale.

A bullet zinged into the tangle, throwing bits of bark into the air. My legs made the decision, and I scrambled onto the pile of decaying trees. It would be twenty seconds before Pike could send another bullet my way.

Brittle limbs broke under my weight as I clawed to the top of the barricade. Two ancient trees, several feet apart, anchored the debris. On my descent over the backside, I gripped the trunk of one for support.

The length of rope, still attached to my left wrist, caught in the fork of a hickory branch as I jumped for the ground. An immediate wrench of pain in my shoulder brought me up short. My toes barely touched the packed earth, and I dangled.

"Here! Over here!" Pike's voice, sharp and angry, came down on me from the heights above. "He's down there. You boys let that snot-nosed kid get away, and it's your head I'll be having, instead of his."

I could hear Logan and Monroe crashing through the woods like a herd of runaway cattle. I was in a heap of panic and bounced up and down, trying to free myself with the weight of my body. The hickory limb cracked, and my feet went flat on the ground. For a brief instant, I caught the movement and heard the clawing of several small creatures deep in the thick brush.

Determined not to be caught like an animal in a trap, I continued the pull, even as I heard Logan's whine from the other side of the barricade.

"I'm…run…out," Logan gasped between spasms of coughing.

"Logan, you worthless…" Pike roared. "Monroe, get up there!"

With a firm grip on the rope and one foot against the solid hickory trunk, I gathered strength and leaned back. I felt the rope slip and allowed my body to sag. The branch gave way. Free from the tree's capture, I fell back, sliding downhill several feet before I could stop.

The barricade shivered with movement. From the other side, a grumble arose as branches snapped and broke under the assault by the bushwhackers. A family of field mice, roused by the disturbance, scurried through the tangle of branches and poured out toward me like a tossed pail of water. They scrambled over each other in waves with shrill squeaks.

I went to beating the ground with the rope to keep from being swarmed before I could get to my feet. The shifting mound of debris towering over me complained greatly. Limbs, by twos and threes, tumbled down. With each loss, the entire pile readjusted, settling with loud moans and snaps. I glanced up.

Monroe appeared over the top, dropped from sight, bobbed back up, arms flaying for a firm grasp of something stable. "There…he…he…" Monroe yelled just as the entire structure shuddered. He disappeared again with a scream.

A tremendous crack signaled the break of the barricade. Years of debris started to move. I turned and half ran, half slid just out of reach of the wreckage that chased behind me—cannon balls of logs and branches, their jagged ends sharp and deadly as bayonets. The torrent careened down the mountainside after me, leaving off the smaller pieces to be caught in bushes or groupings of trees. Large, heavy trunks refused to be stopped, bouncing off obstacles and gaining new momentum as they crashed back to earth.

I twisted around sudden outcroppings of rocks and swung past trees, their rough bark tearing my palms as I fought for control of my descent. The toes of my boots slammed against fat fingers of gnarled roots. I struggled to remain upright, grabbing whatever appeared out of the corner of my eye for support.

Just when I thought my lungs would burst and rip my chest open, the slope of ground eased. I slid up against a great, lichen-crusted boulder, scrambled around the far end, and pulled myself into a ball for protection. The pursuing trunks rolled up and over the rock and bounced on the other side, before settling into a bog of rotting leaves and vegetation.

My heart racing, I couldn't catch enough air, couldn't quell the pain that radiated through my entire body. I coughed until bile rose in my mouth. I had to get control, had to listen, and had to know if the chase was over. Surely, the bushwhackers would give up now. Monroe's scream, etched with pain, echoed about in my mind.

An eternity passed. I willed my breathing into a steady rhythm, straining all the while for sounds not of the forest. Occasionally, a voice, the words far off and indistinguishable, floated down. Must be the bushwhackers were leaving. I unrolled, leaned back, and allowed a heap of aches to subside, even as new pains took their place.

My palms and fingers looked like they'd sprouted porcupine quills. I bent to the task of working out the shards of embedded wood. Blood oozed from the punctures and cuts. Hurt like thunder, but it was better than a bullet wound. I worked my wrist free of the shreds of rope.

"Guess I showed those filthy, rotten, egg-sucking, pea-heads." I leaned against the rock and closed my eyes for a minute's rest. "Yeah, I showed those lily-livered, black-hearted polecats you can't kill a Fears boy."

I put my brain to thinking on the problem at hand. I wasn't at all sure how far north I was. The surprise attack was planned for tomorrow morning. Unless I could get to the wagon train before the bushwhackers, they'd go swooping down with their confounded banshee yells, bringing the devil right up out of hell to ride along with them.

A breeze rustled through the upper branches of the tallest trees, the black oaks and the hickories and spindly pine trees, strong with the scent of resin. The forest seemed to relax. Several jays fussed, scolding the disturbance that the avalanche had caused.

Something brushed past my hand, and I looked down in time to see a lizard whip through the dirt. My fingers, now sore and swollen as if I'd pushed a plow for a week straight, would scarcely bend. Small cuts bled anew. I pulled a handkerchief, made from a square of Ma's petticoat, out of my back pocket, and tied it around my hand.

Logan's unmistakable whine carried on the breeze, and I froze. From somewhere up on the mountain, branches broke and snapped. Moments later, small rocks careened onto the boulder with a clatter.

Merciful heavens, don't those murderin' scum ever give up?

Chapter 29

I couldn't tell how far up the trail the bushwhackers were without peeking over the boulder. I pondered the risk. Pike and Logan crashed through the underbrush as they descended the trail blazed by the avalanche. Must think I'm dead, seeing as how unconcerned they are about announcing their presence. Near or far, they'd be down soon enough.

"No, sir," Logan yelled. "Don't see we have to tramp…" his voice dropped to a mumble, and in the span of a heartbeat, rose again "…down just to fix our eyes on a dead man."

"Shut up!" Pike shot back. "It's a stupid man don't see the job finished."

"Monroe's leg looks busted up bad…shouldn't leave him…"

"I swear, Logan, you're getting as sissified as Taz." Pike's voice dissolved into a series of grunts, as more stones bounced down the mountain and came to rest on the boulder.

I hunkered against the giant rock and eyed the three great logs in front of me. Only the stubs of once-fat limbs protruded from the trunks. Bark had long since crumbled, leaving the core of the trees. Balanced with one atop the other two, they'd come to rest in a muddy bog between me and escape. Going over them would mean a sure bullet in the back.

Nothing to do but keep my head down and belly-crawl around them. Foliage thickened on the other side, slender trees growing so close together that their branches locked and grew indistinguishable from each other. Maybe I could lose myself in the greenery and shadows. As the voices drew near, I stretched forward, snaking from the boulder's protection.

Layers of leaves, continually moistened into a stew by rainwater that poured down the mountainside or oozed from its pores, settled in the land's crevice. My elbows sank in the spongy mire, rich and black with rot. The stench of decaying vegetation rose in putrid fumes.

I stretched long, mouth clamped shut, and pulled myself forward, each movement accompanied with a liquid slurp. The stew oozed through my uniform, sucking me deep. I sure enough wanted out of there. It was in my mind I would be spitting mud bubbles if I tarried. I wiggled around the tentacles of roots riddled with insect holes to the other side of the logs and squeezed under a thicket of thorny rabbit bush, crawling until the earth felt solid again.

"Where is he?" Logan shrieked. "Where is he?"

The ruffians must have been closer than they sounded. Flat on the ground, I stretched an arm forward and moved a broken limb to the side. Crawling through dead leaves would not be a silent accomplishment. Pushing the toes of my boots into the dirt, I inched deeper into the shadows.

"I told you, didn't I?" Pike roared. "I told you a man is never dead until you lay eyes on him."

"Maybe he didn't fall all the way to the bottom," Logan offered.

"Did you pass him on the way down?" Pike asked,

his voice cold as a well bottom. "Don't stand there like a dummy. That boy didn't just sprout wings and fly off."

In the dark of the forest, down where the sun's rays seldom caressed the dirt, the ground was cool and soft. The stench of the bog cleared my head.

It was a spot, not unlike the ticky place back at the natural dam, where hungry ticks clung to the undersides of hanging leaves, just waiting for a warm body to pass. I could almost feel the crawl of little skiddies beneath my mud-soaked uniform.

"Here!" Logan called. "Here's a piece of rope."

Pike's answer was unintelligible. I pushed to my feet. Even a gobshite would know a person wouldn't get far crawling through the woods. Tired as I was, I had to keep moving. Maybe they wouldn't cross the bog. At least now, there were only two on my trail.

Spindly saplings grew like weeds under the tall hawthorns, oaks, and warty hackberries. They slapped against my pant legs, beating clumps of mud free. I scanned the ground, stepping over tangles of brush and slabs of rock. Big Jolly said Indians know how to make their bodies light, how to move without sound through the forest, how to walk on silent feet.

Holding my breath, I pulled up tall, stepping as lightly as my brogans would permit. The crunch of leaves and twigs underfoot sounded like cannon fire. I stopped and stared at a pile of brown bullet-shaped droppings. Flies buzzed around the fresh leavings. Deer! The trail would most likely lead to a stream. I'd had but a dipper of water in ever so long. The thought pushed caution to the back of my mind, back behind the thirst that left my mouth dry and throat tight.

Pike and Logan's voices faded from hearing. I broke into a trot, eyes scanning the ground for the occasional heart-shaped hoofprint. Jasper bushes grew thick, fresh branches encasing each previous year's growth, until they were half as tall as a man.

A deer exploded from the center of the bushes, leaping straight up and over the thicket. The movement was so quick, so unexpected, that I yelped before I could dam the offending sound. A bird startled from its perch, then within seconds the entire flock took wing, arcing high into the sky.

The roar of rifle fire filled the air. I ducked and spun around to scan the forest behind me. Several clumps of branches hit the ground. A shower of leaves, in brief flashes of greens and yellows, sifted down. The shot was wild, too high to have been aimed. I strained to catch sight of a flash of color or movement amidst the dusty gray of close-knit trees. Thin shafts of sunlight cut through the foliage and sliced across tree trunks.

The forest settled into an uneasy quiet. No squirrels chattered or birds fussed or animals moved. Above me, a tall hickory shuddered, almost as if protesting the loss of a branch. A scant breeze carried with it the unmistakable growl of angry voices, still only a mumble in the distance.

Crouched in the bushes, I took a deep breath, willing myself to think. The bog would have shifted, filled in all traces of my passing, almost as soon as I crawled through it. Logan and Pike would have to wade through the mud and skirt around the logs to find my trail. Logan wouldn't go to that much trouble, but Pike was another matter. The man was mean to the core. The only question now was which was more important to Pike—the planned feast back at camp or killing an escaped prisoner?

A beam of sunlight blinked as two figures moved into sight. Damn that Pike! What kind of man would rather kill than eat?

I pushed backward, turned, and, still crouched, picked my way around rocks, avoiding broken limbs and leaves banked in mounds against tree trunks. My legs felt trembly, ready to disown me. I forced them to move, pushing through veils of hanging vines, swerving around trees, following a faint trail toward what I hoped would be a stream.

I concentrated on the pull of air in and out of my lungs. On flat terrain, the act was automatic, but the jar of uneven ground kept me huffing. My tongue was dry as an old piece of leather.

The blue-green of pine needles blended with the green of scrub oak and hickory leaves until colors melted together into a blur. The ground tilted. I stumbled, leaned into a tree trunk for support and slid to the ground, each gasp of air like sandpaper in my throat. Might as well wait right here for a bullet as to die of thirst.

At first, the sound was almost indistinguishable from the rustle of leaves, the creak of shifting branches and buzz of insects, but when I listened hard enough, I caught the liquid bubble of slow-moving water. There was a fresher smell to the air, too, suggesting the growth of moss and clumps of water grass. I pushed to my feet and staggered forward, following my nose.

The trail opened onto sandy ground trampled with the visitation of forest critters. Small hand-like prints of raccoons and skunks crisscrossed over deer and wolf tracks. Several inches of water trickled over a bed of rocks, pooling in depressions scoured by torrents of spring rain.

I dropped to my knees in the middle of the stream, where the water would be purest, bent, and gulped great mouthfuls, taking in bits of debris and sand in the process. I drank until I choked. Ma always said a thirsty man can founder on too much water, blow up like a toad, burst his stomach and flood his insides.

Water changed everything, gave renewed life, and suddenly, I was back to listening for footsteps, not content to wait for a bullet.

East! If I kept eastward, I'd intersect Telegraph Road which ran down from Cassville and into Fayetteville. Somewhere along that road, the wagon train would be strung out like a sitting duck, confident in a faulty report from Shilo Riddle's spies—one a traitor; one decked out in a dead Union soldier's uniform.

With another gulp of water, I rose and followed the curves of the creek bed, stretching to step on the largest stones. No use making it easy to follow my footprints. Wispy branches of a willow hung over the stream. I ducked under them and squatted in the shallow water to listen.

Pike and Logan were still following, sure as the sun was setting in the west. It was a feeling, a whisper in the trees, a snap or crack or splash that wasn't quite right. The knowing lifted the hair on the back of my neck. Right now, I could swear, even the trees had eyes.

Long supple willow tendrils brushed across my face. Despite the humid heat, their spidery touch sent chills down my back. It was then that a hand slapped across my mouth and squeezed. I clawed at the hand and felt myself being pulled backward, deeper into the tree's shadow.

"Shush," a voice hissed in my ear. The smell of sweat and waxy pomade filled my nostrils.

Big Jolly leaned over my shoulder, grinning big as a possum. "Good thing I'm not snake," he whispered.

I reached out to touch my friend, afraid he was one of those ghostly apparitions that crazy men see. The boy was real, warm, and solid. The best thing I'd seen in a month of Sundays. It was just like Big Jolly to jump down out of nowhere.

"What you got to go scaring a man out of his wits for?" I whispered when I found my voice. "I'm being chased, in case you don't know."

"I know." Big Jolly shrugged and whispercd back. "You white men make much noise, whole forest knows."

"What're you doing here anyway? Not that I'm not glad to see you, 'cause I surely am. Your father here, too?"

"Father and brother with cattle, north of here, over in next valley. Hear many gun shots. First, not sure it was Ebby I see. What you do to make those men mad at you?"

"Bloody bushwhackers. That's Pike Benton back there. Him and Shilo Riddle are part of the scum that come to our house and threatened Ma. Remember? The same bunch that attacked us when we camped with old man Casey. This morning, at daybreak…"

I had to stop a minute. The whole shameful affair was painful to admit. "Sleeping like a baby, and I got taken prisoner. Tazewell's a miserable Sesech. There's a whole passel, hundreds of them camped on the other side of the ridge, over by that waterfall."

"*Ahay*, we see their smoke." Big Jolly nodded, voice low as the shudder of a breeze through the trees. "Yesterday we move north. Lots of men coming from all over."

I looked through the veil of willow branches. "That Pike can track near as good as any bloodhound I ever saw. He's bound to kill me." I glanced back at my friend, who was squatting against the stream bank, arms around his knees. "You got anything to eat? I'm so hungry I could eat the bark off a tree."

"No." Big Jolly shook his head. "Ebby come back to camp. We have food, beans, cornmeal, dried apples. Maybe, father trap another rabbit."

"Can't. I've gotta find my way to Telegraph Road, east of here. There's a supply wagon coming down from Cassville. My brother is on it. Those no-good Sesech aim to ambush it tomorrow."

A blackbird squawked a warning. Another, closer to us, answered.

"I gotta keep moving. Gotta warn the wagon train." I parted the branches, then stopped, and looked back. "Proud as a tick to see you again. You get back to Fayetteville, tell Ma I was thinking on her. She was a mite upset when I left. Saw some signs in the coffee grounds…"

I swallowed back the rest of the sentence. No use admitting I ignored her warning. Indians were superstitious about such things.

Big Jolly scratched his head and took a deep breath. "I go, too."

"It's not your fight. Your pa said so."

"I think maybe this war everyone's fight. I help you find wagon train." He peered down the stream and around at the tangle of trees. "'Sides, we race, maybe I win back fish charm."

"Don't much reckon so," I whispered as we slipped from the willows and started on a trot along the stream bank.

An arm's width away, Big Jolly kept pace, hopping over tree roots and scrubby brush with ease. His long dark hair flounced on his shoulders.

My muscles warmed to the exercise, and I fell into a familiar rhythm—heel down, roll forward, push with toes. This was something I knew how to do. Big Jolly, running next to me, was a comfort, gave me fresh energy. It was like old times. Between the two of us, we were sure to find the road, even in the dark. Nothing could keep me from reaching the supply wagon now.

The woods thinned to barren trees, trunks most likely blackened from a lightning fire. We dropped to our knees at the edge of a meadow that ran the width of the valley. Knee-high grass, festooned with clouds of daisies, swayed in gentle ripples.

"Well, if this don't beat all," I said when I could get my breath. "There's still a touch too much daylight. We'll be sitting ducks getting across to the other side. Gotta belly crawl through the grass, or go around."

I listened for any sound that would mark Pike's progress, but could hear only my own deep breathing. How that old man had the energy to keep up the chase, I didn't know.

Big Jolly touched my arm and pointed across the sea of golden grass to the charred skeleton of a giant tree. It stood in the clearing's center, a lonely survivor of the long-ago fire. Halfway up, a black bear straddled a fat limb, with all four legs dangling.

"Him sleep." Big Jolly nodded toward the far side of the clearing and leaned close to whisper. "Run fast. I beat Ebby to other side." He pushed to his feet.

"Wait!" I grabbed at Big Jolly, catching only a handful of weeds for my effort. Nothing to do but follow. I jumped forward, planting one foot ahead of the other and batting at the hordes of insects that flew up out of the grass. From the corner of my eye, I watched the snoozing bear, stretched out along the branch.

Within a few strides, I was even with Big Jolly, matching my friend's pace. The air, taken in great gulps, was sweet with the smell of summer. Razor-edged grass tore at my pants as I forged a path through the thickness in awkward bounds. It was like wading quicksand, and I was relieved when we drew near the forest's edge.

Thunder boomed, multiplied in volume until it blotted out thought and memory. I glanced back in time to see a large flock of blackbirds lift from the tree tops and fly over, casting broken shadows in the waving grass.

Fear dropped me to the ground. My eye, drawn by a wispy column of smoke, found Pike and Logan standing at the edge of the meadow—the very spot where we had been minutes earlier. Logan screamed, pointing, not at us, but at the bear sliding down the tree trunk.

Big Jolly rested on his knees in the deep grass. "Run!" I shouted. "Get to cover before he's reloaded.

Run!"

Big Jolly rose, took a few steps, and stumbled.

"What's the matter?" I yelled and grabbed the front of his shirt. A bright red splotch blossomed down his sleeve. "Aw, no! What'd you have to go and get shot for?"

Big Jolly's eyes squeezed shut, his lips pressed tight. He pushed back to his feet.

"That's right." I slid my arm around his back and willed our bodies forward. "Come on, I got you."

The rifle roared again, followed by the bear's shrill howl.

"Shoot him! Shoot him!" Logan screamed above the bear's raging.

I didn't look back as I plunged into the tree line, staggering under the weight of Big Jolly. "Gotta keep going long as you can," I told him. "Didn't see which way that bear was gonna run."

Scorched trunks sprouted fresh green branches. Shadows deepened and patches of sunlight faded, becoming hazy as it filtered through trees untouched by the fire. I kept pushing forward, half dragging Big Jolly deeper into the tangle of overgrown bushes and knobby trees. Distance muffled another shot.

Exhausted, we slid to the ground. "We got a minute. They're still back at the meadow."

Big Jolly's breathing labored, quick and raspy. He gasped when I peeled the bloodied shirt off. Bone flashed through the torn flesh of his upper arm. My fingers trembled, pushing the wound closed to stanch the flow of blood.

"Big Jolly, listen to me. You got to hold your hand over this hole in your arm. You're losing a bucket of blood."

Big Jolly nodded.

"Bullet went clean through, I think." I dug in my pocket for the fish charm and, with its sharpened edges, hacked a long strip from his bloody shirt to bind up the wound. Ma always said to find the good in something bad that happened, and I tried. "Don't reckon you got to worry about a rebel bullet rolling around your arm like Josiah does."

"Ebby, maybe brother bear run away, not kill those men." Big Jolly lifted one side of his mouth in a weak grin. "Maybe those men kill bear, now they hunt us again."

"Yeah. Maybe that flea-bitten animal is cousin to the fish-stealing bear your uncle killed, and he decides to come after us instead of those bushwhackers." I tied the arms of the shirt together to fashion a sling, and scanned the trees ahead. There hadn't been another rifle shot for a few minutes, but it was best to keep moving.

"Ebby. Go on." Big Jolly shook his head. "I run no more."

"Go on? Leave you alone? What kind of crazy talk is that?" I hoisted my friend up. "Pike'll kill you, too, just for the pure fun of it."

Chapter 30

I readjusted my grip on Big Jolly's sweat-soaked body, guiding us through the thick growth of scrub oaks and hickories. He barely kept pace with the walk, sometimes lifting his moccasin-clad feet, other times shuffling. Layers of leaves, laid down by the passing of seasons, crunched and rustled underneath. Dust, heavy with the odor of mold and rot, lifted and hung in the air.

"I thought you Indians didn't make noise," I complained. "Sounds like a herd of cattle tromping through here."

Big Jolly grunted and stumbled over a tree root. I struggled to stay on my feet. It was no use wearing my friend out, using precious energy neither of us had to spare. The bear delayed Pike some, maybe even killed him, but that wasn't a for-sure thing. We needed a hiding place, somewhere for Big Jolly to rest, and we needed it before it got any darker.

The ground sloped upward, made walking more difficult, but the trees and underbrush thinned, admitting a flush of fresh air. The craggy face of a cliff rose in front of us. I caught sight of a spot of darkness.

"Hey, by gum, we got us a hideout. See there?" I squeezed Big Jolly against my body, willing him to look up. "I do believe that's a cave. What say we rest a spell?"

Big Jolly lifted his head and nodded. He leaned to

the task of climbing, as if the prospect of rest gave him a spurt of energy. Rocks crumbled and shifted beneath our feet. Bracing my body against the stubby trunks of shrubs that grew in the crevices, I pushed Big Jolly ahead. Sweat rolled off me in the unrelenting heat and effort of the climb.

"Here." I panted when we reached a wide ledge just below the cave. "Rest here a minute. I'll take a look about, run out any critters."

Big Jolly eased back against a boulder and closed his eyes. "Pounding stick, Ebby," he muttered.

"Yeah, intend to get me one." I said. "And here be a likely-looking pounding stick, too." I tested the strength of a half-dead laurel bush, before deciding on a limb riddled with tiny holes. It broke away with a loud crack. Big Jolly needed to be hauled out of sight in a hurry.

I scrambled atop the overhang and ventured into the opening, sweeping the cave's floor with the laurel branch. If I was going to disturb a barrel snake or a rattler, it was best to do it at the end of a good ol' pounding stick. Lots of things thrive in the Arkansas hills, all manner of snakes and spiders and insects. Rumor was, if a man lay down for a nap in the underbrush, he'd likely wake up with fingers gnawed to the bone by coffin beetles and such.

The cave's recess was taller than it was deep and reeked of mustiness and animal leavings. A moistness in the stale air suggested the seep of water from the mountain's bowels. My thirst was back—not the earlier raging need, but a thirst, nonetheless, and I moved to the rear of the cave.

In the shadows, a telltale drip guided me to a

fissure. Oozing water glistened on the cave's limestone surface. Running my palms down the wet rock, I followed its path to the floor, where it gathered in a shallow depression before disappearing into the ground. I dipped a cupped hand into the small pool and drank the limestone-tainted water. My eyes adjusted to the dimness. Bits of fur and gnawed bone joints littered the floor.

They'd come back, the wolves and coyotes, dragging their kills. When the creeks were dry, they'd come back for the water that was always at the rear of the cave. Hair bristled on top of my head, and I hurried toward the cave entrance, anxious to get Big Jolly hidden.

"C'mon," I said and hooked my hands in Big Jolly's armpits, lifting him to his feet. "Just like home up there. Even has fresh water."

"Fresh?" he questioned when we finally made our way into the cave.

"So sweet you can almost taste the sunshine." I hesitated, "Well, maybe not exactly sweet. Wet, anyway." We lay on our backs and studied the smoke-blackened ceiling. Here and there it appeared lightning bolts had been scratched into the surface.

"Spirits live here," Big Jolly said.

"How can you tell?"

"Spirits always live in caves." He pointed a blood-smeared finger upward at crude lines and circles drawn on the ceiling. "Many years ago, someone's ancestors lived here."

"Yeah, friendly or unfriendly?"

Strands of hair stuck to Big Jolly's sweaty face. He shrugged an answer.

I sat up and glanced out over the canopy of treetops. Across the valley, a flock of birds swooped and circled, finally disappearing into the greenery. A swatch of pink light tinted the sky and held back the evening darkness. No sign of Pike.

"Water's at the back of the cave. Best shelter in before it gets night." I helped Big Jolly settle next to the shallow pool.

"Your bandage is sopped clean through. Here, I'll tear another strip off what's left of that shirt."

What an almighty mess. First time I get sent out on an honest-to-goodness mission, I get myself traitorized and captured and near shot. Now, I let my best friend take a bullet that was sure enough meant for me.

Big Jolly clamped his mouth tight with the movement of his arm. His bare chest heaved, and a groan slipped from his lips.

The blood-soaked bandage reeked. "This will draw critters," I said, wrapping the fresh bandage tight. Big Jolly's strength was sapped out, that was certain.

"I'm sorry about getting you in this fix. Reckon your pa going to be mad as the dickens at us? He didn't want any part of the war. Even if he gives me the evil eye, I wish he was here right now. He'd know what to do."

"Father come. Tomorrow. Next day. Father look for me." Big Jolly leaned against the rough surface of the cave wall and attempted a grin. "Wish we had old man Casey's Springfield."

"Yeah," I agreed and started gathering nearby twigs. "Ol' Hickory would even the odds a bit. Remember how those bushwhackers hightailed it when Casey blasted them? Now that was a sight!"

I crouched at the entrance, with one eye on the rocky approach to the cave, and reached for several dead limbs. Still no sign of Pike. What was it that polecat had said? A man isn't dead until you see him dead.

"That Pike's meaner than Mr. Flanagan when he gets himself all bound up. Least with Flanagan, that meanness is a sometimes thing. With Pike, meanness is an everyday happening." I squatted and stacked the wood into a pile.

"Father say man has two wolves live inside him. One good. One bad." Big Jolly cradled his injured arm close to his chest. "Wolves all the time fight."

The brittle crack of wood echoed in the hollowness of the cave as I broke limbs into short lengths and studied my friend. Stories were usually the business of Big Jolly's twin. Often you had to figure out the meaning for yourself, unless you knew the right question to ask.

"Two wolves fight, huh? Which one wins?"

"Whichever one gets fed the most."

"Well, I reckon Pike has been feeding the bad wolf all his life, 'cause meanness like his don't just happen overnight. One thing's certain. Unless Pike got himself ate by that bear, he's still out there aiming to stop me informing on their ambush. Shilo Riddle, most likely, doesn't even know about my escape, so he's not apt to change his plans."

An image of the bushwhacker, atop his large prancing roan, flashed through my mind. "Shilo was a raving madman, letting loose in an all-out hell-fire rant. He's whipped those Sesech into a real fury by now." Big Jolly closed his eyes, and I wasn't sure he was still listening to me. "Shilo's set to swoop down on the supply wagon with nigh on to five hundred men for sure. I wouldn't give those Union soldiers a plugged nickel for their chances. None of them."

I dipped what was left of the torn shirt into the water and bathed Big Jolly's face, which woke him up. The boy didn't look good—eyes sunk a mile in his head, jaw set tight. Not much chance he was going to regain enough strength to keep ahead of Pike. Even if Pike wasn't still out there, we would have to move fast to reach the wagon train by morning.

A knot welled in my stomach, one harder and bigger than the fist of hunger already pulling at my insides. How could I leave my friend? How could I let fifty soldiers, including Josiah, ride into Shilo's ambush? I swallowed hard against the bitter answer and looked my friend full in the face, into dark eyes that shone like polished glass.

Big Jolly, body trembling despite the heat, nodded slightly in response.

"You cold?" I asked, looking for a diversion to what needed to be said. Big Jolly's skin felt clammy, like the underbelly of a fish on a stringer.

"I be all right, Ebby." Big Jolly reached up. I caught his hand and pulled it to my chest.

"You know I gotta do it, don't you? I gotta leave you and go on." There. The words were out, like they were telling me what to do. My throat tightened. "Lord knows I don't want to."

Big Jolly squeezed my hand. "Father can track snake over rocks, Ebby. He come. I be all right."

"Sure, sure you will. I'll get back soon as I find the wagon train. Ought to take a day or two, at the most."

An ache blossomed behind my eyes. I stood and unbuttoned my shirt before a tear could escape and roll down my cheek. "Here, wrap up in this. It's a mite smelly. Maybe keep the critters at bay. You got water handy right next to you."

I tucked my shirt around my friend's shoulders. "You got flint in your pouch, don't you?"

Big Jolly nodded.

"That's good. That's good. I got you a wood pile here." I propped the pounding stick against the wall. "And this." My voice wobbled, and I stood. "This pitiful weapon might be of some use."

I scooped the bloody bandage up and took a last look at my friend. "I won't forget where you are."

Big Jolly, stretched out on the ground and looking helpless as a newborn babe, raised his hand briefly before letting it fall to his side.

"No, I won't never forget where you are," I whispered. "I'll be back." My vision blurred as I slipped over the ledge and hunkered there. I had to do it. If there was any hope of finding the wagon train, I had to leave my friend with nothing more than a pounding stick and a few cave spirits. Anybody could see that.

Before I could question the decision, I picked my way down around boulders and scrub trees. I stopped to listen, boot propped against the stub of a tree trunk to adjust for the slope of the mountain

Up and down the valley, locusts serenaded against the heat, in choral waves. The soft rustling of bushes and trees became an exaggeration of noise, but as I strained to sort the sounds, no groans of labor or soft curses or dislodgement of stones met my ears. Quiet as

I could manage, I inched down on the seat of my pants.

Pike was out there, I felt sure. It was a knowing that came over me the closer I got to the valley floor. I stopped at the base of the slope and studied the jumble of trees. In the semidarkness, they were all alike—hickories and oaks and maple, with miles of thick scrubby underbrush and waist-high weeds—nothing at all remarkable about the landscape. How would anybody find this particular place?

A thought popped into my head, like it was waiting for just this moment. I dug in my pocket for the arrowhead—the fish charm that drew brownies to the hook by pure magic. I reached for a slender branch of an oak, about eye level, and jerked leathery leaves from its woody flesh along the entire length. A thumb-sized knob on the branch made a perfect place to hang the arrowhead by its rawhide strip.

If Pike found it, it would have no meaning. But Levi Standing Corn with his keen eyes would know. He would know the meaning of such a sign. I studied the charm, the glass beads dull until they caught a fragment of sunlight. Yes, Levi would know his son was close, unless Pike found it first and jerked it down.

Chapter 31

I stared at the fish charm, memorizing how it hung inches from the branch. How very ordinary the gray arrowhead looked, like it was nothing at all special. And the glass beads, how they near blended into the foliage. I took several careful steps backward, fixing the shape of the young tree in my mind. Patches of faded sunlight became hazy, blurred outlines. With another couple of steps, the arrowhead disappeared from sight.

It wasn't enough. Such a small sign would be too easy to miss. I shifted the bloody bandage to my left hand and reached for a fist-sized rock with my right, then pulled back before touching it. Dried blood caked my hands. Big Jolly's blood. Best not leave the scent this close to the cave.

A commotion from deep in the woods—perhaps a rabbit flushed from its burrow or a wild turkey disturbed from its perch—broke the steady hum of insect sounds. It was hard to make out the noise. It sounded like a cackle or grumble or flutter of heavy wings through thick foliage. Or it could have been none of those things.

Quickly, I rolled rocks together with the toe of my boot—five or six, not so many as to be an obvious pile. One last chore remained. I turned, stretched one leg out and came down heavy on my heel. The effort sent a spiral of pain through my foot as blisters grated against leather. Another few deliberate steps. I glanced back at the prints left in the dirt. Maybe the discovery would be enough to lead Pike away from Big Jolly.

"These'll be the last easy signs I leave," I muttered, hoping to convince myself of the certainty. Then, I pushed ahead, skirting piles of leaves and twigs, all the while listening, sorting the sounds into friendly or unfriendly.

Every few feet, I scrubbed the bloody fabric along a tree trunk or over a large rock moving farther and farther from the location of the cave. Pike wouldn't pick up the faint trace of blood, but other hunters would—the four-legged kind.

A scrubby old hackberry, its girth as big around as Othella Johnson's ample body, sheltered a profusion of springy saplings. I jumped for a limb just above my head and pulled it down far enough to tie the bandage to it. The limb shuddered as it lifted back into place. In the dark, Pike just might miss this sign. And if he didn't, it wouldn't matter. All it would tell him was that somebody had been hurt.

The trees grew taller in the rich soil of the valley, the shadows darker. Once the sun was gone, it would be pitch black. Hunters often found they'd gone in circles trying to move about in the night. To avoid such a mistake, I'd have to go higher up the ridge again to get my bearings.

A stream of water lazied through the valley floor. Frogs, hidden in the stalks of razor-edged water grass, tuned up their croaking for the night's competition. An ideal spot for crawdads and tadpoles for sure. On the opposite side of the stream, a slab of limestone, several feet in diameter, created a small dam. I took a giant step across the pool of water to the top of the rock and hopped to another flat rock before setting boots to the ground.

In the deep shadows, a man would have to look close to see the moist footprints. If I was lucky, Pike would miss where I'd changed directions. The frogs fell silent for a minute. Before I was more than a few feet into the tangle of brush, they resumed their bellowing.

Trees crowded together so thick even the full moon barely lit the shroud of darkness. At first, the soft touch against my nose was light, a mere hint of something unseen. I ran a palm across my face, feeling the unmistakable grab of a finely-spun thread, and walked right into the thick scaffolding of spider webs stretched between trees. Whisper-thin strands caught in my hair and eyelashes.

It was a fight to break free of the giant web's clutches and peel the clinging threads away. Hairy spiders, big as owls, could spin webs that would catch a man up. Before he could get loose, the spider would inject his poison and wait for the man to collapse. Then the man-killer would suck the juices right out of the paralyzed victim, leaving nothing but a shriveled pile of bones. I'd never actually seen such a critter, but Big Jolly swore it was true.

With a shiver, I scanned the shadows, wondering if the itch on the back of my neck was a bite. In the distance, the frogs fell silent. Their silence was louder than their bellowing, and I held my breath until they resumed their serenade. Most likely, Pike was still on the trail.

When the ground began an upward slope, the going proved easier. Trees and underbrush thinned and visibility improved. I scrambled over rocky outcroppings, climbing higher, until I could look out over the canopy of treetops that had grown dull in the early dusk of evening. I'd have to hurry, be on my way as soon as I had my direction.

Outrunning a bullet wouldn't have much meaning if the wagon train fell into the hands of Shilo Riddle and his like. Somewhere out there, the wagon train would be settled in for the night, horses picketed, campfires blazing, soldiers sharing stories over fatback and beans, not knowing they would be targets come morning. And Josiah would be with them, most likely rubbing liniment on the arm still bothered by a rebel bullet.

The rising moon, pale, crisp, hovered above the scalloped edge of the horizon. It was nearly full, a round disk giving out an ample portion of light. An unlucky thing since the spiders had made their webs high, which was a sure sign there would be no rain to wash away my tracks. If I could see, so could Pike.

A rocky ledge provided a good resting spot. I picked at the stick-tights, pulling them from the wool fibers of my pants. Shadows crept up the mountainside. If Pike was keeping to the hunt, he would leave the valley floor, too, and climb higher for better visibility. My stomach rumbled. How long since I'd shared bacon and pea soup with Tazewell? Thirty-two hours? Longer? Torn flesh, foot blisters, heat, and assault by insects were nothing compared to being hungry.

Overhead, a star winked to life, the north star. I stood, arm outstretched, hand spread wide, with my thumb to the brightness, and turned, looking for the Big Dipper off the tip of my little finger. There it was, its handle pointing the way west. I sighted a definite notch in the west horizon, a wide spot where the hills sloped down. It could be the channel for Sugar Creek or the natural break in the landscape where the road to Cassville had been forged. Either way, it was my destination.

A sharp crack of gunfire echoed along the valley, and I dropped to my belly. Something followed, perhaps a muffled yell. Yet there'd been no smack of a bullet into the cliffs or broken tree limbs nearby. Pike was shooting wild, and I thought to call out he ought to give up, that I'd bested him. A few weeks earlier, I'd have done such a fool thing. Not now. Now I was a lifetime older and a whole lot smarter.

I scrambled along the rocks, around scrub brush and misshapen trees, always walking on the edges of my boots to maintain balance. Legs trembling by the time the terrain began to ease downhill, I sighted into the distance, searching out my landmark again.

The scent of overripe fruit floated in the night air. Blackberries! What I wouldn't give for a bowl of blackberries, drizzled with honey and drowning in milk. Back home, vines like these were alive with hordes of bees, the fruit being enjoyed by skunks and all sorts of critters. Every once in a while, a bear followed his nose and had himself a feast.

The ground leveled into a definite path, worn smooth by all manner of animals. Close to the valley floor, where breezes seldom stirred the air, the aroma hung strong. Bees and such weren't about in the dark. With poor eyesight, bears tended to sleep through the night. It was worth the risk of disturbing a skunk or a snake to satisfy my stomach's complaint. Waist-high blackberry bushes covered the hillside in the moonlight.

Even in the dark, I could pick out the clumps of fruit hanging from long tentacles that stretched in every direction. Each berry, large as a thumb, slid free of its stem with the slightest tug. Using both hands, unmindful of the thorns plucking my skin, I filled my mouth with the tart berries. Juice stung a thousand tiny scratches as it ran down my arms and escaped the corners of my mouth.

I pushed farther along the path, lifting vines for the berries hidden deep in the thicket. Something fluttered at the disturbance and flew off into the night. I paused and looked around to study the shadows, pushing the accumulation of seeds around with my tongue. A noise, like a snort or huff, rose from the thicket, but the sound was gone when I listened again.

Imagination, most likely, putting wary thoughts in my mind. I lifted a heavy cane with hand-sized leaves. The best berries grew on such sturdy vines. I continued stuffing them as fast as I could in my mouth.

Stripping the fruit within easy reach, I parted the canes in search of more berries and stirred a musky odor, wild and strong. A warning, unmistakable in its meaning, rumbled from the shadows. For an instant, I froze, unable to move. Carefully I pushed the vines into place and stepped backward several paces.

The bushes exploded with a high-pitched growl, and a black bear stumbled up, standing on short wobbly legs. He wagged his head and roared again, long strings of slobber swinging with the motion.

I snatched up a big stick in my retreat, eyes glued to the angry animal. A handful of berries refused to go down my throat, stayed balled on my tongue, juicing my mouth until I feared I would choke and was forced to spit, spewing berries everywhere.

"Steady there. Don't mean no harm, fella. You can have them berries all to yourself." I took another step backward, my heart pounding in my chest.

The bear raised his paws, claws spread wide, and yowled. The long red scars inflicted by the ancient bear claw on Curly's face flashed before my eyes. A rush of pure fear raced through every bone in my body.

Everything I'd ever heard about bears crowded my mind. Stand still. Face him. Don't try to outrun a bear; it won't work. Climb a tree, and he'll be at the top, waiting for you. Skull's thick enough to bounce a bullet; got to place a knife between his rib cage and rip up into his lungs for a kill.

The bear dropped to all fours and huffed, swaying from side to side, his breath hot and sour with fermented fruit. The animal swung its head and yowled again. Lips quivered above jagged teeth, and, in that instant, I knew the bear's own fear—whether to run or make a stand.

Flapping my arms like wings, I hollered, "Haw, haw, get on out!" Maybe the ruse would make me appear a giant. Most times, a bear won't attack something bigger than itself. At least, that was what I'd heard.

"Get on, now!" I hollered again and whipped the air with the stick.

The bear spun and galloped along the narrow path, tearing through weaving tendrils of blackberries and brush tangles. It disappeared in the darkness, its retreat marked by the sound of snapping branches.

Not more than four or five feet tall, a two-year-old

most likely, lost or driven away by its mother, and near scared to death—one that didn't know its teeth were just as deadly, its claws just as sharp, as its mama's. I sank to my knees, thankful for the animal's ignorance. I needed a minute to steady my heart, calm the pounding in my head.

Twice now, I'd avoided bullets and bears, and it seemed unfair, somehow, to still be breathing. Ma said bad things always happened in threes—injuries and sickness and death. If her superstition was true, I wouldn't be so lucky the next time.

A wolf howled in the distance. Above the bushwhacker's encampment, lay Amos and the others, their blood summoning creatures that lived on death. By all rights, I should be there, too, body bloated in the July heat and gathering flies like the deer carcass in the bushwhacker's camp.

Big Jolly would be huddled in the back of the cave, hearing the same howls and wondering how soon the wolves would find their way to him. I stood with unsteady legs, the ache of fatigue and fright heavy in my mind.

Cutting a path clear of the blackberries, I trotted into the underbrush, whacking with the long stick at the bramble that hung from tight groups of trees. Branches, slender as grass blades, slapped at my face and bare chest, raising long whelps. I pushed on, pausing now and again to determine the easiest path.

Each time, I heard a whisper urging me forward. It came with the rush of wind through the leaves or an animal's distant howl, like Uley's ghost was still pleading with his captors—like Uley didn't know it was all over for him. The thought gave me energy, the energy to warn the wagon train and get back to Big Jolly. I kept trotting where I could and wading through briars, one careful step at a time.

The forest opened to a small pool, admitting enough moonlight to silver its surface. I squatted at its edge, skimming scum with the back of one hand and scooping up a palmful of water with the other. It smelled of mud and moss. Dragonflies darted back and forth, making circles in the water where they touched the surface. Insects rose from the weeds to gather at the bloodied welts on my body. On the other side of the pond, a female deer stepped through the trees and paused. I hunkered down to watch her.

A slap, like that of skin on skin, sounded in the forest behind me. Or perhaps it was the sharp snap of a limb, but in that instant, the deer turned, the white underside of her tail flashing as she disappeared. I forced myself to stay where I was, to look over my shoulder at the tree line. Was it another bear, another deer? Was it Pike?

Foliage moved in the dark recesses of the trees. I rose, bent over to make myself a smaller target, and ran around the pond to put the water between me and whatever moved in the night. Without stopping, I plunged into the bushes.

Crickets sawed in the banks of dead leaves, and locusts whirred in the treetops, but nothing was as loud as my own breathing. I concentrated on keeping it even, despite the jar of uncertain ground. Wisps of fog snaked through the undergrowth, whirling up like forest spirits as I moved through it.

The earth rose, and I bent to the climb. With my feet rubbed raw by leather boots, each step sent waves of pain up my legs. At the top of the ridge, I sat down, pulled off my boots, and massaged my feet. Above the tangle of thick vegetation, fresh air carried the scent of honeysuckle in its currents.

A glorious array of bright stars blinked in the pitch-black sky. I searched out my landmark. The notched ridge looked close enough to touch. A couple more hours of walking, as the crow flies, would put me there, if my feet held out. It would take longer if I had to crawl.

An owl hooted, reminding me that death roamed the forest, that it wasn't safe to rest. I peeled a grimy sock off, holes worn in the heel and toe, and picked threads from the oozing blisters. A slab of bacon would cushion the rub. Silly to wish for such, seeing as how hunger would most likely overrule the blisters.

I pulled the socks back on, with the holes twisted to the top, eased into my boots, and packed grass to cushion the heel. It helped, barely. Even protected from the leather, the pain of blisters throbbed deep.

I took one last look at the distant ridge, to fix it in my mind, and descended the hillside into the valley. A layer of fog lifted halfway up the trees. In the crush of foliage, the absence of light was near total.

Minutes stretched into long hours. Sounds distorted in the thickness, and I couldn't tell their direction. I stopped several times to study the faint paths made by animals. Each time, I thought I could pick out the labored breathing of something in the darkness.

Pike, unable to leave a chore undone, followed. I was sure of it. It's a stupid man don't see the job finished. Pike was many things, but stupid wasn't one of them.

Stars had disappeared by the time I topped a slight rise, and a red streak edged the horizon. Dawn was minutes away. Below, patches of fog obscured the landscape. As I stood to catch my breath, to wait for the sun, I glimpsed a hard-packed dirt road, cut through a wide swatch of land. Tree stumps, on either side of the road, poked up through the fog like stubby fingers. The scent of burning wood was in the air. With a stick for balance, I half slid down the incline in my rush to gain the road.

A sense of urgency pushed me along. I thrashed my way free of the forest's grasp, free of the brambles and briars and nameless sounds that came with each puff of wind.

An unmistakable aroma, faint and teasing, stirred the rumble in my stomach. I lifted my head and sniffed. No one but the army had coffee—couldn't be more than a half-mile away, most likely around the far bend.

Grass flourished in the open area on either side of the road. I waded through its height, stirring fog into misty towers, and knelt at the side of the road, trying to read marks in the dirt. The ruts were old, edges rounded over, not sharp, and I guessed the wagon train hadn't made it this far. Limping into the center of the road, I stopped. Plain as day, two horses left hoofprints in the dew, heading north. Scouts from the train? Or scouts from Shilo Riddle?

Hair lifted on the back of my neck. A knowing spilled over me, the certainty that something watched. Standing, naked of cover, in the middle of the road, I was marked—marked for a bullet. I turned to scan the edge of a group of trees swagged by layers of vines.

"I know you're there," I called out. "You shoot me,

you'll rouse up those soldiers 'round the bend yonder. Can't you smell biscuits and bacon? Coffee brewing?" I stepped backward a few paces, putting distance between me and the trees. Every few feet made a difference in the accuracy of a bullet, evened the odds. "They'll be warned you're here, just as sure as if I told them."

A motion under a giant blackjack caught my eye, and I concentrated on the spot. Slowly, a man inched from the shadows and raised his rifle, head angled to sight down the barrel. Copper red hair sprouted from under a rumpled hat. Pike!

Chapter 32

Ma's saying come back to me. Bad things come in threes, and this was sure enough the third time I'd had a rifle aimed at me in the last twenty-four hours. My death might warn the wagon train, but it wouldn't make me any less stone-cold, worms-eating-on-your-bones dead. I struggled to push down the fear, to think of something to say, and took another step backward.

"Got to hand it to you, Pike, you're like a regular high-dollar bloodhound. Couldn't throw you, could I? About the time I think I'm free, here you come, creeping through the bushes, breathing down my neck." I continued to shuffle my feet, inching backward. "Yes, sir. A regular high-dollar bloodhound, that's what you are."

Pike stood poised, rifle aimed. Why didn't he shoot?

"Aw, now," I continued, searching my brain for Pike's weakness. "You're not a stupid man. No, sir. Make more sense to slide back into them trees. Use the time to get away. You know how slow the army is. By the time I get to that wagon train, and the soldiers get mounted up, you could be halfway back to camp, maybe still get yourself some of those beef ribs or a deer steak."

Still backing up, one slow step at a time, I stumbled on the edge of a deep rut. I steadied myself and glanced back at the trees. A vine hanging from the blackjack twisted where Pike had stood a moment before, fog swirling in his absence.

I turned and limped down the center of the road, the blunt end of the stick digging holes in the dirt as I leaned into it. I expected a bullet to bore its way into my back at any minute. The feeling followed me, so strong it overrode the pain of my blisters. I couldn't be cut down now, not when I was this close to warning the wagon train.

The encampment of soldiers was such a welcome sight, I bit back the urge to cry out. A semicircle of wagons occupied a meadow to one side of the road. Cook fires sent up thin columns of smoke. Men in various stages of dress worked at striking pup tents. Some stood, coffee cups in hand, their conversations a low hum amid the clank of metal plates. Horses, tethered to a rope line, buried their noses in their feedbags, long tails flicking at flies on their rumps.

Campfires burned away the layer of early morning fog, pushing it back into the loose boundary of trees. I swayed, the ground beneath my feet uncertain, rolling. A spot between my shoulder blades still burned with the anticipation of a bullet as I surveyed the knots of men, looking for Josiah or an officer, someone in authority. Someone who would know what to do.

At the edge of the activity, a guard looked up from the opposite side of a big roan. "Hold on there," he called. His thin face scowled as he smoothed a blanket over the horse's back. "Identify yourself, fella."

"I have to see the captain." The need to warn the man was strong even if he wasn't the one in command. "We're going to be…"

Familiar laughter at a nearby campfire drew my attention. Two men sat with their backs to me, hats balanced on their knees, heads bobbing in animated conversation. The cook tossed biscuits from the pan to several upheld hands. Another round of laughter rippled into the air as the hot biscuits juggled from palm to palm.

I gripped the walking stick, anger fueling strength to my legs, and staggered toward the huddle of men.

"Wait a minute," the guard said and hurried forward. He grabbed hold of my arm just as I reached the circle of men eating breakfast.

"Like I said, looks like clear going between here and Fayetteville," a redheaded man said in a voice dripping with a Virginia accent. He sopped bacon grease up from the edge of his tin plate with a biscuit.

I jerked free of the guard and lowered the stick, poking the end at the base of Tazewell's neck. "Why, Taz, surprised you don't choke on them Yankee biscuits."

"What the—" Tazewell dropped his plate and twisted away from the sharp jab. "You?" He gasped, face reddening. In the span of a heartbeat, surprise turned to bluster, and he pointed his finger at me. "Shoot him, boys. He's a rotten bushwhacker."

"Why, you lying…" I sputtered, unable to get the words formed in my mouth.

The guard hooked his arm in my elbow and pulled it back.

Tazewell, voice raised, commanded, "Shoot him! Shoot him!"

"He's the bushwhacker!" I shouted back and pushed my elbow into the guard's stomach, twisting and turning to no avail. "Listen to me…"

In an instant, several soldiers had their guns leveled, unsure where to point, who to cover. One turned on his heels, yelling for the captain.

Greenbrier, dribbles of coffee glistening in his thick beard, bolted to his feet. He scrambled to pull his revolver as his cup tumbled into the smoldering campfire, sending coffee hissing along the hot stones.

That guard was on me like a badger, and I pulled him with me as I lunged forward, the stick still in my grip. Greenbrier abandoned drawing his weapon and grabbed at the stick. It cracked with the strain and broke into pieces.

"Hold it right there," the guard commanded, his grip still tight on my arm. "One of you boys take that man's gun until the captain gets here, and we get this straightened out."

Tazewell's rantings took a new turn as another soldier grabbed Greenbrier's gun. "See there! See there! Did you see that boy try to stab my brother? He's loco, I'm telling you. Touched in the head. Why, you can't believe a word he says. Better gag him before he starts accusing one of you of being an enemy."

Unable to shake free of the guard, I kicked at Tazewell. "You can't gag me fast enough to keep from telling these boys how you're one of Shilo Riddle's men."

"Whaaaa." Tazewell, eyes like saucers, sucked in a mouthful of air. "If I was one of them bushwhackers, me and Greenbrier would be pretty foolish to be sitting down for breakfast right in the middle of you men! Look at me." He spread his arms wide. "Do I look like a bushwhacker?"

If he isn't slick as goose snot, I thought. My head ached with the knowledge stored there. It was going to explode if I didn't get it all out.

"A rattler might have fetching colors," I shouted, "it's still a rattler." I twisted to face the guard. "These are two of Shilo Riddle's men, all right, decked out in our very own uniforms. About now, Shilo's bushwhackers are lined up down the road apiece, waiting for you to fall into their trap." I turned and pointed at Tazewell and Greenbrier, "And these boys have been doing a fine job making sure you do just that."

Tazewell stepped backward. His eyes sought out the Springfield he had taken from me. It leaned against the side of the wagon a few feet away.

"Stop him!" I shouted, pointing at the Springfield. "That's my rifle!" Spurred to action, several soldiers grabbed Tazewell and Greenbrier and wrestled them to the ground, knocking boxes and plates in all directions.

"Get your filthy hands off me!" Tazewell yelled, squirming like a worm on a hook.

A captain trotted up, his revolver flapping at his leg as he fumbled with the buckle. "What's this about bushwhackers?"

Tazewell kept struggling, all the while shouting. "That man is a traitor. A sure enough bushwhacker. Best shoot him before he gets away."

"Settle down," the captain ordered. "There's not going to be any shooting until I get to the bottom of this ruckus." He turned to his aide. "Sound the bugle."

The bugle blared, and men rushed for weapons, the encampment suddenly alive with activity. A soldier ran past, leading a brace of horses to be hitched to a wagon.

"Captain, I thought I was dead, and some of our men are," I blurted out before remembering to stiffen my back and salute. "I been running all night to get here. Shilo Riddle is intent on this wagon train. He's out there right now with more men than we got, waiting at Butcher's Bend."

Once I got started, saying what had been pushing me to run, I couldn't stop. Words poured out of my mouth. "He sent these two spies in to give a false report to catch you unprepared. They were supposed to tell you that the road to Fayetteville is clear."

I pointed at Tazewell. "That fellow right there signed up with me. Shared my tent, but all the time he was passing information on. That's his brother, Greenbrier Benton. There's a whole passel of Bentons, all Sesech-bent."

Tazewell reared back, eyes bugged. "A bold-faced lie he's speaking, sir. I've been a faithful recruit to this army for a considerable time. I'm telling you, this runt is trying to confuse you, for some unknown reason, and slander my good name while he's doin' it."

"Tazewell Benton," I retorted, "you lost your good name all on your own."

"Wait a minute," the captain said, glaring at me from under bushy brows. "Speaking of names, what's yours, and why should I believe you over these scouts?"

"You can believe him because he's my little brother, Captain." Josiah pushed through the crowd of men and saluted. He nodded toward me. "Though he does look a mite untidy now, I reckon I'll claim him."

Chapter 33

A wave of relief surged through my body, and I felt myself tremble. For an instant, I was afraid tears would gush forth and shame me. I turned from Josiah's sympathetic face to the captain and took a deep breath.

"I'm Private Ebenezer B. Fears, sir. Tazewell and I were sent out on a scout to see if we could find the whereabouts of a band of bushwhackers assembling back in the hills. Taz betrayed me into their murderin' hands. Me and four other soldiers got took. It wasn't hard to hear about the attack. That's all they were talking about. Like I said, Shilo says hitting this wagon train and plucking supplies from the Union Army will be like a Sunday School picnic."

"Well, Shilo Riddle, is it?" the captain glanced around at the activity. "Sunday School picnic, huh? Butcher's Bend? I guess you might have put a crimp in his plans." He patted my shoulder. "At ease, soldier. Good work. Know how many men are waiting for us?"

"Rumor back at Fayetteville was five hundred men banded together. Buck Brown's men joined up with Shilo Riddle's bunch. There were a heap of 'em strung out along the base of a sheared-off mountain with a cave and a waterfall. Can't say for sure there were five hundred, though. No time to count how many."

I shifted my weight to ease the pressure of the blisters and searched for anything else I could tell the captain. "Saw mostly Arkadelphia rifles. Said they'd have lots of ammunition once they hit this wagon train, so I suspect bullets are in short supply for them."

"Huh!" The captain pulled at his chin, running his fingers over the stubble of a beard, and turned to a soldier next to him. "Lieutenant, go to my tent and get my maps. Sunday school picnic, indeed. We'll see about that." He looked down at Tazewell and Greenbrier, sitting cross-legged in the dirt, with rifles aimed at their backs. "Tie 'em up. And see them boys are gagged and secured in the back of a wagon. Might be they won't think being shot at from the trees is so funny."

Backing away, the captain nodded to Josiah. "Seems your little brother just messed up a bushwhacker picnic. Done a fine job, too."

"Wait, Captain. One more thing." I swallowed hard, pushing back the tears that burned behind my eyes. "Pike Benton tracked me through the night and caught up with me about a half-mile back. Don't know why he didn't shoot me. He sure enough shot four other scouts, unless it's 'cause I word-bested him into thinking on how a gunshot would alert the wagon train and likely get him caught. He could be gonna warn the men at the bend."

"All night, huh? He on horseback?"

"No, sir. I think he's on foot, like me. But I don't know that for sure." I took another deep breath. "And, sir, there's a friend of mine bad hurt back there. Took a bullet meant for me. I left him in a cave. I need a horse and someone to go with me to find him."

The captain scrubbed his face with a burly hand. "Son, we can't spare a single soldier. You've done a good thing here." He patted my shoulder. "I'll see it gets in the report. We'll send someone back as soon as this train gets to Fayetteville, safe and sound."

"Just a horse, then. I can go back alone if'n I had a horse." I took hold the captain's sleeve before I thought better of it.

"We can't spare any horses, either. Even if I had a spare horse, you're not in any condition to go back out." The captain pushed my hand away. "You won't do your friend any good if you pass out trying to find him."

I felt myself go lightheaded. I'd poured out all I knew about the attack. The burden of knowing was lifted, passed on to someone else, and I should have felt relief. Instead, all the aches and wounds of the night came surging back. A cramp wrapped around my calf, tightening like a vise. I winced despite my best efforts.

"Here now." The captain nodded to Josiah. "Take care of that brother of yours."

Roaring orders as he went, the captain retreated toward his tent. Soldiers scattered, pounding me on the back as they passed, their words of praise falling over me like sunshine.

"Cy." I grabbed my brother, panic welling in my chest again. "It's Big Jolly that's hurt. I can find him. I know I can."

"Big Jolly? What's he doing out there?" Josiah lifted one of my arms to examine the welts and scratches and insect bites.

"Him and his pa and brother took to hiding their livestock back in the mountains. He heard all the shooting and came down to investigate. We was racing through this meadow when Pike sure enough shot him.

274

He's hurt bad. I got to go back."

"Ebby, you'll go back. I'll loan you my own horse," Josiah said, running his fingers over the injuries. "Just not today. You heard the captain. Today we got to keep all these supplies from falling into Shilo Riddle's hands."

"You don't understand. I promised. I promised Big Jolly I'd be back." Heat welled behind my eyes. A lump as big as a fist lodged in my throat.

Josiah shook his head. "Ebby, you're a soldier now, and soldiers take orders. Don't mean you got to like them." He nodded toward Tazewell and Greenbrier, who were sitting on the ground, hands bound. "Didn't you say that was your rifle? What's it doing in the dirt like that?"

I stood for a minute, staring at Tazewell, the cause of all my misery. If it weren't for him, I most likely wouldn't have been captured and Big Jolly wouldn't be laying in a cave waiting to be rescued. I limped over and reached for the Springfield, wishing for all the world I could pound it over the traitor's head.

"I'll just take this, Taz." I knelt and pointed the barrel at him. "Seeing as how you're not going to need it anymore."

"Why, Ebby, I was only taking care of that old rifle for you." Tazewell pushed his lower lip out and blew at a lock of hair in his eyes. Garlic wafted in the space between us. "It was a might careless of you to lose it like you did," he added, a note of the old tease back in his voice.

I stood to escape the odor. "Pardon my bad manners for not thanking you proper like." Coldness replaced the heat of threatened tears.

A soldier bent to the task of tying a handkerchief around Greenbrier's bobbing head. The bushwhacker struggled against the gag as the soldier grunted in his effort to secure the tie. Tazewell, hands behind his back, looked up at me and allowed one corner of his mouth to lift in a half grin.

"I still think you ought to change that name of yours, Ebby." He tilted his head, and the grin slid away. "You gotta tell that captain I never actually killed anyone. I tried to steer you clear of Riddle's boys. You tell them that, you hear?"

"Taz, it won't make a whit of difference what I tell them. You know wearing that uniform and working for the enemy makes you a spy. There's men dead 'cause of you. I was nearly dead, in case you forgot that fact." I cradled the rifle in the bend of my arm and ran a finger back and forth along the oily smoothness of the barrel. I was looking at a dead man now. No matter how mad I was, the realization roiled in my stomach.

"Reckon you know what's gonna happen to me. I'm likely to meet Skinny's fate at the end of…" Tazewell's sentence was cut off as the soldier poked a handkerchief in his mouth. Unspoken words growled up from his throat to be caught by the gag, and his face went red again.

I was held by the grasp of Tazewell's golden eyes, deep and intense, pleading without words. I watched as soldiers hauled the two captives to their feet and pushed them toward a wagon.

Josiah put an arm around me. "Hard thing when a man's friend turns out to be a traitor."

I leaned against my brother, glad for his strength. "Far as I know, Taz never killed nobody. But I reckon

276

he's gonna hang for the company he keeps."

"Prob'ly. Let me see your hands." Josiah nudged me toward the campfire. "Aw, now, them puny scratches are hardly worth noticing."

"Well, I thought for a while I was likely to have me a rebel bullet to brag on, like you, but seems I outran the thing. Ran all night, and got a heap of blisters to prove it."

"That so?" Josiah scooped bacon grease from the bottom of a pan with his fingers and began to massage it into my palms. "Sit down. Let's see those blisters."

"I had nary a mouthful of berries to eat and maybe a few locust and crickets on the side and sucky pond water. Tried to kill me a bear, but it got away. No matter though. I'd have had to eat it raw." I sat down and with tremendous effort lifted one leg.

Josiah tugged the boot off, trailing the shreds of bloody sock with it. Broken blisters oozed across my toes, the ball of my foot and heel. I fell backward, gripping the rifle against the burn of air on raw skin, and groaned.

"Now lookie there, Cookie," Josiah declared to the cook, who was dismantling his ovens, storing them in wooden boxes. "The boy thinks these are blisters. Why, I've had bigger sores on my behind from sitting a horse all day." He reached for another gob of grease before the pan was whisked away to be stored with the ovens.

Cookie, one cheek bulging with a chew of tobacco, paused and squinted an eye at my quivering foot. "Saddle blisters are nothing. Wagon blisters, now, those are worth complaining about. Bouncing up and down all day long, driving your tailbone up between your shoulders, blisters as big as plates on your bum."

He dropped a cloth bag on my chest. "A sourdough sandwich, with a couple rashers of bacon and a slice of onion, will have to hold you until we get to Fayetteville. Want more, you should'a got here earlier."

I pushed up on my elbows. The smell of bacon, strong under my nose, stirred the ache in my stomach. "Much obliged."

Cookie spat a stream of tobacco juice into the smoldering coals and turned to watch a detachment of soldiers, riding two abreast, trot past. "Got an empty flour sack that might make good bandages for those feet," he said to Josiah. "Then best get that boy in the back of the wagon. Let him find out what real blisters are like. Have a feeling we're going to make double time all the way into Fayetteville."

I patted the Springfield. "Willy finds out I near lost this rifle, I'll never hear the end of it."

"Willy finds out you got yourself captured and near shot, you'll never hear the end of it," Josiah said and chuckled as he tore the flour sack into strips. "In fact, Ma finds out you got yourself captured and near shot, you might as well settle in for a lecture longer than a Sunday sermon." He whistled through his teeth. "Wooeee."

"All I had for protection was Big Jolly's fish charm." I winced as Josiah wound a strip of fabric around one foot. "It must have worked 'cause I never did get shot."

"Seems to me, Ebby," Josiah said, "that's all you needed." He smiled. "That and them big feet of yours."

Chapter 34

Fine clouds of white flour escaped their cloth sacks with each bump in the road. Soon, I was coated in the stuff like some ghostly haunt. Still, resting on full bags made a softer bed than the ground I'd most recently slept on.

I waved the air and coughed. The sourdough sandwich sat heavy in my stomach, and I wished for a sip of Cookie's burnt coffee to settle things down. Not mentioning my blistered feet, every bone, every joint, every muscle ached. The thought of Big Jolly back in the cave, waiting for rescue while blood leaked through the hole in his shoulder sobered my thoughts and made sleep impossible. Damn Pike's devil bullet!

Like some old man, I grunted and groaned crawling across the bags to hang out the supply wagon's back gate for air. Hardly worth the effort, being the fourth in a line of five wagons all rattling over the same ruts stirred not only dust, but all kinds of tiny torments disturbed by the passing.

"Hey, little brother." Josiah's voice boomed, interrupting my misery. "Haul yourself back inside."

"Aw, Cy, I can hardly breathe in there." The complaint came out a whine, and I hated the sound.

"Word is, there isn't a road bypassing Butcher's Bend that's suitable for loaded wagons. Looks like we're going to plow straight through what's most likely to be a blizzard of bullets." Josiah ran a sleeve across his forehead and resettled his hat. He leaned from his horse to rap the top of my head. "I want you to keep your noggin down."

I reared away from a second rap. "You're not my commander, Josiah. If there is any fighting, I guess I'll do my share. In truth, there's nothing I'd like better. I'm itching to get a shot at them ruffians." I glanced back at my Springfield resting atop flour sacks.

"Now see here, little brother. You've done enough getting the word about the ambush to us. I'm not worried about my commander; it's Ma I'm thinking on." He gathered the reins, ready to skirt the wagon and ride ahead.

"Wait, Cy. This train'll need all the help it can get. You'll be out there, easy target for them bushwhackers. I'm gonna be in here, which gives me an advantage over you. I'm a good shot, and you know it. But I don't know where the cartridge box got to, and I can't shoot nothin' without bullets."

Josiah stared hard at me, chewing his lower lip, which meant he was thinking on the reasonableness of my argument. With no way to use my rifle, I'd have to keep my head down like he wanted.

"Every man will count goin' against five hundred bushwhackers," I said in case he'd forgot.

Taking a deep breath, Josiah nodded and lifted a cartridge box from his shoulder. "Aim for the body, bigger target. Don't get in a hurry. Make sure you have a clear shot. Our boys will be riding alongside the wagons. Remember, once you pull that trigger, you can't call a bullet back." He leaned out to swing the pouch to me. "Be a shame to hit a boy in blue, 'cause it won't make a bit of difference whether a man gets took down by Sesech or Union fire."

I stretched to grab the black leather box. No sooner than Josiah let go of it, he rapped me another time on top of my head before he spurred his mount away, and I swatted back nothing but air.

"Remember!" he called over his shoulder.

I hauled back inside the wagon, dragging the pouch with me. Must be something about being an older brother that made them think a lecture should accompany every howdy-do. I wasn't some empty bucket. Of course I'd not let loose a bullet until I knew where it's going. I grabbed one of Cookie's towels and went to polishing flour dust off my Springfield.

When I lifted the flap and peered inside the pouch, there weren't but ten paper cartridges neatly tied up and tumbling about inside. Ten. Against five-hundred.

"Hang on, boy!" Cookie's voice carried back to me. "Get ready. Butcher's Bend up ahead." With that, he bellowed, "Come on, you lazy mules. Move on out." The wagon lurched, rocked wickedly to one side, then righted. The wheels protested with a loud squeal, and I feared they might spin off with the next big hole in the road.

Despite bounces that lifted me inches off the wagon bed, I stacked two flour sacks against the sides and hunkered behind them. I retrieved a cartridge, tore the paper open with my teeth and steadied the rifle stock between my feet and barrel under my nose. There wasn't but a spoonful of powder in the paper. With the rough ride, it was a trial to pour it down the barrel without losing so much as a speck. Ten chances was all I'd get to set things right, and I aimed to make each one count.

I heard the unearthly caterwauling first, even before the sound of gunfire ahead. Awful screeching, whooping and hollering—enough to bring Skinny, trailing the hangman's noose around his neck, up out of his grave to join them devils in their fight. I near forgot what I was doing before I remembered to drop the minié ball in after the powder.

The ramrod seemed welded to the underside of the rifle, and while trying to stay upright in the wagon, I fumbled with the contraption. "Dad-blasted, infernal, pitiful piece of rotten metal." The good cussing must have worked, 'cause the rod let loose. I went to pushing the minié ball down the barrel and worked the percussion cap into place.

With the Springfield steadied on the flour sacks, I labored to cock the hammer back as far as it would go and stay on my knees. I no sooner spied a brute rushing down off the hill straight at me, then a bullet tore into the sack, spewing a cloud of white dust into my face. I was blinded and went to coughing and snorting and spitting. Worse than swallowing a mouthful of gnats, the stuff made paste in my mouth and near gagged me.

Just like my finger didn't have a lick of good sense, it gripped the trigger so hard the rifle exploded when the wagon hit something, sending me sprawling backward.

I struggled to sit up surrounded by the dull thud of bullets hitting sacks and sharp crack of them splintering the wagon's wooden slats. Above it all, Cookie cussed the mules, until he didn't.

Fluttering a layer of flour off my eyelashes, I blinked back the sting in my eyes and chanced a look at

Cookie, who sat hunched forward while the mules plowed ahead mindless of his silence. Some might think mules don't have a lick of good sense, but except for Othella's crap-critter, they do. Unless they were tight-reined, it would be just like the lead mule, a big black long-eared mongrel, to jump the road and head straight into the woods for cover.

I clamored across sacks and boxes and shifting barrels to get to Cookie. "You hurt bad?"

"Get ahold them reins down there, kid," he growled, the stub of a cigar clenched in his teeth. His boot held the westbound reins to the floorboard, while his left arm hung limp, a gush of blood soaking through his sleeve. It was a relief to find Cookie still had a tight grip on the reins threaded through the fingers of his right hand. I'd never handled a brace of six mules before, and for an instant, I wished for the lucky fish charm again.

I climbed the seat and stooped to gather the tangled bundle of leather, each strand tethered to one of the three stampeding mules hitched on the left side of the wagon tongue. A bullet smashed into the wagon inches from my hand, which angered me considerably. Words I didn't know I knew spouted out my mouth. I feared my arms would be jerked free of my shoulders until I got situated next to Cookie who found his hollering box once more. Between the two of us, those mules kept running, following the wagon in front.

A riderless horse raced beside us, and I hoped it wasn't Josiah's. Mostly I kept my eyes on the animals, but once or twice I glimpsed a fellow in gray, waving his revolver about or pointing it our way. Whether I wanted to or not, I'd duck for an instant. Big as he was, why Cookie didn't get hit again I don't know, 'cause he never flinched. Or maybe it was those miserable sneaking scoundrels were rotten shots and finally ran out of ammunition, like I suspected would happen.

As suddenly as it started, it ended. The banshee yells died away, and except for a bang or two, all I could hear was the pounding of hooves, rattle of misused wagons, and loud jangle of metal hardware on the tracings. That, and maybe, the deathly pound of my heartbeat inside my chest. Cookie was hollered out, and I could tell he was wilting.

Looking like a rumpled angel, Josiah galloped alongside the wagon. "You all right, little brother?"

I nodded. If I'd opened my mouth I probably would have started blubbering.

"If you're all right, how come your hand is bleeding?"

The sting came alive with the discovery. Two splinters the size of a nail, sprouted from my left hand, and I was angry all over again. Cookie slouched onto my shoulder, his breathing raspy. Ahead of us, the wagons were slowing. Last thing I wanted was to have sole control of wild-eyed mules running up the back of another wagon.

"Cy, this don't hurt much, but Cookie's bleeding like a stuck hog, and I don't think I can handle six…"

Before I could finish, Josiah was aboard, taking over the reins. "Get something to stop that bleeding," he ordered. "Wooo-oop, wooo-oop." Josiah's holler was near as good as Cookie's, and the mules slowed to a mere trot.

Cookie's head lolled back. Squinting one eye at me and cigar still firmly between his teeth, he croaked, "A bit o' flour to pack this hole would be helpful."

"Yes, sir." I tumbled over the cargo to retrieve a towel. Several bags were ripped open, flour everywhere. It wasn't hard to scoop up a handful.

As soon as I'd patched Cookie and near dragged him off the seat to the back, I took a care to my hand. Blisters and splinters looked to be my lot in this war. Still, I wasn't anxious to have a bullet to brag on like Josiah, and now Cookie.

A sergeant trotted up and informed us to keep moving, stay tight, and stay alert. We might have spoiled their ambush, but unless the bushwhackers were entirely out of ammunition, they'd most likely hope to at least pick off the last wagon or two.

Nine paper cartridges remained. It was a mystery where the first one ended up. I readied my rifle, dreading another attack. The day wore on past noon, then into the night without a stop for food. I was luckier than most, riding in the cook's wagon had its advantages. I might have been swatting away fine white clouds of flour every little bit, but a tub of left-over breakfast biscuits made up for the inconvenience.

Night brought out more than coyotes. Now and again, a Rebel would raise cane from the tree line, warbling an unearthly howl, and pretty soon, another and another would join until the whole woods seemed alive. One of our boys would let go a shot or two in that direction. I did, too, until Josiah hollered to stop.

"The scoundrels aim to get the boys to empty their cartridge boxes at shadows. Hope to even the odds a bit." He snapped the reins, but his heart wasn't much in it. "These poor animals are about done. We won't be able to outrun another attack. Just hope to make

Fayetteville."

Through it all, Cookie snored away, sprawled out on the flour sacks. His unlit cigar, smoked to a stub, teetered on his lower lip. I plucked it off to toss away, until I thought better and tucked it in his pocket. Then I settled next to him, determined to be ready should we suffer another attack. The Springfield grew powerful heavy, just like my eyes which still smarted, and I thought to close them for just a bit.

****

"My gosh, he does look a mite chewed up, don't he?" Willy's voice roused me. I attempted to sit up, but nothing responded, not even my eyes. They were pasted shut.

"Let's get this flour dusted off, else Ma'll think she's seeing a haunt," Josiah said. "First he's gotta let go that rifle."

"I'm not lettin' go!" Why I mumbled that, I can't fathom, 'cause the rifle slid out of my arms like it was buttered. Willy's hands, strong, sure, dragged me over the wagon's back gate and hefted me across his shoulder.

"Not countin' getting yourself captured, Ebby, you done good," Willy remarked to my hind end, but I heard him clear enough. Dangling like they were, the feeling was coming back to my arms and hands. Willy carried me to his horse and hoisted me into the saddle. I scrubbed my face awake with my good hand—the one not poked full of holes.

Torches lit up the night as dozens of our boys, all chattering about the attack, led the lathered-up mules away and unloaded the wagons. It appeared the bushwhackers took a toll on our soldiers, as many limped toward the hospital tent. Best I could, I looked for Tazewell while Willy and Josiah wove the horse through the activity. Maybe it was just as well I didn't see him.

What do you say to a traitor, one that had been a friend?

Word spread quick enough to Squatter's Field, and folks rushed out to meet us in their nightclothes, all asking if we knew this fellow or that and whether they might be hurt. No wonder poor Ma fretted herself ragged with nothing to remark on except the war. I resolved I wouldn't worry her with blisters and the like and straightened myself in the saddle.

I saw the lantern come on in our tent while we were yet a few yards away. By the time we got to the campsite, Ma had lifted the flap to peer out.

"We brought Ebby home, Ma." Willy's voice was almost whisper soft. "Don't reckon you got any coffee about, do you? We could do with a cup."

"Ebby?" Gripping the collar of her night shift with one hand, Ma stepped out and lifted the lantern high with the other, frosting her hair in a golden glow. She was a mite frowsy-headed at first, but right away her eyes went wide, and she gasped as I slid off the horse.

"'Tis a haunt come to see me in the image 'o me youngest son." She let go her collar and reached out. A bit of flour puffed from my hair with her touch.

"No, Ma." I shifted from one foot to the other, trying to relieve the ache of blisters. "I'm fine. It's just flour."

Ma rubbed her fingers together. "Flour? Ye been rollin' in flour?" She blinked, then frowned as she continued an inspection of my arms. "And crawlin' in bushes again?" She set the lantern on the ground and grabbed my punctured hand. Even in the dim light, or maybe because of it, my hand took on a ghastly look, blood-crusted and bruised to the wrist.

"What be this? An injury?" Questions rolled over one another. "I knew it. Ye were shot, weren't ye?"

"Shot at, Ma. Shot *at*," Willy interrupted before I could set Ma's mind to ease. He nestled a bucket of water and coffee pot in the coals Josiah stirred to life.

Mindless of my sweat and grime, Ma pulled me to her, near hugged the breath out of me and didn't let go. I could feel the tremble in her grip, and though she didn't say it, I knew what she was thinking.

"The signs were wrong, Ma. Settle your mind about an unlucky name. A hundred bullets come my way, and not one found its mark." I let Ma guide me to her rocking chair because of a sudden, I was feeling wobbly. "In truth, I'd say my name was a touch lucky."

"That so, Ebby?" Ma's voice took on a severe tone. "Then, what happened to ye boots? Ye were wearing them, sure enough, when ye left." She squatted and plucked at the ragged bandages on my feet, peeling them away, exposing oozing blisters to air. I stifled a yelp and flopped back in the rocking chair.

A gossip of hang-abouts went to whispering with the excitement me and the boys brought to the camp. Several women passed judgement on my blisters, one stating she knew someone who lost a foot with carbuncles like mine.

Ma rose to her feet. "There'll nay be talk like that." She tossed the limp bandages into the flames, causing them to spark and flare.

Willy swished a finger in the bucket. "Water's

warm. Best we get those blisters cleaned before they turn ugly. Hate for little brother to lose a foot."

"I'll hold him, Ma, while you scrub." Josiah chuckled and fed another limb into the blaze.

A hand rested on my shoulder, and I was of a mind to shake loose, but when I looked up it was Martha standing beside me. I forgot the hurt, forgot everything, but the fact I was gonna have to tell her about Big Jolly.

Chapter 35

Martha stood still as a church column, hand to her mouth, and I could tell she was holding back tears when I got to the part about having to leave Big Jolly in the cave. *Alone*. I hated the sound of the word. It made me feel like a coward, like somehow I should have hoisted him over my shoulder and carried him home.

"As soon as it's light, I aim to go back." I looked down at Ma, who'd finished washing my feet, greasing the blisters, and dusting them with calomel powder before wrapping them with strips torn from a clean towel. She sat back with the same horrified look on her face as Martha.

"Ye nay be walking on these feet for a bit." Ma's eyes welled with sympathy. She shook her head, brushing a lock of burnished hair back, and went to tying up my injured hand.

"I won't have to walk. Cy's gonna loan me his horse. He promised." I glanced across the fire at my brother.

Josiah took a deep breath, lips tight. "After that run today, she's played out, Ebby. I'll do what I can to get you a fresh mount, maybe a mule if nothing else."

Willy tossed the last of his coffee in the fire and stood, a tin cup dangling from one finger. "Should you ask, at daylight I'll be on my way to Fort Smith with dispatches. I have the captain's ear, Ebby. Before I go,

I'll…"

"I find son." Levi's voice was deep, startling, especially since he was standing in the shadows as was his custom. I didn't know he was even in the vicinity.

"I'll go with you, Levi." I pulled up to test my feet. Wrapped neat the ache was tolerable. "Don't know where my boots got to, but my old ones are in my tent, back at camp. You'd get them for me, wouldn't you, Cy?"

Levi's nose flared, and he crossed his arms. "I go fast. Alone."

"I won't hold you back, Levi. You need me. I know you're the best tracker in these parts, but I know where I left Big Jolly." I looked around at Levi, Martha, and Ma, standing with my brothers, and a few of the camp's residents, all staring at me.

"I'll go by myself, if I don't go with you, Levi." I'd left my friend, and I wasn't going to be denied going back to get him. "My boots, Josiah?"

Martha ran a sleeve across her eyes and laid a hand on Levi's arm. "The boy won't slow you down if he's riding."

"Ebby, you'll nay pull boots over those swollen blisters." Ma's remark had neither command nor sympathy to it, and I wondered if she saw my side to the argument, then she added, "Ye best let them toughen a bit."

"I've something better than boots." Martha turned and hurried toward her wagon. Levi snorted and stomped after her, prompting the hang-abouts to wander back to their tents, too, all chattering about the ambush.

"Now, Ma. Ebby may have got himself captured, but that's not entirely his fault what with Tazewell proving to be Sesech." Willy frowned at me, then set his empty cup next to the coffee pot. "I had my suspicions about that foul-smellin' Josh, always skippin' out on chores and such. I should have took a care to who his family was. Otherwise, little brother done all right. I reckon if Big Jolly has a chance, Ebby needs to go with Levi. No one I trust more in these woods than the Indian."

My mouth dropped open. Willy siding with me against Ma?

Ma shook her head. "I nay like the odds o' him goin' out there again, hurt like he is."

Josiah squatted to poke the fire. "You know Ebby's bound on finding Big Jolly. He goes with Levi, and they run into any bushwhackers, they'll not think hard on an Indian and scroungy kid."

Josiah siding with me against Ma and making an even better argument than Willy? My mouth was still agape, and I gasped, drawing in a flutter come to the firelight. I coughed and gagged, spit most of the moth out.

"I'm not hurt much, Ma." I cleared my throat, wiggled a sore foot to prove the point.

Ma stood there, turning the Calomel tin over and over in her hands. We all knew it was best not to hurry her when she was ruminating on things. Squatter's Field was coming to life in the fading darkness. Several campfires sputtered into blaze.

Willy looked around. "Best they go now before dawn. Never know who is friend or foe these days."

"Aye, and I suppose you'll be needing this." Ma handed me the Calomel tin. "I'll fix a poke to take. Ye'll be needing bandages and last night's corncakes."

She drew herself up, the spark back in her voice. "A clean shirt. I'll nay be havin' a son o' mine half naked and lookin' like a ruffian." She disappeared in our tent.

The boys turned to go.

"Wait! Willy…Josiah. Ma would never have…"

Willy stepped toward me, put his face close to mine. "Don't make me sorry, Ebby. I don't aim to answer to Ma should somethin' happen to you. Out there Levi is the boss. Do as he says, you hear?"

Willy turned again and reached for his horse's reins. "I'll tell the captain you're on sick leave."

"And don't be a dunderhead," Josiah said and rapped me on the noggin before I could duck.

I watched them leave, weaving their way back to the road, their heads bobbing in conversation. The night had grayed and would soon be gone.

"Ebby?" Martha was at my side. "Sit and let's see if these aren't better than boots." She held out a pair of moccasins—soft brown leather, warm and smooth to the touch, inside the dark imprint of a foot. A beaded design of three crossed arrows pointing different directions decorated the top of one.

"Did you do the beading?" I asked while stretching open one of the moccasins and easing my foot into it. Snug, but not tight. I breathed a sigh of relief. Ma wouldn't have been happy with me leaving with nothing but bandages on my feet.

"I did. When Levi and I were first married." She motioned to me. "Let me help."

I held out my other foot. "How come only one has arrows?" I figured it meant something or other. Most Indian doings did.

"Oh, I ran out of beads," she said, reaching down

293

to run a finger along the design. "These beads are very old—belonged to grandmother's grandmother." Martha tugged the back of the moccasin over my heel, smoothing the leather along the side of my foot.

Now and again the glass beads caught the firelight and winked to life in soft hues of rose and blue. There was something about them. "Are these like…"

"Like the ones on the fish charm?" She nodded. "The same. I pondered taking more off the charm, but old uncle said words over them." She brushed back a tear. "Maybe the moccasins will be lucky, find path to Big Jolly."

Ma ducked out of our tent, a cloth poke dangling from one hand and mended shirt in the other. She studied my feet and remarked on the crossed arrows. "Aye, 'tis a good thing to keep the spirits confused. They nay know which direction ye be heading."

Levi led his horse over, a leather water skin hooked to the saddle pommel. I hurried into my shirt and touched Ma's cheek, wishing to banish the worry-lines away.

"I'll be fine. Maybe, just having the Fears name is lucky. Jim and Willy seem…"

"Ye be forgettin' about Josiah." Ma transferred the poke to my shoulder.

I sighed, bent, and hugged her tight. Ma was bound to worry, no matter what I said. I just hoped she didn't go tossing out anymore coffee grounds looking for signs.

Martha and Levi stared at each other for a minute, didn't say anything, which didn't surprise me none. I barely hauled myself in the saddle before Levi started walking, and I nudged the mare to follow him, weaving past wagons and tents to gain the road.

A mile past camp, I brought the horse up next to Levi. "See that path? Up there is where we turned off." He nodded and soon we were in the tangles, ducking under branches and such. Every so often, Levi paused, studied the ground, a broken branch, or sniffed the air.

I sniffed, too. Except for the pungent aroma of molding leaves and dead wood, broken by the occasional fresh breeze through the trees, I didn't smell anything of note. Maybe Levi was part wolf. I laid myself along the horse's neck and closed my eyes trying to bring the past two days alive, remember our twists and turns.

"Boone's Holler," I called out to Levi. "That's where we camped the first night by a poor excuse for a creek. We tramped up and down the holler, but we should have gone on through." The memory of Taz's misleading hunches and my being so gullible gnawed at me, until I thought on the traitor's present circumstances and wondered if he was stretched yet or not.

It was midmorning when we came upon a long-dead campfire. I slid off the mare, swallowing back a groan when my feet settled on the ground. Levi bent, held up a chicken bone.

"Ah ha. This is where we camped first night out, ate fried chicken. See here." I snatched a chewed garlic wad from the dirt. The dried mass still held a touch of stink. The discovery gave me energy, and I pulled myself back on the horse. "We need to follow that pitiful stream to where it branches off Little Coon Creek. Then cross the creek. There's tracks on the other side."

Levi nodded, and I nudged the horse into the stream to follow him. He wasn't much for conversation, so I hushed my mouth. The hum of insects grew loud in our silence. A thick crowd of powerful trees, oaks and hickories, gave way to frilly willows stooped and waving, reaching for the water bubbling over stones in Coon Creek.

"There, just like following breadcrumbs." I said, louder than intended when Levi showed me several wads of garlic. He tossed the chewed bits into the bushes, held up his hand. I leaned forward and whispered, "Tracks of three horses, other side."

I paused to let the horse drink its fill, then urged him on across the creek and past the hoof prints, now dried, near gone. Broken branches, trampled grass, horse leavings, clearly marked the path, that and egg shells. The thought of hard-boiled eggs bargained off Tazewell set my mouth to watering, and I reached into Ma's poke for a corncake. Then remembered Big Jolly hadn't eaten in two days and put it back.

Soon enough we were upon the place of Tazewell's treachery, the ring of stones piled high with the ashes of a bushel of leaves that brought my capture. All thought of eating banished, gave rise to a bitter taste in the back of my throat. Levi had his nose to the air again.

"The main camp is just ahead," I whispered as we followed the path, remembering the cold dread that settled over me while being marched at gunpoint into the bushwhackers' lair. It was a fair day, just like then, only now the afternoon was alive with the squawk of birds coming and going overhead.

I ducked when Levi led the horse into the foliage. The smell of woodsmoke was strong, and I knew the miserable, murdering, thieves were back, hopefully licking their wounds. We were close, and the spill of water down the cliffs near drowned the grumble of voices rising and falling. Levi nodded, and I dismounted quiet as possible, hoping the moccasins were why Indians could walk on silent feet.

Levi lifted a branch to better view the meadow. Raggedy men clustered in groups, not nearly as many as before. Some stretched out on the ground, and I hoped they weren't just tired, but maybe hurt enough to be no threat. The skeleton of Greenbriar's deer still hung, even from a distance it was black with insects. Clouds of birds—vultures, hawks, blackbirds, jays—funneled into the air and down again on the ridge. I knew they feasted on what was left of Uley and the others, what might have been left of me. My stomach lurched, and I swallowed hard.

"I come down off the ridge on the other side," I whispered to Levi. "That's where I met up with Big Jolly."

Voices drifted to us, and I froze. Levi pulled the horse's head down, snugged its nose to his chest. A short distance away a group of men broke through the woods into the meadow, several riding, some walking. They were still coming in from the attack, but now there was no bluster, no laughing. I felt hard in the heart and hoped they'd left a lot of their comrades behind for birds to feast on over at Butcher's Bend.

Levi eased the branch he was holding in place, looked back at me, black eyes speaking his command. Walk silent, don't talk. I followed the horse, stepping past twigs, over pebbles, keeping to the soft dirt. It was as much to cushion the bottom of my feet as for silence, for they ached with each step taken. Every little bit, Levi stopped to listen, sniff the air. Usually, up ahead, a fellow or two would crash through the underbrush and limp into the clearing.

It seemed a hundred years before we skirted the valley and rounded back to where I'd come off the ridge followed by a slide of rocks and ancient tree trunks.

"Best we cross the ditch here, Levi. There's a bog that'll suck you under up ahead. The other side of the bog was where me and Big Jolly met up." It was the first I'd spoken all afternoon, and my whisper came out raspy.

Levi looked back at me, nodded. "You ride now, Ebby. Forest quiet."

He waited while I pulled into the saddle, glad for the chance to rest my legs and feet. Gripping the reins, he led the mare on a trot across the ditch and into the tree line. It was late, going on supper time, and the trees cast long shadows. I worried what would happen if we lost the daylight. Despite the bumpy ride, I closed my eyes again to picture the whole sorry chase.

"It was a pretty fair stream, said you and Little Jolly were camped just north in the next valley. Headed east until we came to a big meadow."

Levi swept his head side to side, and though he didn't look back, I knew he heard me. The trees all looked alike, and the worry came back to me that I might not recognize where I left the forest and hauled Big Jolly up into a cave. Before I had a chance to think on the matter too hard, we were at the stream. We followed it along to the sandy bank where I was surprised to see me and Big Jolly's footprints. That was where we took off racing. Me and Big Jolly. Racing to warn the wagon train. A lifetime ago.

A sudden stop unsettled my thoughts. Levi stood stock still, nose to the sky. He handed me the reins, the message of danger plain in his stance. I followed his upward glance. Several vultures circled above, and then I caught the stink of death, faint, unmistakable. I could barely breathe. Lots of things die in the forest. Rotting flesh, animal or human, surely smells the same, though I couldn't be positive of the fact.

Crouched with knife in hand, Levi moved ahead. I nudged the mare to follow, but she balked, clearly unnerved and not willing to follow my command. I watched as Levi paused, parted the scraggly vines of gopher bushes, then stood and motioned me forward.

Must be an animal carcass. Relieved, I slipped out of the saddle, landing as soft as I could to spare my feet, and with reins wrapped around my good hand, tugged the horse along.

"You know?" Levi pointed to the ground.

The gristly sight near turned my stomach. That was no animal carcass.

Logan.

At least I was pretty sure it was Logan, though the face was near ripped off. One eyeball stared, unblinking, straight at us. A hand, fingers clawed as if reaching for help, caught on a branch and hung suspended. The other hand, gnawed clean off. Blood, no longer bright, soaked his shredded shirt, soaked his torn pants, soaked the ground and made a feast for the hoard of flies buzzing about.

Pulled back by the horse, I turned away. "Must have been the bear," I muttered to Levi, nodding toward the meadow where the creature was last seen. It was then I sighted a big shaggy mound a few feet beyond. Something scurried away and set the weeds to trembling. Groundcover was trampled, ground rumpled and showing an occasional boot print, or huge paw prints with nails digging holes deep enough to plant corn.

"Big Jolly was shot just the other side of this meadow." I pointed the direction. "We didn't make it too far after that."

Levi grunted and left on a trot, sun-dried grasses slapping at his legs. I remounted to follow, passing the lightning-struck tree the bear had used to sun himself. A creepy feeling tickled the back of my neck. I knew it was memory making my skin crawl, giving me the flutters inside.

We crossed the meadow, Levi all the time scanning the ground, finding his son's blood on blades of grass, then our footprints before entering the forest's dappled shade. I leaned from side to side, on the lookout for the pile of stones I'd left. Evening coming on, it was getting harder to read signs, and I felt frustrated. We were close. I could feel it.

"Should we call?" I whispered. The wind had quickened, rustling the branches.

Levi bent, picked up a stone, then another. "Someone kick, maybe trip over, stones here."

"Then he's hereabouts." I could hardly keep the excitement out of my voice, hope rising that Big Jolly was near. I turned the horse in circles, searching the trees. Around and around, back and forth. A gust of wind set the branches rustling. It was then, in a flash of daylight, I spied a faint sparkle among the leaves and pointed. Levi saw it, too, and reached up, plucked the fish charm out of the tree, brought it to me, grinning. It was the first sign of relief he showed.

"He's up there." I dismounted, the sharp pain of blisters barely noticeable. "There's a cave beyond the ledge, hard to see from down here."

Levi put a hand on my shoulder. "Wait. I go first." He reached for his water skin and saddle bags.

I was of a mind to argue, but Levi was right. If Big Jolly was dead, I didn't want to look on my friend like that. Levi disappeared over the ledge, dislodging pebbles in his wake. I shouldered Ma's poke, staked the horse, and waited, rubbing the arrowhead for all it was worth. The dangling string of ancient beads clicked softly with the motion.

"Ebby, come." Levi reached his hand down as I struggled with the climb and hauled me up past the ledge, into the cave.

"Is he…?" I couldn't finish the question.

Levi smiled, jutted his chin to the back of the cave.

Big Jolly, face pale, eyes sunk deep, lifted a hand and let it fall. "Wagon train?" he asked, voice weak, a mite trembly.

"Safe," I said, feeling like I could walk on air. Big Jolly was alive. He smiled, and I could tell he wanted a story like Little Jolly might relate. I did my best. "Tazewell and his brother got there before me, but I told them a thing or two. Sitting, eating Yankee biscuits, lying through his teeth about how the road was clear. All I had was a walking stick, but I poked his back with it, made him think it was a gun…"

Soon enough, Levi had a small fire going, and we dug into Ma's corncakes and Martha's dried apples and fried pork rinds. Food never tasted so good.

Finally, Levi unwrapped Big Jolly's bandaging, releasing the awful smell of old blood. He grimaced as his father poured water over his wound, the hole now pitiful bruised and puckered. I talked as fast as I could telling him about Pike and the ambush and the run for Fayetteville, so he wouldn't feel the sting so much.

With darkness on us, the fire made shadows on the walls, jumping and wiggling about. I was talked out, and Big Jolly seemed stronger with the food, or maybe it was with the company. We leaned against the cave walls. I studied the moccasins on my feet, the old beads gracing the top of one, and decided they were lucky, pulling us toward those on the fish charm.

"Remember that bear?" I asked. "He saved our lives. Gave us time to get away. Just wish it was Pike got caught instead of Logan. Pike didn't even bury his brother, just left him there for the critters." I shivered despite the wave of heat coming off the flames.

No one said anything. We listened to the drip of water seeping out of the limestone walls and hitting the shallow pool. It sobered me to think Big Jolly had nothing more for company than that.

"Were you scared? 'Cause I was scared all the time I was running."

"No. Not scared. Someone's ancestors waited with me." Big Jolly nodded toward the drawings across the ceiling, and Levi grunted agreement.

We sat for a long while, watching out the cave entrance at the forest below. Every so often, off in the distance, a wolf would set up a lonely howl. Then when stars winked to life, I dug in my pocket and pulled out the fish charm. I fingered the arrowhead and string of small glass beads before I laid it in Big Jolly's lap.

"I think, maybe, it was spirit of old uncle keeping you company."

A word about the author…

M. Carolyn Steele enjoyed a career in journalism and commercial art before retiring to pursue a love of writing and genealogy. She has short stories published in seventeen anthologies and has won a number of awards, which includes nomination for a Pushcart Prize.

Her writings reflect a childhood steeped in Civil War history and Indian lore. Carolyn presents a variety of programs designed to inspire others to commit family stories to paper and authored the non-fiction book, *Preserving Family Legends for Future Generations*, a 2010 First Place winner for Heartland New Day Bookfest. A fictional book, *Spirit of the Crow*, dealing with a half-breed's quest for acceptance is set in 1836 Indian Territory.

http://mcarolynsteele.com